FROM A SEA ABLAZE

Ray Murray

BLUE JACARANDA
>P U B L I S H I N G<

Blue Jacaranda Publishing Ltd: Reg No 7790913
The Old Coach House, 14 High Street,
Goring-on-Thames, Reading, RG8 9AR, UK
www.bluejacarandapublishing.co.uk

Printed & bound in the UK

A CIP catalogue record for this book is available from the British Library

Cover design: Steve Banbury
Cover background: National Maritime Museum, Greenwich, London

ISBN: 9780957076686

Dedicated to the Roseland Peninsular in Cornwall
and all who are lucky enough to live there.

1
La Invincible

The seaman stowed the leather-bound chest beneath the bunk bed and touched his forelock. "Is everyone aboard?" Diego de Olivarez, standing in the open doorway, asked curtly.

"Most of them, sire."

Diego stepped inside the tiny cabin, crossed to the tiny glass-paned window, and stood gazing out at the surrounding activity. "When do we sail?" It palled him to have to ask this common seaman but there was no one else here to question. The quarterdeck was empty

"Two more days, perhaps three. Stores are still being loaded, sire."

Dolt! Diego could see that for himself. His impatience to get aboard meant that he was here two days before he needed to be. He could have stayed with one of his father's friends in much more comfort. Too late to be thinking that now. "Where has my manservant been put?"

"In the forecastle, sire. At the front."

The dolt thought him ignorant of seafaring terms. "Watch your tongue. I'm well aware of where the forecastle is. Too far, I want him nearer. Much nearer. Tell him to sleep in the passageway, outside my door, so that I can call when I want him."

"Yes, sire."

Diego dismissed the man and glanced round the cabin. He had expected it to be larger, but with every inch of the ship taken up with men and stores, he was lucky to have a space to himself. The squadron's flagship had been full and Don Miguel de Oquendo, the squadron's commander, had personally arranged for him to sail on this, the San Salvador, with the privacy of a tiny cabin as compensation.

The room measured a mere nine feet by six. Along one side was a wooden bunk. A stool, water pitcher and bowl, standing on a table bolted to the wall, were the cabin's sole furnishings. Above the table, a second tiny window looked out across the quarterdeck. Through the salt-scoured glass of the starboard window, Diego could see a blurred image of the rest of their squadron lying at anchor. He opened the window. To their right, the galleons of Castille; in the centre, the royal galleons of Portugal and the great San Martin of the Duke of Medina; out of Diego's immediate sight, rode a host of others ships. One hundred and thirty vessels, carrying more than thirty thousand men. The greatest fleet ever assembled. A constant stream of smaller boats ferried messages, men and stores from ship to ship, and shore to fleet, while the constant sound of ropes clattering through pulleys, hawsers creaking, voices shouting instructions, echoed and re-echoed across the harbour's stirred up water.

Diego watched the activity spellbound, pride in what he was seeing rising chokingly to his throat. Never had so much might been concentrated into one fighting force. And this was just the naval fleet; they had yet to pick up the invading armies from France. This time, nothing, he mused, would stand in their way.

***

The lumbering Armada inched its way slowly northwards, the lead ships cutting their speed in order to keep the fleet intact, the slower vessels trying desperately to gather in every breath of wind and not get left behind. They were now halfway across the infamous Bay of Biscay, where the last invasion attempt had foundered, moving slowly towards a point northwest of the French coast. Here, they would begin to cross the wide mouth of The Sleeve that the English with their intrinsic arrogance referred to as the English Channel, skirt Lizard Point, sail on to meet with Parma's army at Calais, re-embark with it, cross the narrow stretch of water, and march on London. There, finally, they would see that accursed arrogance wiped from their faces.

Diego, wearing a new velvet doublet, silk hose and soft leather breeches, a jewelled dagger at his belt, stood on the raised deck above the stern castle, gripping the rail. Below was the quarterdeck, below that the main deck, packed with Spanish, Flemish and German soldiers, many of them sick from the constant motion of the sea. So far, he had managed to keep his stomach under control, but it had not been easy.

The excitement of weighing anchor, moving out towards the open sea, of being part of this great enterprise, had at first made the movement bearable, even mildly pleasant.

But on leaving the shelter of land and heading out into the Bay, the motion had become a sickening roll, emphasised by the fleet's cumbersome, slow pace.

"You look pensive, Senor."

Diego turned to face the speaker: an overweight, middle-aged merchant and wine grower, aboard as a guest of the captain. He wore a plumed hat to which he clamped his hand, keeping it from blowing away. Diego thought he looked fat and ridiculous.

"I was thinking of the coming battle," Diego said stiffly.

"Not with concern, I trust."

Diego's chin lifted, "Certainly not. With pleasure."

"You expect it to be pleasant?"

"The English have much to answer for: they have plagued us for years. I can assure you, paying them back will be extremely pleasurable."

The wine grower smiled. "Ah, yes. The captain has told me of your feelings. He said your family once lived in England. Is this true?"

Diego reddened uncomfortably. "How does he know that?"

"I believe," the merchant said, "that the admiral, Don Miguel, may have mentioned it to him."

"It is possible. The admiral is a close friend of my father."

"But your father has not come on this venture?"

Diego flushed at the upstart's questioning tone. "He was on the first attempt, in the Spring," Diego said. "The storm they suffered spoiled his appetite for more."

"I'm not surprised. I hear it was very bad."

The first Armada had been twenty days out from Lisbon before there had been enough wind to clear Cape Finisterre. By then all the food had gone, the drinking water had turned bad, and they had yet to reach the English coast. When the storms finally turned them back, half the crew, by all accounts, had been too ill, too idle, or too scared to do more than lie where they'd collapsed. "Waves higher than the mastheads, they say. He and my brother were lucky to survive. A second voyage, he thought, would be tempting fate."

"Yet he allows you to go."

"I had already pledged my presence to the Blessed Virgin. He was angry but could do nothing about it. I was not going to be left behind a second time to sit and await news with the women. Now we sail much strengthened and this time it will be successful. This is God's way of weeding out the weak so that the Armada lives up to its name - La Invincible." He waved a dismissive hand. "Not that I'm saying my father and brother are weak, but simply that they should have persisted more strenuously. It was their duty to be standing on English soil, raising the Holy Father's flag, not running before the wind, tails between their legs, back to Spain from where they started."

"I think you are maybe being a little hard."

"It is the army as a whole I criticise, not individuals."

"Even so."

Diego shrugged. "Perhaps." What did it matter what this fat overweight upstart thought. "It has had its benefits. I would not be on this great enterprise if the first attempt had succeeded."

"True. So why then, Senor, are you not aboard the admiral's ship?"

"The flagship was already full. The San Salvador was the best that Don Miguel could arrange in the time."

The merchant smiled. "Not such a poor consolation."

"No, it is very good. I have my own cabin. On board the flagship I would almost certainly have been forced to share."

"And your brother?"

"He has joined the Duke of Parma in France."

"A much shorter sea crossing. I wish I'd had his good sense."

Diego frowned. "He is not afraid of the sea. It was simply more convenient, and he will be in the forefront of the battle when we land."

"Tell me, Senor, why do you dislike the English so?"

"They have left the Holy Church," said Diego in some surprise.

"Some have; others have stayed true. You misunderstand me: what is it that you hate about them. Did they treat you badly when you were in their country?"

"On the contrary, we were accepted to the point of being ignored."

"Ah!"

"And what does that mean? Ah?"

The wine merchant waved a hand. "Just a middle-aged man's way of speaking. So, how long were you there?"

Diego teetered on his heels as the ship rolled. "Five years. I was seven when we arrived, twelve years of age when we sailed home to Spain."

"Permit me to say that you are still a young man."

Diego bridled. "I am seventeen. Not too young to fight if I am called."

"But not on this venture, I gather. Like myself you are here to enjoy the spectacle."

"That is true, but I would not be afraid to fight if circumstances dictated."

"Let us hope that we will not be called upon to do so," said the merchant dryly. "And where was 'there' when you were in that accursed country?"

"A seaport called Penryn. We will possibly sail past it. If we do, I will point it out to you."

"Most kind. I shall be interested to see it. Do you speak the language?"

"Yes."

"That might prove useful. We will need people with such knowledge to rule the country when we have conquered it, shall we not?"

"There are English Catholics sailing with us now who can do that."

"You think we will trust them that far? I doubt it."
A sudden gust of wind lifted the wine grower's hat, He
grabbed it and held fast. "So, tell me, Senor, what is it like,
this England you dislike so much?"

"In winter it is icy and wet. In summer cold and damp.
Even when the sun shines it has no warmth. Without doubt,
the dreariest country on God's earth."

"And the people?"

"Arrogant. More arrogant than you can possibly imagine.
Even the peasants believe they are better than anyone else."

"I have noticed that in the English who sail with us. They
are of the faith but show little humility."

"They never do, and never will. It is not in their nature."

"So what was the reason for your being there? Five years
is a long time to be away in another country.."

"Today, back home in Spain, my father is an important
landowner of some standing. Then, he was a successful
merchant, selling wines to the few there with any breeding."

"Ah! Perhaps he sold mine."

"It is very possible. In fact, if you sent your wine to
England, it is almost certain that my father would have
handled it."

"And he took you, the family, with him?"

"Yes. And made a considerable fortune. But, unfortunately,
my mother became ill. The damp air. Each winter she would
suffer. In the end, we came home so that she could live in the
sun." Diego paused, then said angrily: "In my opinion, we

should never have gone there in the first place. England has turned my mother into an invalid, and I shall not rest until they have paid for every cough that racks her body."

***

Diego came out on to the quarterdeck. The day had dawned bright and clear but his head was still muzzy from the previous day's terrible weather. Blinding squalls, blowing out of the north, had turned in the night and swung round to the south-west, increasing in violence, the resulting heavy seas being more than his stomach could stand. He looked around: the Armada's squadrons had mainly managed to stay together but it seemed some forty or more ships had been forced to part company with the Duke of Medina's fleet, including the entire Andalusian squadron.

The captain of the San Salvador came out on the quarterdeck and nodded to Diego. "A rough night, Senor. But it seems to have passed. We now have the task of rounding up those who have got themselves lost and also of finding Don Pedro de Valdes, commander of the Andalusian squadron."

Diego nodded.

"You slept well?" the captain asked.

"Very well," Diego lied.

"I'm pleased to hear it. Not many will have done."

Over the next few hours, three pinnaces were dispatched by the San Martin to round up those who'd become separated from the main group; the Andalusian squadron eventually being found anchored off the Isles of Scilly. Reunited, except for five ships in need of repairs, the Armada sailed majestically on up the Channel, seeing only one English ship, a barque, sailing windward, at speed, towards Plymouth Sound.

Anchoring off The Lizard, the Duke of Medina called the squadron commanders to a Council of War, many of whom voiced a desire to sail into Plymouth Sound and capture Drake who had long plagued their fleets and merchant ships. But the Duke insisted this was against King Philip's orders, which were to sail directly on to France, embark the Duke of Parma's invasion army and transport them across the Channel to England.

All this, Diego heard from the San Salvador's captain as the Armada weighed anchor once more. War, he was told, was now imminent; they could see the distant coast of England, and Diego could feel the excitement inside building to a crescendo. How he wished he could take part rather than be just an onlooker.

The wine merchant came on deck. "So, Senor de Olivarez, this is the England you speak of so harshly," he said, gazing at the distant blue smudge that lined the horizon.

"No more harshly than they deserve," replied Diego sharply.

The merchant nodded but made no comment.

"You do not agree?" pressed Diego.

The merchant looked at him and shrugged his shoulders.

Diego noticed that he was still parading the plumed hat, and still having to hold on to it in the stiff breeze. "Neither do I disagree, Senor," the merchant said. "I am content to await developments."

Waiting was for women and old men, thought Diego, his lips curling visibly in derision. He was here and he wanted action.

2
Waiting

Bess sat on the headland, high up on The Jacka, gazing seawards towards the Eddystone rock. From across these waters, everyone was saying, was where they would come from. But, gazing at the placid expanse, it was difficult to imagine the menace - a kind they'd not known for five hundred years - that lurked beyond the summery haze hovering over the distant horizon.

Below, in the fishing village that had been her home and of the Trevanion family for longer than most could remember, there was an excitement in the air and Bess wasn't sure there should be. Expectancy, certainly; apprehension, yes; fear, probably. But excitement? Somehow it didn't seem right. What if they were vanquished? She pushed the thought aside. Vanquished meant beaten and she couldn't imagine that happening. Invaded, yes. But Robert and his like would bravely drive them out, back into the sea that had brought them here.

From the shore came the soft swish of waves breaking against rocks. It was Sunday. And on Sundays the Reverend Ffermer preached his usual diatribe: this Sunday proving no exception, as the vicar yelled dire warnings of what they could expect should the Spaniards ever succeed in landing. Not that Bess believed the warnings to be untrue; she just wished they didn't have to be constantly reminded of them.

It always seemed sad to her that their beautiful St Veryan church, erected to the glory of God, should echo to such wild rantings. The interior of their parish church had always fascinated Bess. She'd sat there often, imagining her grandfather, great grandfather and the scores of Trevanions, Blameys and Trudgeons who'd worshipped there over the centuries. Some, especially the older members, found the building cold and unwelcoming: the floor sucked up dampness from the ground, leaving the stone paving constantly covered in a film of moisture. Today, it being mid-July, the interior had been cool and unlit; in winter, alter candles reflected warmly off wood panelling handsomely carved to represent cloth hanging in folds from a pelmet of Tudor roses. At the foot of one such panel could be found the initials WT, proudly cut there by Walter Trengrove's great grandfather who, according to legend, had spent a large part of his life shaping the wood in memory of a wife, dead through childbirth, just ten months following their marriage.

There were times when the Reverend Ffermer had spoken of removing the panels on grounds that they displayed an ornateness more in keeping with popery: a proposal angrily resisted by the Trengrove family, with the vicar eventually accepting the Squire's more tactful comment that the building would seem even colder without them. Unfortunately, their vicar had not given in so easily over the alter, and the carved and painted structure that Bess's father, Henry, remembered as a boy, had long since been replaced by a simple oak table, as had the mural painted walls, now lime-washed a stark and glaring white.

"Thought I'd find you up here," said a voice.

Bess turned. Her heart missed a beat and a brief flush of desire swept through her.

"Up by the beacon, keeping watch?" queried Robert Williams.

"Only until my father comes. It's his turn."

Robert plonked himself down beside her. "Seen anything of the enemy?" he said with a grin.

Looking seawards at this perilous time was an activity in which the whole village was involved. As was every man, woman and child the length of England's coastline.

"Why?" she said. "Don't you think they'll come? Or is it that you think it's a man's job to tend the beacon."

"They land on Cornish soil, we'll make every man jack of 'em wish he'd never been born," he replied, his brave words making Bess's heart skip a beat. "As for tending the beacon that's a task for every person in the realm, young or old, man or woman."

Bess knew that, like all Cornishmen, he'd face the enemy bravely when the time came. At seventeen years of age, he was big enough for two Spaniards: well-built, handsome as a courtier with it, each time she looked at him her heart slipped its moorings. Though nothing had been announced, she tended to think of him as her Robert. Did he think likewise? The truth was she didn't know. He'd not spoken;

18

they'd never talked of the matter. It was just accepted.

"Jep Trist tells us that the whole of Truro's buzzing like an upturned hive," Robert commented. "With the militia there urging citizens to watch for papists signalling the enemy. Hang 'em, I say, then they don't need watching."

Bess smiled. The only papist she knew was an old man living over in Porth East, as proud of being English as anyone. She couldn't imagine him signalling any Spaniards.

Robert climbed to his feet. "Here comes Henry. I'll leave you to your watch."

Bess glanced east: her father was approaching along the cliff path, accompanied by Nicholas, her young brother. "No need to run," she said.

Robert smiled. "I'm not running. I have things to do other than pass the time on idle talk with pretty maidens."

"It's Sunday," Bess protested. "God's day of rest."

"And Sundays I like to stretch my legs. If I'm to be called for the militia next month I'll more than likely be expected to walk to Plymouth Citadel and that's seventy miles or more."

"Robert," greeted Henry, halting next to them. "Keeping Bess company?"

"Aye, not that she needs it. She's content with her own self but I was passing and stopped to say hallo."

Nodding to them, he strode off along the cliff top towards The Dodman and Bess watched him go, his long legs striding out. Was he off to meet someone? A maiden? She hoped not. Henry was saying something, waiting for her reply. Bess

19

looked at him. Nicholas was grinning. "Sorry, Father, what was that?"

"Never mind," he smiled. "You just keep ogling Robert Williams."

"I was not," Bess replied quickly.

"You were, too," said young Nicholas. "Enough to turn our stomachs."

Bess reddened angrily.

"Oh, come on," grinned her brother. "We're teasing. If that's what pleases you, carry on ogling. It's Robert we should feel sorry for."

***

Later, Elizabeth, Bess's mother, accompanied by Jep Trist, arrived with food. "Saw 'Lizabeth down at the harbour," Jep said by way of explanation, "and thought I'd 'company her." Bess smiled. More likely he smelled her mother's baked fish.

Jep sat himself down. "Know what you're thinking, and it ain't true. I've eaten. Kate gave us cold herring."

"Well, Jep, you know you'd be more than welcome to share what I've brought," Elizabeth told him, unpacking a basket.

"Well..." Jep started to say.

"Oh, for goodness sake," Henry interrupted, "join us, Jep. I'm sure there's enough for one more."

"I'll allow it does smell good."

"I'm afraid, as it's Sunday, it's cold but I can vouch for its goodness," Henry said: Elizabeth was renowned for her cooking.

"Well, if you think…"

"Pass him something," Henry said, "or he'll go on like this all afternoon."

Nicholas laughed, Jep grinned, and Elizabeth passed round fish, bread and ale.

"No ships in sight," said Jep, gazing out to sea. "Spanish or English."

"They'll come," said Henry. "And the beacon'll be ready when they do."

Bess glanced at the woodpile. The beacon they tended comprised a large iron basket much like a giant brazier, filled with brushwood and tinder, mounted on six feet tall iron legs. All around the country blacksmiths had forged similar baskets, with the selected high points chosen by the militia to create a chain of communication leading to London and other principal towns and cities. It was these chains that would finally warn England of the Armada's approach.

Yes, they were ready, thought Bess. But no one knew exactly what to expect. The afternoon passed peacefully and Bess lay on the cliff top, dreaming. Gulls that had swooped round them looking for crumbs from their meal had decided to seek elsewhere, and a Sunday afternoon quietness had settled over the headland.

"Stranger coming," Jep remarked softly, taking a grass stalk out of his mouth. Henry looked up to see a giant of a man striding up The Jacka towards them.

"Henry Trevanion?" the man called as he approached. "Villagers told me I'd find you on the headland. Will Bligh, from St Mawes with news of son Thomas."

"Dear God, how is he?" said Elizabeth, going pale.

Jep said softly: "I'll keep watch. You go and see what it's all about." Henry nodded his thanks and all four rose to their feet to meet the man.

"Calm yourself, Mistress Trevanion," Will Bligh said. "It's greetings I bring, not ill news." Henry extended a hand for him to grip.

"And this must be Nicholas and Shrimp," the barrel-chested giant said, doffing his hat and extending his hand to both. Bess coloured at the nickname given her by her brother. Will Bligh's expression softened. "Thomas must have poor eyes: you're no shrimp," he said. "Or if you are, then you're the prettiest shrimp I've had the good fortune to meet." And Bess's face reddened even further.

Bligh turned to Elizabeth. "Forgive me, Mistress. I did not mean to cause alarm. Having been transferred to St Mawes Castle just this week, Thomas asked me to pass on his good wishes and this is the first chance I've had."

Bess gazed at this man towering over her father. He spoke with a rolling burr that sounded from Devon or Dorset; his light brown hair, roughly trimmed beard and hazel eyes, making both his looks and speech quite different to their own. Cornish fisher folk were mostly dark haired, blue-eyed, as she was, and shorter and squatter in build. It was their Celtic blood, her father said. Bess liked to think it was also from a lifetime of looking at the clear blue sea and sky. Her gaze dropped to the giant's rough clothing. Unless an officer in the militia was wealthy and willing to throw his money around, most soldiers called up in the muster wore their own clothes and Will Bligh, dressed in britches down to the knees, wide brimmed hat, and a leather jacket over a loose fitting shirt, proved no exception.

"So how is Thomas?" Henry asked him.

"Well enough. He misses you all. And in that respect is no different from any other soldier called away to serve his Queen. But I'll wager many will be sorry to see him leave Plymouth when this war is done, and they won't all be maidens."

Henry smiled. "Aye, he was always well liked. Excuse Elizabeth, she worries about him."

"'Tis to be expected. But you have my word, Thomas is fit. If it weren't for the fact that he misses home, I think he might even be enjoying the coming war. He's a great one for making the best of a situation. Few days go past without us laughing at his antics."

"Aye, he was always the jester," Henry said, his voice soft and husky. Bess knew her father missed Thomas greatly. She did what she could to help harvesting their catch but she was a woman.

Will nodded. "Today's the first day they've let us out since we arrived, so I felt a need to stretch my legs."

"You walked from St Mawes?" queried Bess.

"Tis but eight miles. But they're putting me in charge of fetching supplies and I'll get given a cart and horse. Having promised Thomas to keep you informed, next time it'll be easier." He indicated the pile of brushwood and tinder. "That's a fair beacon you've built there."

"The whole village, not just us. We had praise from Sergeant Wills when he came. Said it was the best hereabouts."

"Sergeant Wills from Plymouth? If he said that, it was praise indeed. He's not one to offer such lightly, as Thomas well knows."

"Thomas knows him?" asked Elizabeth.

Will Bligh smiled. "More the other way round. But enough of that. I've told you he's well and that he wishes the same of you back home. I'll gladly pass on your good fortune to anyone making the journey to Plymouth." He turned: "So, how's young Nicholas?"

"Well enough," said Nicholas eagerly. "Looking forward to the coming battle. We should see it well from up here."

Will Bligh frowned. "Aye, you'll get a good view. But I'd rather it wasn't happening."

"We have no choice," Nicholas said forthrightly. "Our vicar tells us they're the Devil and must be destroyed."

"And what of you, Bess? Are you betrothed?"

A fleeting image of Robert's smiling face flashed before Bess's eyes.

Henry laughed and Elizabeth smiled. "Nay, she's but sixteen years of age," Henry said.

"Plenty get betrothed at sixteen."

"True, but she's busy helping me catch fish at the moment. Plenty of time for that when this business is over and the young men come back from the war. Bess is a dreamer, she likes to let her imagination roam."

"Naught wrong with that. So meantime you're a fisherman, Bess. Or should I say fisher lass? Is there such a word? You surely don't look like one."

At first, Henry had said that it was man's work, too hard for a woman, but his protests had been feeble, all the while instructing her on the tasks that her brother had once carried out. Now she was as skilled as any fisher lad, her shoulders broad from rowing and hauling in nets and, unlike the fine ladies of Truro, her skin tanned from wind and rain.

She looked down at her kirtle, or skirt, made of wool, her bodice made of linsey-woolsey, a mixture of coarse linen and wool, the sleeves embroidered with a posy of flowers as it was Sunday wear.

"These are my Sunday clothes," she said. "You should see me when I'm working."

"I'll warrant you still look pretty."

"She does that," said Henry proudly. "Believe me, there'll be no shortage of suitors when the time comes."

"She already has one," said Nicholas. "His name's Robert."

"You hush," Bess said angrily.

Will Bligh laughed, then glanced at Jep, positioned on the far side of the beacon, trying not to listen to their conversation. Will lowered his voice. "So what do you think to this coming war, Henry?"

"I ain't listening," shouted Jep. Henry smiled. It would be difficult not to: only the beacon separated them; under the fire basket and between its iron legs, Jep was in clear view. "You go ahead," Jep called. "Talk freely. Henry Trevanion is a man worth listening to."

"I don't welcome it," Henry said, "but I think it's inevitable. I keep hoping it'll die down, but too many people are stoking the fire."

"Aye, I suppose so." Will paused. "So, have you ever met a Spaniard, Henry?"

"One or two. A few Spanish merchants set up businesses in Penryn during Mary's reign and stayed until the troubles became too bad for them to continue. Why do you ask?"

"Because I've never met one. Perhaps some are as bad as they say, but they can't all be so. Many must be just like you and me. So what is it that makes us want to kill each other?" He gazed across the water at the sea birds perched on Gull Rock. "Thomas never questions such matters. He says the English hate the Spaniards and the Spaniards hate the English and that's all there is to it. If we don't kill them, they'll kill us. But is it as cut and dried as that? I've never killed anyone in my life. If my first is to be a Spaniard will

26

that make it right? Or will God hold me in contempt and commit my soul to hell?"

"I cannot say what God will do. I only know that their faith is not for me," Henry replied. "I was but a boy when Mary Tudor was on the throne but I remember well my parents and those who lived in fear through that reign, and felt its icy breath."

"Aye, but it's difficult when one knows that today's Protestant is sometimes yesterday's Catholic, and tomorrow it could just as easily be the other way round."

Across the beacon, Jep gave a knowing chuckle. Henry eyed Will shrewdly. "That might well be true, but few will thank you for reminding them of it."

Will sighed loudly. "I find it difficult to believe God made us to fight among ourselves for his favour."

"Perhaps so. But you asked me what I thought and I've told you. You must determine your own views. What news do you bring from Plymouth?"

"Of the war? We heard that Howard is back in Plymouth Sound from out in the Bay of Biscay where he's been trying to spy the Spaniards' movements. It seems he couldn't spot them and thought it best to retreat rather than have the Armada outflank him. But that's all. And so far no one has seen hide nor hair of any Dons."

"Oh, they're out there, make no mistake. We might not have set eyes on them but they're there."

"If anyone from St Mawes Castle is sent to Plymouth,

ask them to give Thomas our love," said Elizabeth.

Will nodded. "Aye, I said I would and that I shall. But we don't expect to move much now. It's a case of staying where we are and waiting to see what happens, and be called upon to act when it does. The invasion will happen. As you say, Henry, it's too far gone to turn back. Whether they'll land or be beaten at sea we can only wait for God to decide." He paused, then said: "I'm sorry if I burdened you all with my thoughts, but they've been troubling me for some time."

"Nay, Will. 'Tis only right that you should consider the matter. Too many just meekly follow everyone else. If you find yourself near our village again, call in and see us. You'll be more than welcome."

Will smiled. "Aye, I'd like that very much. I must get back to St Mawes or I'll have the sergeant after me." They shook hands, and watched as Will strode back the way he had come.

Gazing after him, Henry said: "Will Bligh seems a good man. Thomas couldn't wish for a better friend."

"Amen to that," murmured Elizabeth.

Nicholas glanced at them. "The Reverend Ffermer might not agree with you, Father."

Henry sighed. "Yes, well thank God the Reverend Ffermers of this world are sometimes wrong."

From the other side of the fire basket, Jep gave another heartfelt chuckle.

3
"Beacons Ho!"

The plaintive cry came from a fishing boat on their left. The sun was up and the pearl grey light had changed to a warm, soft yellow. Clouds hugged the far horizon, while the sky above remained blue and clear, and land edging the Roseland peninsular and Falmouth Bay stayed flooded with sunlight. The fisherman raising the cry, was riding waves further out and had a far broader view past the protruding headland and across the wide bay to the rocky Manacles beyond.

"And another... And another... There goes Nare Head," cried Bess excitedly as one after another the beacons leapt into life, spreading their warning message with the speed of light.

"Right," cried Henry. "Pull hard for the shore." Just that moment, they had harvested a lobster pot and were on their way to the next. All around them, fishermen hastily dropped pots over the side, racing for the sanctuary of the harbour.

Bess silently willed Jep, whose watch it was, to light their beacon. Come on, she urged, strike the tinder and catch the straw. A wisp of smoke drifted up into the blue, grew into a plume and burst forth at its base into yellow flame. She dropped her oar and leapt to her feet. "There goes ours," she yelled. "There goes ours."

"Sit down and row before you have us both in the water," cried her father.

Bess grabbed the floating blade; there was no time to hoist the sail. Replacing her oar, she glanced east towards The Dodman and saw smoke climbing into the sky. The message was being carried across the country with unbelievable speed. She stared fascinated as she bent her back into pulling for the shore. "At this rate it'll be in London before the day's out," she cried.

"Sooner. It's travelled more than twenty miles in ten minutes."

Bess gazed at the beacons as they rowed. "That's two miles in a minute," she calculated, breathing hard. "More than a hundred miles in an hour," she gasped in awe.

"Aye, faster than a swallow on the wing, or a hare on the run. Now stop gawping, girl, and row."

The boat ground into the shingle. Around them, vessels jostled each other in the entrance to the cove. Jep Trist was standing on the jetty, jumping up and down with glee as much as trepidation, surrounded by a huddle of excited women. "They be coming this time," he yelled at Bess and Henry. "This time there be no mistake. This time they be here for certain."

"Aye, it looks very much like it," cried Henry. Jep should have stayed on The Jacka to watch that the beacon stayed burning. No matter, they'd built it well: once lit it would remain so to the last embers. He turned to Bess. "Leave the boat. I'll pull it ashore. Run to the top and see what you can spy."

Bess jumped into the water, ran across the wet sand in bare feet and began scrambling up the rock face. Fifteen feet up, grass and fresh bracken took over with a path worn bare through to the headland's peak. Ahead of her, the beacon was blazing, shooting sparks high into the air. She was now high enough to see across the bay. She halted, breathing heavily. Her heart sank. Nothing! She swore roundly and unbecomingly: all along the coast, beacons were blazing away merrily; it would take days, if not weeks to rebuild them.

Then, on the horizon, far to the south-west, the sun reflected off white sails. Not one, not two, but a forest of canvas packed so thick that, if the alarm hadn't been raised, she would have thought it to be no more than a low lying cloud. Heart in mouth, she brushed her hair away from her face, and turned to the south-east, squinting into the sun, searching for Drake. Except for a lone fishing boat racing towards Mevagissey harbour, the sea was as empty as a tinker's purse.

"Can you see anything?" panted Henry, leading Jep and a straggling line of villagers up The Jacka's steep slope. Bess could see Nicholas, her brother, among them, along with young Francis Bosawen, racing each other to the top as if this was a game.

"Aye, just. But they're still well down on the horizon."

"Where? I can't see a thing."

"I lit ours as soon as the Nare went up," babbled Jep.

"Over there."

"I struck the tinder and up she went."

"What, that white haze?"

Henry squinted his eyes. "Aye, that's them."

"Holy Mother of God!" muttered Richard Pyne. "How many are there? There must be hundreds."

"A sizeable number, that's for certain."

"If it was me, I'd sail up the Fal and take Penryn. That way they'd cut off Pendennis."

"Sergeant Wills says they aren't likely to land in these parts, but will sail up the Channel, pick up Parma's men and land them at Dover."

"Drake'd never let them do that. He'll tackle them long before they reach France, mark my words."

"So where is Drake?" queried Bess. "Far as I can see, there's no sign of him."

"It won't be easy getting out of Plymouth in this wind," said her father.

"If he waits too long, they'll land for certain."

Slowly, they fell silent, watching the distant fleet hug the horizon. A feeling of apprehension settled over the group. Finally, Henry said: "Jep, it's your watch, you stay here." He turned to the two elder Bosawen brothers: "Walter and Harry, keep an eye on our beacon and make sure no sparks catch the grass. We don't want to fight a brush fire as well as the Spaniards. The rest of us had best get back and comfort the women. Anyone wants to go back out into the bay, stay within hailing distance. The rest, pull your boats up onto the hard, it may prove our last catch for a while."

"Can I stay here and watch?" asked Bess eagerly.

"No, your mother may be fretting. You can return later if she agrees."

"What about the arms in the sail loft?" asked Will Pascoe.

Henry, on instruction from Sergeant Wills, had organised a collection of available weaponry, from pikes to pitchforks, muskets to ancient crossbows. "Leave them for the moment. There'll be plenty of time to hand them out when we know which way they're headed."

Reluctantly, the men turned and made their way back down to the village. The enemy was in sight at last, but they weren't being called upon to do much more than watch.

***

Diego, the wine merchant, officers of the San Salvador and of the various troops on board, were clustered together on the quarter deck, gazing at the land they had been sent to conquer, still with no sign of any enemy fighting fleet. Just once, for the briefest of seconds, a lookout in the topmost mast had shouted that he thought he'd glimpsed white sails out towards the Eddystone reef, but nothing had come of it.

Diego gazed round at the Spanish fleet with pride. Spaced roughly in a crescent, two hundred yards apart, ships on the port point were now a mere two miles off shore; those on the starboard tip, four miles further out. In the centre of the formation, three large galleases, rowed by banks of oars, preceded the Duke of Medina's great galleon flying the huge square flag that had been blessed by the Holy Father. Flanking the flagship were more galleons and ships bedecked with banners and pennants, some so long they hung from masthead to deck. Tucked away, safely in the centre, were dozens of supply ships protected by more galleons and with a host of smaller boats to their rear. What a magnificent sight, Diego thought with pride. Truly La Invincible.

By early afternoon, the giant fleet, having passed both St Mawes and Pendennis castles with no sign of a counter attack, was now level with the village of Portscatho, pointed out to them by the captain on a map he produced and laid on the deck while they all gathered round. The shore was now so near they could see figures lining the cliff tops.

Diego went back to his cabin and strapped on a sword. Back on deck, he drew the steel from its scabbard and flourished it at the distant figures.

The captain smiled. "You are preparing yourself, Senor?"

"Of course. I may be only an onlooker of this great enterprise but I am prepared to fight if it comes to close quarters."

The captain nodded his approval. "I'm sure you are. And you'd be a welcome recruit if that were to happen."

Diego was pleased.

"But there seems to be no sign of Lord Howard and Drake's ships as yet," the captain said dryly. "With the tide and wind as it is, they will find it difficult to leave harbour until we have passed Plymouth and, with such slow progress, I'm afraid that is not likely to happen until tomorrow."

Waiting, waiting, waiting, thought Diego, slapping his sword back into its scabbard. That's all they seemed to do - wait.

***

Three times Bess standing on the cliff top tried to count the invading fleet, each time missing some and counting others twice. The approaching bank of sails was so thick that it was often impossible to distinguish one ship from another, giving the Armada the appearance of a floating island, ringed by white cliffs. Even allowing for errors in counting, there must be between a hundred and a hundred and fifty ships, Bess thought with alarm.

They had managed to follow the Armada along the coast, but keeping pace had proved less easy than first thought. Its slow progress was deceiving, and every few yards they found themselves breaking into a trot. Along the way, anxious villagers from Caerhays, Boswinger and Penare stood gazing silently at the spectacle.

Arriving at the high point of The Dodman, Bess saw the beacon there had now died to a shimmering heap of white ash beneath its giant iron brazier. Men, women and children from St Goran and Porth East crowded round, seeking news but, as Henry told them, they knew no more than those questioning them.

"Drake'll not get his ships out of Plymouth without

being towed by rowers, and that'll take hours," one man murmured, knowingly.

"Maybe the Spaniards'll sail past, then Drake can come out and take them in the rear," said Harry Bosawen who, along with his twin brother Walter, had followed Henry, Bess, Nicholas and Richard Pyne along the cliff path.

"They know he's in the Sound; they'll not let him gain the weather advantage that easy."

"They'll have no choice once past Plymouth."

And so the nervous chatter went on. But a nervousness, Bess noticed, that was laced with increasing excitement. The nearest Spanish ship was now less than eight hundred yards off shore. They could see decks crowded with figures; the late afternoon sun glinting off helmets and breastplates. Along the ships' sides, gun ports stood open, cannon muzzles protruding from the square openings. Trumpets called to each other, relaying commands; occasional drum rolls and distant shouts added to the commotion.

Then, as the Armada rounded The Dodman, the trumpeting and shouting increased, sails were furled and the rattle of a hundred anchor chains rolled like thunder across the water.

Bess and the others watched in excited anticipation, any moment expecting to see troops being ferried towards the shore. But the ships remained stationary, the activity slowly dying as it became obvious to the watchers that the fleet was now anchored for the night.

"We'd best stay and watch," murmured Henry. "In case

they try landing under cover of darkness."

A man from St Goran said: "We'll leave someone from our village, too."

"We're staying with you," announced Walter and Harry Bosawen promptly.

"What about me?" asked Bess.

"Your mother will want you home," said her father.

"I'll be more use here," Bess pointed out. "If they land, I can run back and warn everyone."

"That's all right, let her stay," said Richard Pyne. "Elizabeth'll be fine, I'll go back with Nicholas and we'll see she's told the news." The Pynes lived next to the Trevanions.

Henry glanced at Bess. With the Armada poised ready to invade, it was every man, woman and child's duty to do everything to resist. "Aye," he said finally. "You can stay."

To Nicholas, about to argue the point, Henry said: "Your mother will need you, Nicholas. You'll be the man of the house in my absence, so take charge. Come back in the morning with food."

"There'll be nothing to see before dawn," Bess told him.

Reluctantly, Nicholas nodded.

***

Bess, Henry, the Bosawen twins and the man from St Goran, lay on the grass gazing in wonder at the thousands of torches and lamps reflecting off the water. The sea glowed and sparkled, flashing back a thousand fragments of light as waves lapped the anchored fleet, while an occasional small boat, moving between one vessel and another, stirred the reflections into dancing necklaces. The beauty so fascinated Bess that she found she was inclined to forget its dire purpose. Never before had she seen so many ships gathered in one spot, and the fact that these were enemy ships was gradually becoming lost in the spectacle.

Two brief sightings of their own navy had been granted them before darkness finally fell. Once, towards the Eddystone reef, the evening sun glinted off sails that could only belong to English ships. And later, just as the sun was setting, they spied a group hugging the coastline east towards Plymouth, beating their way into the wind, past Gribben Head. The Spaniards, failing to see the first group, had obviously sighted the second and four of their pinnaces sailed to investigate.

Gradually, silence settled over the Armada. One by one lights were extinguished until all that remained was a single lantern on the stern of each vessel. The five watchers arranged sentry duty among themselves - one to remain awake, the others to try and sleep, then to change round. But it was a long while before Bess, who'd opted for first duty, was to hear the sound of steady breathing.

4
First Blood

Diego woke, raised his head, and looked out his cabin window to find the sun's rim breaking the eastern horizon. Landwards, its golden light crowned the Cornish cliffs and inland hills. Dressing hurriedly, he stepped out onto the quarterdeck, wet a forefinger and raised it above his head: the wind, shifting in the night, was now blowing west-north-west. A quick glance round showed that none of the galleons and supply ships appeared to have moved from their moored positions - all was as it should be, as God intended. La Invincible was ready for battle.

Suddenly, the sound of trumpets broke the morning's stillness, echoing across the water. Sailors appeared, hurrying about the decks, and began climbing the riggings. Within a very few minutes the yardarms were dotted with men; sails were lowered, ropes tightened to catch the wind, anchor chains winched in, and the Armada began moving across the wide mouth of what the captain, referring to his map, had said was St Austell Bay.

The cluster of English ships that had been sighted the previous evening still hugged the coast, again trying to beat to windwards, with every gun on the Armada fleet trained in their direction.

The quarterdeck rapidly began to fill with officers and passengers anxious to see what if anything had developed during the night. Very little, it seemed to Diego. "If that's all El Draque can muster, it hardly seems worth the journey," he murmured to the wine merchant alongside him. "We could have sunk them with less than a single squadron."

The captain, standing at the ship's rail, overhearing Diego's remark, smiled and said: "Drake's fleet will be a great deal larger than a dozen ships, Senor. That may prove to be part of the English fleet but it is by no means all of it."

Diego turned to him. "So where are the rest? Skulking in Plymouth harbour, or running before us out of reach?"

"With Drake one never knows. But I'll wager we'll find out soon enough."

Diego stared. "You speak of the devil as though he were some favoured compatriot."

"I wish he were, Senor," the captain sighed. "I wish he were."

"The man's a pirate," Diego said angrily. "A coward who'll run at the first broadside. And I'll wager it so."

"Keep your money, for you'll surely lose. Drake may be a pirate, a heretic, many things, but a coward he is not. I've seen him fight."

Diego, brushing aside the wine merchant's muttered caution, tugged angrily at the purse attached to his belt. "Five gold pieces says either we do not see him today or, if we do, he runs like a dog before us."

The San Salvador's captain shrugged. If the admiral's impetuous young friend wanted to throw his money away, who was he to refuse. "Done," he replied.

***

From their high viewpoint on top of The Dodman, Henry stretched out an arm, pointing a finger out to sea. Far away, on the distant horizon, a fleet of sails was outlined mistily against the blue.

"Spanish stragglers," Harry Bosawen murmured.

"They're not Spaniards, they're English."

"It's Drake," cried Bess excitedly. "He must have sailed round the Eddystone reef to gain the wind. How the devil did he manage that?" She switched her gaze to her left. The cluster of English ships sighted the previous evening was still hugging the coast. "And the Spaniards haven't seen them," she said excitedly. "They must think that's the English fleet, over there."

Henry eyed the three groups, calculating their distance in terms of wind and tide. "Aye, and it'll be two hours or more," he murmured, "before Drake's close enough to make a challenge."

"If it is Drake," said twin Walter.

"Who else can it be?" asked Bess.

Henry turned. "The villagers will never forgive us if Drake sets to and sinks them and they haven't seen it with their own eyes." Everyone hesitated, knowing full well he was right but loathe to miss any action. "It'll be three hours," Henry pressured, "two at least, before a shot can be fired."

"I'm away." The St Goran man leapt to his feet and

disappeared down the cliff path.

Walter said: "Straws to see who goes." He broke off three blades of grass: one just over two inches long, the others nearer four. Placing them behind his back, he arranged the blades so that less than half an inch of each was showing. Bringing his hands to the front, he offered the tips to Bess: "Maidens first. Long lengths stay, short length goes."

Bess reached out and drew a blade from between Walter's fingers. It was difficult to tell with the first drawn whether the length was short or long. Harry drew his. Bess grinned, it was definitely shorter. Harry groaned. Walter opened his hand to show his was also long, his grin joining Bess's: "Nothing'll happen, while you're gone," he argued.

"It's ten miles, there and back," Harry moaned. "It'll take all of two hours."

Walter scoffed. "Pooh! You can run that in less than an hour."

"You were supposed to be the one running to warn everyone," Harry said to Bess, crossly. "That's why you stayed."

Bess grinned. "Straws, remember? We drew straws. Blame Walter: it was his idea."

"Straight forward two to one chance," Walter said loftily. "All honest and above reproach."

Harry's face dropped. "I'll have to sit through the Reverend Ffermer's sermon," he pleaded.

They'd forgotten it was Sunday. "Aye. And it'll be good

for your soul," Walter grinned.

"Soon as he knows the battle is about to start, my guess is he'll put off any service until this evening," Henry said. "Routing the papists? Our vicar won't want to miss that."

Harry's face lit up. "Aye, you're right." He glanced out to sea. Drake's ships were still hull down. Bess doubted whether the Spaniards, down at sea level, would spy them for another hour. "Right," Harry said. "Tell them not to start without me."

***

The English ships hugging the coast opened fire, splashing wasted shot into the sea a half-mile short of the nearest galleon. Jeering Spaniards cheered the fusillade, continuing to train their cannons on the few English ships within their sight. A full half hour passed before it was realised that the fusillade had served its purpose by causing them to neglect their seaward side. A ship on the Armada's outer flank fired a gun, signalling English ships approaching from the south-west. The Armada tightened its formation. The Duke of Medina's flagship, directly astern of the galleases, once more hoisted its huge battle flag, and an impetuous galleon, turning to face the new enemy, was immediately pulled back into line by trumpet calls from the command ship.

"Where in God's name did they come from?" asked the wine merchant, seeing the English fleet bearing down on them.

"I told you to never underestimate El Draque," muttered

the captain with feeling. "Now the devil has gained the weather gauge."

"Poof! La Invincible will still out sail him," said Diego.

"But how did he do it?" pressed the wine merchant.

"Not only him, but Lord Howard, Hawkins and the whole English fleet," said the captain, eyeing the number.

Diego hurried back to his cabin and once again buckled on his sword, his stomach churning with excitement and laced with a faint tremor of fear.

Back on deck, Diego saw the Armada was now level with Gribben Head, and that having struggled against a headwind throughout the night, the English ships hugging the coast were at last able to sail round them and join up with Drake in the Armada's rear.

As soon as the two fleets were joined, a lone English ship sailed towards the Armada, fired a single cannon shot at a towering galleon, heeled over, darted back to the waiting English line, and a hundred battle standards rose to Spanish mastheads as the challenge was accepted.

***

The lone cannon shot heralded Harry Bosawen's return. Accompanying him was Robert Williams. They thrashed through the bracken and threw themselves to the ground.

"Dear God," wheezed Robert, splayed out alongside Bess. "I'm dying. How many of the bastards have we sunk?"

Bess, her mouth suddenly dry, found herself flushing hotly at his nearness. "None, yet," she said. Her fingers began untangling her tresses, which had become knotted by the salt-laden air. She was conscious that although it was Sunday morning, in all that had happened, she still wore her work clothes.

"None? How could we miss? The sea's covered with the scum."

"There's a devil of a lot of them out there," said Bess's father.

"With this wind, they'll be out of sight before the battle's even started," moaned Robert.

Ten minutes later, young Nicholas panted up the hill, closely followed by Richard Pyne. Nicholas thrust a bundle at Bess and collapsed on the ground. "Here, mother sent food," he gasped.

"Where are the others?" Bess asked.

"Don't worry." Richard Pyne sucked air into his lungs in great gulps "Every man in the village is on his way to some vantage point or other. They wouldn't miss this for the world. The Reverend Ffermer is vexed as a wild cat: the women got together and insisted on saying prayers for the English fleet. I warrant it'll prove the quickest meeting they've ever attended."

The bundle contained a barley loaf and a flagon of ale. Bess broke the loaf in two and passed half to her father as Jep Trist and alehouse keeper Will Trudgeon joined them.

"Which one is Drake?" gasped Will.

Richard Pyne, who had once sailed with Hawkins, shaded

his eyes and pointed. "That looks like Drake's Revenge leading the starboard attack. That's definitely Hawkins' Victory, and there's Howard's Ark Royal."

The English fleet closed the gap to cannon range, swung broadside on and pounded the Spaniards. Hull planks splintered as English shot went home. Spanish galleons went about, and ran parallel to the English line, matching broadside for broadside, but their cannons were angled towards ships of a similar size and the shot flew high.

**

The San Salvador, along with the rest of Miguel de Oquendo's Guipuzcoan squadron blasted away at the English line, the resulting tumult making everyone's ears ring, the galleon heeling over with the force of the firepower. Diego was immediately enveloped in smoke, the smell of gunpowder making him choke, his eyes smart. He clung to a rail as the squadron wheeled smartly about, ready to reload their cannons for a second pass.

To the San Salvador's left, a Spanish ship abandoned the formation, enticing English ships to come alongside and fight hand to hand. Ignoring the offer, the English ships proceeded to circle the brave ship, pounding it with cannon shot. Diego saw a spar fall in a tangle of rigging causing marksmen, seated astride the spar, to fall screaming into the sea where they were left to drown, their shipmates too busy to rescue them. Meanwhile, Drake's squadron was sailing back and forth, pounding the lone galleon with each pass. Within a short time, the Spanish ship's foremast had been smashed, her rigging tangled by the falling spar, her sails holed like netting, while part of her forecastle showed gaping holes.

No ship, thought Diego, could take that kind of punishment and remain afloat for long. After an hour of bombardment, the Duke of Medina's San Martin, assessing that its smaller sister had suffered enough, bore down on the English ships, and Drake, coward that he was, dodged out of range, and the rescued galleon was escorted bravely back into position.

As if in revenge, the Spanish squadrons turned in formation, leaving their supply ships to sail on unescorted, and for the first time bore down on the English in an organised counter attack.

"A battle at last," Diego said with satisfaction. But the galleons were soon finding themselves no match against the English when it came to speed. Diego, watching the enemy ships heel over sharply as they turned, noted that they were much more agile. They might lack the fire power of the Spanish but with their cannons angled lower, they could blow holes in the sides of the larger, slower galleons, all the while dodging in and out of the smoke of battle like jack rabbits.

"They are like a pack of cowardly jackals attacking brave lions," Diego shouted to the wine merchant, the whole scene enveloped in horrendous noise. "Why don't they come alongside and fight like men?"

As he watched, Howard's ship dodged neatly away. The Spaniards rushed at Drake, then again at Howard. Each time the English captains literally danced their ships out of reach, staying to windward, not once willing to lock their ships together with grappling irons and engage in hand-to-hand fighting.

Diego, waving his sword about in angry defiance and with no enemy at hand to stab, heard shot whistling over his head, peppering their sails, and realised that he, who had come only to watch, might be killed without any chance to kill an Englishman in return and thus glory in the telling.

A round shot hit the deck and three sailors fell screaming with pain. A cannon ball blew a soldier's head off as he watched, a fountain of blood spraying out of the severed neck. The noise made any pretense of order a thing of the past: the flash of flame, the smell of exploding gunpowder, the stench of spilled blood, the smoke swirling around, created a hellish nightmare Diego felt he was unlikely to ever forget.

Suddenly the English fleet withdrew. Quiet settled over the scene and Diego found that he was trembling; his legs shaking so much he could hardly stand. He gripped the ship's wooden rail. The wine merchant said something to him. But Diego's ears were still ringing from the deafening noise of broadside after broadside being fired, and heard nothing but a roaring in his ears. He looked: the wine merchant had blood on his face and Diego saw a splinter of wood had torn a gash in the man's cheek.

***

Stones rattled behind Bess. The Reverend Ffermer rode into view, horse and rider sweating from the steep climb.

"I came as quickly as I could," the vicar puffed. "But the women needed comforting." He lowered himself to the ground, tucking his cassock under crossed legs. "What's happening to our gallant seamen? Have they sunk the papists yet?" He peered towards the horizon. "Is that them? They're a long way out; I can't tell one from another."

"They anchored here all night, so near we could see sailors walking the decks," Bess told him eagerly.

"The damned dogs are changing position again," yelled Will Trudgeon. "Begging your pardon, Reverend Sir."

"Don't beg my pardon. Dogs they are and damned by God they certainly will be, so you speak nothing but the truth."

From the corner of her eye, Bess could see the Reverend Ffermer eyeing the empty ale flagon. "Battles certainly give one an appetite," he murmured. "Has anyone a morsel of cheese or a piece of bread?"

"I'm afraid that's all there was," apologised Henry. "We were ill prepared."

Bess suddenly felt sorry for the old vicar. Sixty or more years to her sixteen, this was the man who, in the village school, had taught her to read and write; who'd recited psalms, rolling the words across his tongue, his eyes filled with joy as he savoured their beauty. Now, such feeling had long been replaced by a hatred of anything Catholic; his one remaining pleasure that of his stomach.

"It seems they've broken off the attack," Robert shouted.

Bess turned her gaze back to the bay. The ships were now little more than dots on the horizon.

"Looks as though they're heading up Channel, after all," said her father.

"They could still land at Torbay."

"Aye, there won't be much to stop them there."

The sky was suddenly lit by a flash of yellow.

"Storm over yonder," murmured Jep.

Thunder boomed across the bay. Way over, on the horizon, an orange glow spread its dull light on the underside of clouds.

"That was no lightning," Henry said. "'Twas more like a great explosion."

To Bess it looked as though the whole sea was afire.

"Let's pray it wasn't one of ours," said the vicar fervently.

"Amen to that," responded Richard Pyne.

***

Pain knifed through Diego's body. He opened his mouth to scream and seawater filled his lungs, choking him back to consciousness. He flailed his arms, striving to keep his head above water. The quarterdeck and poop deck, indeed the whole of the aft portion of the San Salvador seemed to have erupted in a great explosion that had lifted him high

50

into the air and dumped him into the sea. Around him were screaming men, lifeless bodies and flaming debris. Burned raw, the nerve ends in his legs shrieked a frantic message to his brain as saltwater bit into the torn flesh. "Dear Mother of God," he moaned, "where are you?"

His thrashing arm found a broken spar and his hand wrapped itself thankfully around it. Fingers brushed against torn unmoving flesh. He blinked swollen lids and found himself peering into sightless eyes that stared blankly past him. He prised the dead man's fingers loose and let the body float away.

With water-filled eyes, Diego gaped at the surrounding horror. The San Salvador was a blazing hulk, its centre deck afire, its stern ripped out by the force of the explosion. Flames leaped high into the air; sails and rigging gone in the first searing flash of heat. One mast was a pillar of fire. It burned fiercely, then toppled to crash down on the deck, sending showers of sparks hissing into the sea. Two hundred men had stood on the foredeck watching the battle; a further fifty had stood on the now non-existent stern castle. The sea around was filled with them; some alive, some in shock, the vast majority maimed or dead.

A hand grabbed at Diego's singed hair. He reached back and forced the scrabbling fingers to let go. A despairing face slid past, silently beseeching him to help. Recanting, Diego stretched for the reaching hand. Wet fingers slithered, slipped and drifted out of reach. Eyes still fixed upon his, the body slid beneath the surface. Diego sobbed. As though summoned by his compassion, the body rose again further out, but this time unmoving, floating face down.

Long boats, launched from galleons nearest the stricken San Salvador, moved among the fallen, picking up those still alive, the low viewpoint making the rescuers look very near. Diego called to them and was shocked when they didn't seem to hear. He called again, disbelievingly. The cry, so loud in his own ears, a mere plaintive bleat drowned by the shouts of those nearer and less injured.

Other men in long boats were trying to take the blazing San Salvador in tow. To the west, English ships hovered out of cannon range. And the sea, which had seemed so crowded from the San Salvador's afterdeck, was suddenly very empty.

The Armada was continuing to move steadily away. Diego watched the great fleet diminish in size as the distance increased. A rush of water and an English ship sailed past him, then another. Diego raised an arm in silent plea. Everyone on board was gazing towards the Spanish fleet. A sailor, leaning over the rail, glanced down at the floating bodies, saw Diego's raised hand and spat into the water.

Then, as quickly as they had arrived, the English ships were gone and Diego was alone.

***

Darkness had fallen, the sound of surf was near. Diego, tired beyond belief, heard the roar but could gather no more strength. A wave broke over his head and tumbled him towards the shore. His injured leg scraped against sharp shingle, sending pain rasping through his body. His fingers dug into the sand as the undertow tried to drag him back. Another wave broke behind him, lifting him gently on to land. He rolled on his back and faced the night sky, choking and spluttering for breath. Stars spun, then slowly went out as finally he slipped into unconsciousness.

5
Washed Ashore

The pain was excruciating. Beads of sweat ran down his brow. His body, beneath the burnt and tattered finery was slippery with oozing blood and perspiration. Curled up in the shallow angle formed by the bottom of the tiny fishing boat, he lay with one arm across the wooden seat, his head on his arm, feeling too sick to care whether he'd been seen climbing into the beached vessel or not. Gradually, the sickness eased, leaving him shivering with cold. The burn on his leg was weeping badly, and the slightest movement required a concentration that drained his body through the sheer exhaustion of even the slightest effort.

For two days he had managed to avoid contact with anybody in this terrible land; hiding by day, slowly edging his way westward by night. There had been two narrow escapes: one when he had stumbled over a sleeping vagrant; the other when a dog, sensing his presence, had roused the home it was guarding with barks loud enough to wake the dead. Somehow, fortune had stayed with him; no one had been roused, they either lay drunk, fast asleep, or were dead, and he had finally managed to slink away with no one the wiser. But now every inch of his body cried out for rest.

Summoning his remaining strength, he lifted his head to peer over the boat's gunwales. Two more hours, he judged, and it would be high tide. And by that time it would be dusk with the sky deepening with every minute. He prayed to the Holy Mother that the fisherman whose boat this was, having finished work for the day, would find no need to return.

The vessel lay on its side in the thick mud of the harbour bed, attached by a rope to an iron ring in the jetty wall. As much as he feared returning to the sea, any other alternative he found impossible to contemplate. His one chance lay in steadfastly making his way westward; that way he knew he could eventually reach sanctuary.

But the plain truth of the matter was he was in no condition to walk even a quarter of a mile, let alone seventy. Not only that, travelling across country, he was certain to meet with patrols. Fuzzily, he estimated that he must be somewhere near the town of Plymouth, but so far had been unable to determine on which side of the town he'd been washed up.

It was now almost dusk and the tiny cottages lining the harbour stood unlit and silent. As the tide rose, the boat slowly righted itself, and painfully he adjusted his position to each fresh angle. Then, feeling the bottom lift off the harbour bed, impatiently waited until the tide ebbed before casting off. As soon as the boat was clear of the harbour, he would try hoisting the small sail and edge the vessel into the wind. Gradually, slowly, the tiny fishing vessel began to drift seaward.

**

The Trevanions' cottage, small, originally built with but a single room on the ground floor by one of Henry's antecedents, had been extended upwards with the addition of a second storey by his grandfather. Stone built, rather than with the softer earth, clay and chalk mixture called cob and straw roofed; the window openings shuttered, without glass, and covered with greased linen to let in light. The wooden shutters, often closed at night, now stood wide open in the summer warmth, as did the door facing the lane.

The ground floor, single room's sparse furnishings consisted of an open hearth oven with a chimney to emit smoke and fumes, a table, a settle, two stools and a short row of shelves. In the corner, a ladder led to the upstairs floor; a floor divided by wood partitions and curtaining to make three room fitted with wooden cots made comfortable by the addition of straw-filled mattresses and woollen blanket covers. By fishermen's standards it was reasonably comfortable accommodation, less so in winter, necessitating the shutters to be closed to keep out wind and rain, but a good deal better than that of some villagers.

Fishing over for the day, the Trevanion family sat there wondering whether the Spaniards had landed on English soil, had brought Parma's army across the Channel from France and were now marching as a great invading force on London, or whether they were still at sea being slowly decimated by Drake and Howard's smaller but superior fleets, for despite the magnitude of the enemy force seen from the cliff tops, they sincerely believed this to be a possible assumption.

News drifted back slowly and when it did it tended to

be packed with rumour, both true and false. It was now five days following the Armada's initial sighting and the early excitement was waning fast. Bess, fancying to bring back the feeling, had a mind to visit The Dodman once again. When she said this, Henry smiled at her. "You'll not see anything from there: both fleets are two hundred or more miles further east than that."

"I know," Bess said. "But I have a notion that I'd like to rekindle the scene once more in my head before memory goes and it drifts out of reach."

"Aye, you and your imagination were always a one for that. Run along then, but don't keep us waiting for supper."

Nicholas rolled his eyes.

Before her mother could voice any misgivings on wandering alone at this momentous time, Bess was striding alone along the cliff path, her head filled with thoughts as to how she might word an account of the past eventful days. It was important, she told herself, that she not only record the facts, but recapture the mood.

A year back, she'd taken to writing a diary on scraps of paper she found and saved; for clean, virgin paper rarely came to hand. And what had begun as a daily record gradually developed into noting down her thoughts as well as happenings. At first, she'd been sensitive about it; writing by lit candle fat in the privacy of her partitioned-off bedchamber. Then, gaining confidence and feeling that the family's interest was based not on mere amusement, she had begun reading paragraphs that pleased her out loud to them. Unbeknown to Bess, her parents, far from being amused, were justly proud of her literary skill: it was rare for someone in their position to express themselves in such a way. Many fishermen could neither read nor write. But Bess's father had wisely invested in his children's education, happy to spend the sixpence a week for them to attend lessons at the vicarage. By the age of twelve, Bess had left school with a sound knowledge of reading and writing, and a growing thirst to develop the ability. But there was little for her to read: they owned no books, papers or manuscripts. The only item available to them was the bible kept chained to the pulpit in St Veryan church; and any writing she produced was simply a record of what she'd done and what she thought. It fulfilled no purpose, the family may hear her read certain passages to them, but no one had access to it other than her.

Now, crossing the sand at Porthluney, deeply immersed in thought of what to pen, Bess failed to recognise the plaintive cry, putting it down to the call of a seabird. The second mew stopped her in her tracks. Listening, it was near, no more than yards away. Then, having heard no repeat sound and about to move on, she saw a dirt stained foot slowly slide into view from between nearby rocks. No more than the toes and the turn of an ankle, but such was their condition that she felt her stomach churn. The flesh was burned raw, part blackened with soot, the foot interlaced with weeping cracks. Scrambling over rocks, she peered down at the huddled figure of a youth, little older than herself. A nerve trembled in his closed eyelids, his lips parted and the mewing sound Bess had heard just a moment before, issued forth once again.

She stared at the injured leg and, to her horror, saw that the wound spread upwards past the knee, with remnants of scorched clothing making it difficult to tell where blackened skin ended and burnt fabric began. Eyes still closed, the man mouthed words that Bess failed to grasp. She bent down and spoke softly to him: "Hold on while I fetch help."

The eyelids fluttered open; the injured man stared at her blankly; then, to Bess's alarm, his eyes filled with fear as he tried to draw himself away; his injured foot, thrusting against the sharp rocks, causing cold shivers to run up her spine.

"We've got to get that leg cleaned and the wound dressed," she said, "otherwise you'll lose it." The man gave no sign of having understood. Bess frowned, staring down at him. A stranger! She glanced at the burnt clothing: this was no wandering tinker. "Where're you from?" she asked. "You're not from these parts; I know everyone our age for miles around."

The man made no response, his features frozen in fear.

"Visiting kinfolk?" Bess pursued. "So where are you staying? Porth East? St Goran? Mevagissey?"

The man's eyes remained fixed upon her. "A girl," he said finally, and the fear slowly left his face.

"Aye, a girl. But I prefer young woman," Bess replied dryly. She looked back at the leg. "Can you walk?"

The man shook his head. "Too much hurt."

Too much hurt? Not the way someone from the West Country spoke. "Too much pain, you mean."

"Yes, too much pain."

"Can you hop?" The man stared blankly at her. Bess pointed at his good foot. "Can you hop on one leg if I help?"

"A little."

It struck Bess that 'a little' was a curious way to express the fact. She crouched down and smiled encouragingly. Definitely a stranger. "You must be from up country. How did you get here?"

The man pointed to the sea. Bess glanced at the beach. There was no sign of any boat, nor any other means of his having arrived from that direction. The injured man's eyes suddenly blazed with fervour. "I come with Miguel de Oquendo." Bess could think of no one with such a strange sounding name. "We come to claim England for King Philip," he added with fervour.

Bess stared at him. King Philip? It was a full minute before the statement registered. "You're a Catholic?" she cried. Her brow creased: that fact alone shouldn't raise such fears. A dangerous admission, yes but... Then: "No! You're a Spaniard," she said incredulously.

"Yes," the man hissed. "I am a Spaniard. Now kill me and have done with it."

Bess scrambled to her feet. The Spaniard's face paled. She stared down at him in disbelief, trying to collect her scattered thoughts, at a loss as to know what to do. A Catholic would have been different enough but a Spaniard, an enemy, here in Cornwall? She glanced round, the beach was deserted. No help there: the nearest villagers, half a mile away. She gazed down at this man who was her sworn enemy and shivered with apprehension. That, given half a chance, he would kill her without hesitation and consider it a task well done she had no doubt. It had been drilled into them enough times by the Reverend Ffermer.

"So enemy, what will you do?" The Spaniard hissed. "I am your prisoner. You will hand me over to El Draque?"

"El Draque? Who's he?" Bess asked.

"The heretic corsair who leads your miserable fleet."

"Oh, you mean Drake," Bess said.

"Yes, Drake."

"He's at sea sinking the Armada."

"He will never sink the Armada: it is invincible. It flies King Philip's flag. It has been blessed by the Holy Father."

Bess tried to think what she should do. Leave him and fetch help? But where could he stay while she went? He was too badly injured to run away. To the west of the cove was a small cave but it was shallow and wet at high tide. A fisherman's hut built above the shoreline was empty but could always be visited by someone taking shelter from a sudden rainstorm. A derelict barn on the Caerhays estate, no more than a few hundred yards from where she now stood, was unused and had been so for the past three summers. The roof half collapsed…

It was with something of a shock that Bess suddenly realised that rather than seeking a means of arresting the Spaniard, she was searching for a place where he might stay out of sight. What in God's world was she thinking of? The words were out before she could stop them: "There's an old barn, not far from here, you can stay there until morning."

Bewilderment spread across the Spaniard's face, followed by a brief flash of enlightenment. "Ah!" he said. "You are one of our Catholic helpers?"

Bess shook her head.

The bewilderment returned, this time tinged with suspicion. "Why then? Why do you not hand me to El Draque or one of his officers?"

Why indeed? So why didn't she? Bess tried to think of a reason, but couldn't. "We'll talk of that later," she said.

The Spaniard passed a hand across cracked lips. "I would like water."

"There's a stream near the barn."

"Barn? Where is this barn?"

"Just over there. Not far."

The injured Spaniard hesitated; his mouth opened, then closed. Bess could see him fighting not to tell her what he sought. Pride was finally defeated and it burst forth anyway: "I cannot walk," he said.

Bess was surprised at the effort it had cost him to ask for her help. "You can rest your weight on my shoulder," she said. She reached out a hand and pulled the Spaniard up to stand on his good leg. Looking again at his injury, she winced. Then, glancing back at the man's face, saw his teeth were clenched and a film of sweat had broken out on his brow. "Does it hurt?" she asked softly.

Pride resurfaced and the Spaniard tried to pull his hand away. "Leave me. I do not need the help of a girl," he snarled.

"Woman," Bess said and held his hand fast. "Need it or not, you're getting it, so make the most of it while you can."

Tension flowed from the Spaniard's body as quickly as it had flowed in. "You are right. I am your prisoner." He waved his free arm dramatically and nearly fell. "Do what you will."

Bess smiled at the overt reaction. "At the moment, my only concern is for your health."

A flash of shrewdness showed. "Ah, yes, I see. I am worth a fine ransom, am I not?"

Bess flushed angrily. "Your leg needs the help of a physician." The Spaniard stared at her, disbelievingly, opened his mouth to make a retort, then thought better of it. "Put your arm round my shoulder," Bess said firmly. "Now, lean your weight on me and hop on one foot."

"There is hop again. What is hop?"

"Jump up and down on your good foot."

"Ah, yes. Hop."

63

The area around the rocks was strewn with loose shale and they almost fell at the first step. But once on firm wet sand, Bess found they could move more easily. Even so, the strain on the injured Spaniard was immense and Bess could feel the man's body tremble with the effort.

The worst part was yet to come. Above the high water mark, soft sand gripped their ankles, sucking any remaining strength from the Spaniard's legs. They slithered to a halt; tears hovering on his eyelids.

"I cannot move; the land is not good."

Bess smiled. "No, the land is good, but the sand is soft. A few more yards and we shall be on firm grass."

"I am not making fun of your language; my English it is not always good."

"As a matter of fact, it is very good."

The man made no reply: he was gazing towards the firmer ground ahead. The next few yards, Bess realised, must seem like a mile. She kicked off her shoes. "Here, let me carry you on my back."

"You are a girl and not strong."

"Stop calling me a girl: I'm as strong as you. At the moment, stronger."

The Spaniard wavered, pride fighting tiredness and pain. Bess waited patiently. She saw his shoulder slowly droop and tears of frustration prickle his eyelids. Turning her back, Bess said quietly: "Put both arms round my neck and hold on tight."

Bess's back was strong from hauling in nets, even so she was glad when they reached firm ground and the man could take his own weight. For a second, the Spaniard's arms stayed round her neck, his fingers near her throat, before dropping, resignedly, onto her shoulders. Bess turned to face him.

"I could have strangled you, just like that," the Spaniard said, and tried to snap his fingers together. The fingers flicked but no sound came.

"At the moment, you couldn't strangle a rabbit," Bess told him.

The Spaniard's eyes blazed. "Do not think it will always be so." The anger lessened. "But you are right," he muttered helplessly.

The rest of the journey was easier; nevertheless, the injured man was near to collapse by the time they reached the barn, his face grey with fatigue.

"We are there?" The question emerged as a croak.

"Yes, you will be safe here until morning."

"And then?"

Bess pretended not to hear.

The far end of the barn, where the roof remained intact, was dry. Straw from the thatching had blown in, forming a soft layer over the hard packed earth. Bess helped the man sit, legs outstretched, his back against a wooden stanchion post. A full five minutes passed before the Spaniard opened his eyes.

"Why do you do this?" he asked croakily

Bess searched for an answer but could find none that made any sense. "We are the same age. You are hurt," she replied lamely. "I would do the same for anyone I found injured. Friend or foe."

The Spaniard shook his head. "What you say may be true but it is not a reason. I am your enemy. If I had found you in my country, I would kill you…" He searched for the right word. "…without pause."

"Without hesitation," Bess corrected him. "You say that now; you might well think differently should the occasion ever arise."

The Spaniard stared at her.

"My name is Bess," she said.

"Diego de Olivarez." The Spaniard gave a curt bow from his sitting position and winced as the movement sent pain shooting through his leg.

"Bess Trevanion. Where did you learn to speak English so well?"

The Spaniard smiled weakly. "My father is a merchant in Seville. Before that, he was a merchant in your Penryn. We live in Cornwall for five years when I was young."

"Our Penryn?"

"Yes."

"Is that where you were making for?"

The Spaniard glanced at her suspiciously. "Why do you ask?"

"No reason."

"I would like water," he said.

"Please is the usual way of asking."

The Spaniard looked at her, anger glinting in his eyes. "Please," he said eventually.

Bess tried to think where there was a water supply. There would be water up at the manor house; no one would build a house that large without a supply spring; but to approach there would draw attention. Was there a stream? There must be. She recalled other times she'd walked across the beach here. Yes, there had been a narrow stream running into the sea, that is if it hadn't dried up in the summer's warmth. "I'll fetch some," she said. "We must clean your leg before it becomes infected." She searched round for a container. The barn was littered with debris but nothing that would hold water. Her shoes, she thought. They weren't exactly waterproof, made of leather with wooden soles, but she had nothing else. "I'll carry the water in my shoe," she told him. Diego de Olivarez's nose wrinkled with distaste. Bess grinned. "They're clean, quite new, no more than two years old."

Diego moistened his lips with his tongue. "I would drink from them even if you had never washed your feet in your life."

"Don't worry, my feet are clean. They spend most of their time in water. I'm a fisherman."

Diego looked aghast. "Una campesina?" said in such a

67

way that Bess knew it was said with the disdain of someone used to giving orders, not listening to them. "You are a peasant?" he said finally.

"Peasant? I'm a fisherman," Bess responded proudly. "Or rather a fisher lass."

"Women do such things?"

Bess laughed. "Not many, I admit. But I do."

Bess recovered her shoes from the beach, rediscovered the stream, hurried back with the shoe filled with water, and bathed Diego's wounds with strips of cloth torn from her petticoat. The treatment was distressing. Sight of the raw flesh and the pain she imagined the cleansing must be causing, made her grit her teeth as hard as the Spaniard must be doing. Both were trembling when the task was done.

Much of the soot had been removed, but some blackened areas around the wound required more vigour than Bess was prepared to use at this point in time.

"How did it happen?" she asked shakily.

"The ship I am on, it blows up. In the afternoon, on the first day of battle. And I am thrown into the sea. I manage to hold to a piece of wood. In the night, I float to the land."

Bess recalled the explosion they had heard on the Sunday; the sea afire on the distant horizon. "Aye, we heard it. But that was five days ago, way over towards Plymouth. How did you get here?"

"I find a fishing boat."

"You stole a fisherman's boat?" Bess was shocked.

Diego's lips curled in distain. "What would you have me do? Pay for it?"

"Where is it, now?" Bess demanded.

"I hit rocks." He said uncaringly and pointed towards The Dodman. "The boat, it is broken. I crawl the rest of the way." He paused. "I wish to sleep. I am tired."

Bess looked at him: she could see utter exhaustion in his face. "Yes, rest. I'll come again tomorrow and bring food."

"And perhaps the English soldiers?"

"We'll talk of such things tomorrow." She gazed out at the bright sunlight framed by the barn door. "I must think... We must both think."

But Diego de Olivarez was already asleep: the man's breathing, shallow and fast, punctuated by soft whimpers. She turned back and gazed down at him. Five days growth of fine wispy beard covered his chin and upper lip. His skin, where it was unharmed by fire or grime, had a soft, well-cared look. Not her class of person at all. Why then, was she so hesitant to hand him over to the authorities? The man was an enemy, a Spaniard, a Catholic invader. They had nothing, absolutely nothing, in common. Perhaps if he had not spoken to her in English, she might have had less qualms; but, somehow, with language forging a link, she'd judged the man to be in need of help before it had registered who or what he was.

She picked up her shoes, walked to the barn door and gazed out to sea. In her brief life, she had gained enough experience to know it was unlikely that anyone could help her with the predicament she now found herself in. This was a decision she must make alone. Her father had openly stated his distrust of Spaniards and, according to Will Bligh, her brother, Thomas, felt the same, as did her Robert. As for the Reverend Ffermer, he'd have no hesitation in throwing every one of them into the fiery depths of hell. And, if he were to find out about this, toss Bess, for the traitor he would undoubtedly believe her to be, in after them.

Behind her, Diego de Olivarez stirred uneasily.

6
Fresh Fish

Long into the mild Cornish night Bess lay in her cot, wooden
shutters open to the world, greased linen square at the window
unpinned to let in the sea air, gazing at the moonlit square
suspended on her bedroom wall, pondering the dilemma in
which she had entangled herself, her head telling her one
thing, her heart another. The man is an enemy, hand him
over to the authorities; the man is badly injured, show some
compassion; the opposing thoughts twisting and turning
in her head like wheeling gulls as she asked herself: what
would Robert think if he knew? He'd vowed that they'd see
every Spaniard who landed in their fair land, rue the day he
was born - and here she was, harbouring one of them.

She closed her eyes to still the whirling thoughts and lost
all sense of time. Somewhere an owl hooted. Mere minutes
seemed to pass before, on once more opening her eyelids,
she found the morning sun streaming through her open
window, her father up, dressed, and standing over her cot.

"It appears that the excitement of the past few days has
caught up with us at last," he said. "'Tis a full hour past
dawn and no one's moved a muscle."

Eyes heavy with sleep, Bess mumbled her apologies.

"Don't vex yourself. I slept on as well," Henry admitted,
leaving her to dress.

Hurriedly pulling on working skirt and fish-stained

smock, she descended the ladder that gave access to their bedchambers. Bess found her father waiting below, her mother and Nicholas still upstairs in their cots. "'Tis a bright morning for all we've missed an hour of it," Henry said. "The sun's warm and the sky's clear."

Ignoring her father's idle chatter, Bess found herself wondering if the Spaniard had managed to sleep more soundly than she. If the exhaustion on his face had been anything to go by, he would still be out to the world. It was also unlikely that he'd eaten more than odd scraps of food during the past five days, so he'd be as hungry as a starving horse. However, any doubling of her own appetite would gain immediate notice. She must try and hide portions when no one was looking.

"Still, tomorrow's the Lord's Day. Perhaps we can catch up on our rest then, God and the Reverend Ffermer permitting." Bess hardly noticed her father's constant prattle. "For 'tis certain the vicar will have prepared a good long sermon to speed the Spaniards on their way."

Also warm clothing: the nights could be chilly. Her own wardrobe was hardly suitable and anything missing from Thomas's would inevitably be noticed by her mother. No, the Spaniard would have to make do with the rags he was wearing until she could find something more appropriate. She glanced up, suddenly aware of her father's look and the questioning silence.

"Well, what do you say?"

"Sorry, Father. I was dreaming. What do I say about what?"

"Why Truro, of course."

"What about Truro?"

"'Tis obvious you've not heard a word I've said. Truro… going there."

Slowly the meaning sank in. "Today?" Bess queried.

"Well, the fish won't keep till Monday. You know, I'm beginning to think your mother's right: you are thinking of a lad. Nothing else could occupy your mind so fully. She tells me it's Robert Williams. He's a good Cornish lad…"

"When did she say that?"

"Last night, when you arrived home late and failed to say a word all evening."

Bess swallowed as the guilt hit her. "No, Father, 'tis no Cornish lad."

"Well, whatever it is, it must be truly powerful to occupy you so you don't even hear me mention a trip to Truro."

"What about Jep?"

Her father sighed. "I told you. Does no one ever listen? Jep's gone down with a fever. Went sick with it yesterday. And I've said, if he's no better this morning, you and I will take the cart in. Well, I've been down to see him and, if anything, he's worse, so I've told him to stay in bed and sweat it out."

"Well let's hope he takes heed and doesn't make for the alehouse as soon as our back is turned." Bess's thought veered back to Diego de Olivarez. "What time will we be back?" she asked with concern.

"What's it matter? The day's our own. We'll be back before supper. And Jep'll not leave his bed today." Henry studied her. "It's not like you to make a remark like that."

"You're right, it was uncalled for. I don't know what made me say it."

"No, 'twas not uncalled for. It's exactly the kind of thing Jep would do if he weren't so ill. The surprise was in hearing you voice the thought."

"Well, I apologise, anyway." Her mind raced: they'd be back late afternoon; the family took supper two hours before sunset, so there'd still be time to visit the Spaniard before they ate. A journey into Truro was an event too rare to miss and refusing to go would only arouse adverse curiosity. "I was thinking more of how much time we could spend there," she said lamely.

"Now that will depend on how long it takes you to waken yourself up, breakfast, and get the cart loaded. I've asked Nicholas whether he'd like to come, as it's Saturday and no schooling, but he has other plans. It seems he and young Francis Bosawen have an urgent appointment to play at fighting Spaniards with wooden swords, down by the withy copse."

Bess had dressed in work clothes rather than clean skirt and bodice. Not at all suitable for the trip to Truro. "I must change," she announced.

"Change?"

"My clothes."

"We're fisher folk, plying our trade. You're right as you are." He grinned. "The blue of the smock matches the blue of your eyes."

She sighed. "Let me at least put on a clean bodice. There will be fine ladies shopping in Truro. I'll not let them see me looking like a vagrant."

And poor Henry could do no more than shrug and wait.

***

Their route lay through Lamorran Woods, across the head of the creek, then followed the silted-up river through Tresillian. Soon the cart's motion had Bess's head nodding. Henry said little, letting her catch up on lost sleep.

The fishermen's cooperative that he preferred calling an unofficial guild, had been Henry's idea. Previously, they had relied on traders coming to them; with fish going bad while they waited their arrival, and traders getting together to form rings where one man would bid low for the whole catch and the rest remained silent, sharing the proceeds among themselves once out of the village. At first, the so-called guild had met with violent resistance; the fish cart attacked by ruffians on the journey to Truro and the villagers having to fight them off with staves and boathooks. But eventually the traders had tired of this and the cart now travelled unmolested, allowing them to sell their harvest to the populace direct and at a greater profit. And thankful the Porthloe fishermen were, for theirs was a hard business, Henry mused while Bess nodded.

From Tresillian, the dirt road ran uphill, through more woodland, and then zigzagged down into the river valley to finally open out onto quays lining the upper reaches of the Fal. The change from a peaceful tree-lined lane to a clattering noisy town was immediate and dramatic. Pigs and cattle were being driven through the town and up the hill to the slaughterhouses. Farmers, their labourers loaded up with baskets of live chickens, dusks and geese, shouted to the populace to mind their backs. Amidst all this, Henry pulled the mule to a halt and Bess, her tiredness dropping away like a cloak from the noise of surrounding activity, climbed down from the cart and took the halter.

"Take care of the fish while I find a spot to unload," called Henry.

Bess nodded as her father dived into the teeming throng. Every time she visited Truro, she thought it the most exciting place she'd ever seen. A three-sided quay, piled with goods, stretched from the river into the busy centre. Surrounding the quay were warehouses and chandleries; the narrow streets leading off, lined with timber-framed houses that often leaned drunkenly towards each other, and built so close that people reaching out the upper windows could virtually touch hands.

The quayside was crowded with town folk and buyers and sellers from outlying villages and littered with baskets and barrels. Bess watched merchants haggling with tradesmen and women screeching at street sellers. Everyone seemed to talk twice as loud as was necessary, the grate of cartwheels and the clatter of horses hooves adding to the noise. Children and dogs scampered through the throng, cuffed and kicked where they hindered. A net maker, with flashing fingers, was hard at work nearby, and Bess marvelled at his dexterity: fisher folk in their village made their own nets but none with a speed that could match this man.

The tide was out and a dozen boats lay drunkenly in the Fal mud. On the far side of the quay, Bess glimpsed her father pointing across to where she stood. A cart rolled by, blotting him from view; when it cleared, her father had been swallowed up by the shifting crowd. She was still searching for him when he suddenly reappeared at her side. "Right, let's get this cart round there," he said.

Bess tugged at the halter and the mule moved sluggishly forward, her father shouting at people to mind their backs. Slowly they edged their way up one side of the quay and down the other.

Henry indicated a space being held for them by a couple of street urchins and tossed a halfpenny coin at the nearest. "Pull in here." Bess jerked the mule to a halt and tied the rope to a stone block. "Fresh fish," cried Henry, unloading the baskets.

Bess caught up the cry. "Fresh fish, caught in St Veryan Bay."

"How fresh is fresh?" queried an old woman.

"Unloaded yesterday. Pulled in the nets myself," replied Bess. "And kept in a cold cave overnight."

The old woman sniffed at the soles lying on top. "Don't look as though they was caught yesterday."

"Neither do you," retorted Henry. The old crone screeched with laughter. "If you don't want them, mistress, there's plenty who do."

"None caught today?" queried another potential buyer.

"Give us a chance," Henry said. "We were up at dawn to get these here."

In less than two hours, they'd sold the lot: half the load going to traders within the first half hour, the rest in half dozens to passing housewives. During that time, Bess had been too busy to think about anything other than selling their stock. Worse she'd been too occupied to even think of Robert Williams. As the last basket was emptied and Henry began unwrapping the food they'd brought with them, her thoughts slid sideways to the needs of the Spaniard and the bread and cold baked fish her father was offering her.

"Well, take it. It won't eat itself," said Henry.

Bess reached for the food, thinking there was precious little here for two people, and spent the next ten minutes hiding the bread and chewing somewhat theatrically on the fish.

"Hard work always makes a person hungry," commented Henry. "What we need is something to wash it down." He fetched a leathern pot from under the seat. "Stay with the cart and I'll fetch some ale."

Bess watched as he made his way to the end of the quay, to return five minutes later with the tankard filled. "Sup this down. I've had mine. Then we'll see what news has been posted."

The narrow streets leading from the quay to the market place were lined with workshops, their hanging signs swinging and squeaking in the strong breeze coming up the Fal valley. In the front of workshops, open to the public, tables and stalls displayed the goods made inside, while a wench or daughter stood by to entice customers to step in and inspect the wares and haggle the prices. Above these workshops were the craftsmen's domestic quarters where their families and apprentices lived.

Henry and Bess passed the town pillory where a man and a woman were locked together, taunted by passers by. The man had his ears nailed to the post; the woman roped to his side. Hurriedly, Bess averted her eyes: whatever the man had done he didn't deserve this kind of treatment.

Over the years, the Corn Market, a round timber-framed building in the town centre, used for the selling and buying of grain, had also become the centre for news and on its walls and posts were often nailed announcements that the high sheriff, mayor or town beadle felt it necessary to bring to the public's attention.

"There's a crowd here today," Henry observed as they

approached. Thirty or more men and women were huddled round a seal-embossed sheet nailed to a wooden stanchion. Bess and Henry pushed their way to the front. The notice gave the latest position of the war at sea.

"What's it say, lass?" asked an old man standing next to Bess. "I don't have no reading or writing."

"Aye, read it loud so we can all hear," called someone from the back.

Bess glanced at her father. Henry smiled reassuringly.

"'Tis a list of the ships lost in battle."

"We know what it is. Read what it's wrote," said the old man.

Bess cleared her throat. "'By the Gracious Command of Her Majesty the Queen, I am instructed to issue the following statement with regard to the attempted overthrow of her sovereign realm by an invading army sent forth by the King of Spain. In that on Sunday the twenty-ninth day of July, an invading fleet being sighted off Her Majesty's shores, Her Majesty's fleet, under the command of Admiral Lord Howard, did proceed to do battle with…'"

"What about Drake?" queried the old man.

Bess glanced quickly down the notice. "There's no mention of him."

"There must be. Drake's out there chasing them up the Channel."

"It doesn't mention anyone but Howard. '…did to do battle with the enemy forces, driving them forward into the narrow waters of the English Channel by the magnitude of their fire power. Two Spanish ships of war have now been taken, one wrecked by an explosion of gunpowder, the other in fine condition, with the loss to the enemy of two hundred lives and four hundred prisoners taken. All with no loss to Her Majesty's gallant forces. The invading fleet is now under continuous bombardment with great loss of life and damage to the enemy ships, and is being pursued at Her Majesty's command that the entire invasion fleet be destroyed forthwith. Thanks be to God who sees the rightness of our cause. Long live Her Gracious Majesty and death to all her enemies.'" Bess paused. "It's signed, Raleigh, Lord Lieutenant of Cornwall."

"You sure it doesn't mention Drake?"

"Not one word."

"You can I read, I suppose? You're not just making it up?"

"She reads well," Henry said. "And there's no mention of Drake. Why should there be? The fleet's under the command of Lord Howard."

"I sailed with Drake. No man or woman, saving one, God bless her, ever gave him orders. Howard may be Admiral of the Fleet, but it's Drake that'll tell the men what to do and beat the Spaniards."

"Raleigh never did like Drake," yelled a voice from the rear.

"Aye, that's true. And 'tis Drake that'll save us, not some

lackey from Court."

"'Tis precious little news, anyway. We already know about the papist ship that exploded, and the one captured; we heard all that the day before yesterday."

Henry explained: "The farther up the Channel they go, the longer the news'll take to reach us."

"Aye, that's true, Henry Trevanion."

Bess and Henry turned to see Will Bligh seated astride a cart laden with bulging sacks. They pushed their way through the crowd to greet him.

"Will!" cried Bess.

Will Bligh grinned down at her: "I thought I recognised that lilting Cornish accent."

Bess coloured. "They wanted me to read the notice to them."

"Aye, and well you did it, too." Bess and Henry glanced enquiringly at Will's companion. "This is Simon Pugh. Henry Trevanion and his daughter Bess: both good friends." They nodded at each other.

"What causes you to visit Truro?" asked Henry.

"Provisions for the garrison. Prices are better here than in St Mawes so our officer saves money by sending us into town,. And how are the Trevanions?"

"Well," answered Henry. "And you?"

"Well enough. Better for not having to see off fifty thousand Spaniards last Sunday."

"Aye, 'twas an anxious moment," said Henry. "And

still is for those living up the coast. Have you any word of Thomas?"

"Not a word. But never fear, he's well. We would have heard were it not so."

"That's true. Bad news was never afraid to travel. How is life at the castle?"

"Dull and tiring. But mainly dull."

"Is there any news about moving east, towards the enemy?"

"No, we'll not move from St Mawes yet awhile. No unless the Spaniards land and march westwards, which is unlikely, or sail back along the coast and attack Plymouth, which I suppose is possible."

"But also unlikely. 'Tis rare for an easterly to blow for more than a few hours this time of the year. And I'd not fancy their chances of tacking against the wind with a fleet that size."

They continued to exchange views for a quarter of an hour before separating. Will and Simon to make their way back to St Mawes by way of Tolvarne ferry; Bess and Henry back to Porthloe the way they had come.

Bess was thoughtful as they journeyed home, anxious to find out how Diego had fared. By the time they reached Treviskey, shadows had lengthened and it was late afternoon. Bess slid down from the moving cart and said, casually: "I've a mind to walk across the fields and stretch my legs."

Henry halted the mule and gazed at her. "Aye, it's been a

tiring journey."

"My bones are set; a walk will loosen them up." Bess could feel her face flushing. She tried telling herself that it was no lie - the movement of the cart had made her back and thighs ache. Her father's eyes seemed to bore right through her. Bess returned his gaze as boldly as she dare and found understanding in his look.

"If you want me to come with you, I'd consider it a trust and keep it so," he said softly.

Her heart gave a sudden lurch. What did he know? "Nay," she said. "'Tis nothing but a stiffness of the joints." She turned and climbed a stone hedge into an adjoining field. "I'll not be more than a short while."

Henry nodded and waved a hand in acknowledgement. As the cart moved forward, he turned his head and cried: "If you get hungry you can always eat some of that bread hidden in your skirt."

7
"Why Do You Do This?"

Henry's words had taken Bess by surprise. It was obvious that he suspected her of something, but what? It seemed he viewed her hiding the bread beneath her skirt with a degree of amusement but no great concern, and Bess, thinking about it, was inclined to shrug it away.

Down in the valley to the south of Polgrain, where Gabby the hermit lived, she could hear his mangy dog barking. The only other sounds were the soft hum of insects and the sweet song of a rising skylark, high above her head. The barn, when she approached, was equally peaceful. She paused. Had the Spaniard left?

"Diego," she called softly. "It's me: Bess Trevanion."

No answer.

Approaching the broken down door, she peered cautiously in: the straw where he had lain was flattened; other than that, there was no sign that the barn had ever been occupied, and the whole episode might well have been imagined.

Stepping through the open doorway, instinct made her suddenly spin on her heels. The blow struck her shoulder, missing her head by inches. She raised an arm and the second blow struck her elbow. Her assailant staggered forward and fell at her feet, his eyes filled with open hostility, sweat glistening on his forehead. "I will kill you, yet," Diego hissed.

Bess glared at him, her breathing rapid, and kicked the wooden stave from his hand. Diego screwed up his face and, for a moment, Bess thought he was about to burst into tears. "I will not be left a prisoner like a… like a common criminal."

"You're free to leave when you like. No one's stopping you," Bess said angrily. "Go now, if that's how you feel."

Diego's eyes flashed. "And I will not be spoken to like this by a peasant. I am, Diego de Olivarez, your superior; show me respect. In my country I would have you flogged."

"Then all I can say is it's fortunate we're not in your country. Here we don't flog people whose only crime is trying to help their fellow beings." Bess held her shoulder and moved it in a circle, testing whether any great harm had been done. It seemed the blow had lacked any strength, the pain settling into no more than a dull ache. Her breathing slowed.

"Next time," spat Diego, tears of rage glistening his eyes, "I will break your skull."

Bess snorted. "It would take more than a weak tap like that." She pushed the square neck of her bodice to one side: the skin was no more than grazed, a red patch showing the beginnings of a slight bruise.

Diego struggled into a sitting position. "Why do you not strike me back?" he taunted her. "Do not peasants in this awful country have any pride? Do you not realise I am your enemy? At the first opportunity I will kill you and escape this miserable island."

"Try anything like that again and I'll..." Bess paused. She'd what?

Diego sneered. "And what? What will you do? Hand me over to your army? Saying to them, 'Here is a Spaniard. I have been hiding him, but now I have changed my mind.'" He scoffed: "If that is what you think then you'd better do it now, tomorrow it will be too late."

Bess remained silent. He was right. As he was shrewdly pointing out, each passing hour made a change of heart more difficult. The time had passed when she could claim that she failed to realise what she was doing. "Perhaps, yesterday," she said finally, "if you'd spoken in Spanish, with no understanding of English, I might have acted differently. Now I don't know what to think."

"You are mad."

"Perhaps."

"Your countrymen will hate you when they find out, and hang you by the neck. Then you will be dead, and I will be alive, rescued by our victorious army. How foolish is that?" he spat.

"I don't intend that anyone shall find out."

"So, what is it you will do, tell me?"

"I don't know." The truth was she'd not thought through the consequences. "Until now, I've been more concerned with your wounds," she said. Suddenly, she remembered the bread. "Here. This is all I could get. It's not much, but it's good wholesome food. I'll try to get more, tomorrow."

Diego snatched at the food, no word of thanks, and began filling his mouth at an alarming rate. Was this the way foreigners ate? Like animals? With no manners? Watching him, Bess said, "When did you last eat?"

The answer came through a mouthful of crumbs: "Three days ago… four. I cannot remember."

"Eat it slowly or you'll choke," Bess told him.

Diego nodded, stopped stuffing his mouth and began to chew more steadily. "I would like water."

"It will have to be from my shoe again," she said. "Tomorrow, I'll try and remember to bring a flask."

"No matter."

"And don't try waylaying me again."

"Waylaying? What is waylaying?"

"Hitting me over the head."

Diego looked at her accusingly. "I wait all the time but you do not come. I thought you had gone to fetch an officer from your army."

It was with some surprise that Bess realised that she had spent a whole day in Truro, where there was a troop of militia, had even spoken to Will Bligh and Simon Pugh from St Mawes Castle, and yet the idea of handing Diego over to any of them had never once entered her head. "I had to go to Truro with my father."

Diego looked at her and said pompously: "I have been to Truro, many years ago. A dull town, grey with no colour."

Bess, about to say that it was no such thing, decided argument would be useless. The man was totally bigoted. Even worse than the Reverend Ffermer. "Stay here while I fetch water."

Diego's eyes blazed at her tone. "Do not tell me what to do."

Anger flared at his arrogance. "While you are in my care, you'll do what I say," she hissed back at him. She glanced down at his leg: the flesh was raw, oozing puss, and looked hot and inflamed. The anger quickly passed. "Sit over there," she said more gently. "I want to clean your leg… Here, let me help."

She took hold of his hand and pulled him to his feet. Together, they stumbled to the barn's far end and Diego collapsed on the pile of straw. During the next ten minutes, Bess carried back two shoes filled with water; one the Spaniard drank thirstily, the other she used to wash his leg. Refilling one of the shoes for a second time, she set it down at his side. Diego lay back on the bed of straw, his face pale, his eyes closed, sweat beading his forehead. Cleansing the wound had been a painful process for both.

"There's a notice posted up in Truro about your ship," said Bess.

Diego looked at her. "What does it say?"

"That your ship exploded and was captured, and that over two hundred people died and four hundred have been taken prisoner."

Diego snorted. "They lie. We do not have that many people on board."

"Two ships have been captured. I expect the figure is for both."

"What is the name of this other ship?"

Bess tried to remember if the notice had made mention of a name. Or had someone in the crowd shouted it out? "The Rosary. Something like that."

"Rosario?"

"Yes, that was it."

"Pedro de Valde's flagship? It is impossible."

"That was definitely the name."

"I do not believe it. It is a lie to make you think that you are winning. It is a trick, so that you will continue to fight, when you cannot win." Diego lay quiet for a moment. "What news is there of the invasion?"

"None, as far as we can tell. The latest news is that Drake is still chasing the Armada along the coast."

"We have not landed?"

"Not as far as we know. My father says the news'll take longer to get to us, the further east they sail."

Diego nodded. "I am sure if we had landed you would have heard. It must be true: we are not going to land until we have joined up with the Duke of Parma." His eyes shone, feverishly. "Together, they will make the greatest army in the world. We will be invincible. Nothing will stop us. Nothing. Not Drake, not anyone."

Bess was getting very tired of the man's arrogance. "Perhaps. Perhaps not."

"His Holiness the Pope has ordained it."

"That might be important to you, it is of little consequence to us."

Diego stared at her in astonishment and hastily crossed himself. "You do not fear God's wrath?"

"Funnily enough, we think God is on our side. What happened before the San Salvador exploded?"

Diego glanced at her, suspiciously. "Why do you want to know?"

She sighed. "Because I'm interested, that's why. No other reason. Wouldn't you want to know what happened if we'd tried to invade your country?"

"You would never succeed. We would drive you back into the sea."

Bess took a deep breath. The man was making it difficult to even like him, let alone aid him. "What happened before Sunday?" she repeated.

"We sight England on Friday morning, at dawn. What is today?"

"Saturday."

"Eight days ago?" Diego queried in surprise.

Bess nodded. "When did you leave Spain?"

"We leave La Coruna the week before." His eyes focussed on the barn's entrance as his mind recalled the scene. "Ah, what a sight," he said. "One hundred and thirty ships, all with their flags flying, drums beating and trumpets sounding. All around the harbour people are cheering and waving. It is a glorious sight. If you had seen the Armada you would know that it is invincible."

"We have seen it. Last Saturday and Sunday, when it sailed past our village."

"Then you know. Was it not terrible?"

Bess smiled. "Terrifying, not terrible."

"Yes, terrifying. Was it not so?"

"Yes, it was."

"Then why do you continue to fight? You cannot win."

"Perhaps we think differently. Let's go back to La Coruna. You sailed with flags flying. What happened then?"

"I am in the San Salvador, the second most important ship in Miguel de Oquendo's squadron. Don Miguel is a friend of our family and has arranged it personally. For one week we sail north. The wind is good. We see England. Our Admiral tells us to anchor and he holds a council of war.

"He tells us we must sail on to meet the Duke of Parma and help his army cross the sea. Many of the commanders do not agree. They wish to attack Plymouth, but the Admiral says that the King has ordered it and we must obey. Some of the commanders are angry because they know that El Draque is at Plymouth and they wish to land there and capture him."

"You'd never have trapped Drake in Plymouth. He was out of there before you'd reached St Austell Bay."

"We know that now. But we have the wind behind us and

we think that he might not be able to."

"It would take more than wind and tide to keep Drake bottled up knowing that the Armada was sailing up the Channel," Bess stated proudly.

"The man is a devil. We would rather seize him than capture the whole of England."

Bess grinned.

"Please," said Diego, "I am thirsty."

At least he'd said please. Bess passed him a shoe and watched him drink from it. "What happened after the council of war?"

Diego wiped his mouth and handed back the shoe. "We see fires burning all along the land. That is very clever. We know then that we cannot make the surprise, so we take our battle positions and make a big..." He held up his hands with the thumbs and forefingers touching, forming a triangle.

"Arrowhead?"

"Yes, that is very good, arrowhead. But we call it a... Something to do with a small moon?"

Bess frowned. "New moon? Crescent?"

"Yes, a crescent."

"We saw it. You must be good sailors to keep together like that."

"We practice many times."

"Whereabouts was the San Salvador?"

"First there are the three big ships that have both sails and many men." He moved his arms backwards and forwards to indicate rowing. "Then the most important ship of all - the San Martin, with Admiral the Duke Alonsa Perez de Guzman el Bueno Medina Sidonia on board. On each side are the battle fleet - on the right, the Duke's Portuguese squadron and on the left the Castile squadron of Diego Flores de Valdes. Behind him are all the store ships with food and gunpowder; then, at the back, the Andalusians under Pedro de Valdes and the Biscayens under Juan Martinez de Recalde. On the right, Miguel de Oquendo's squadron, in which I sail, and the Levanters under Martin de Bertendona."

Bess laughed. "That's quite a mouthful."

Diego looked at her. "You make amusement?"

She shook her head. "No, I'm not making fun. It's just that the names are long and difficult to say."

"Ah, I see, yes. A full mouth." Diego gave a weak smile. "I must remember. A full mouth, perhaps, but what magnificence. All the troops are lined up along the sides, ready to fight, the drums play, we look so brave and everyone is so excited. We are here to avenge all the insults made by your English pirates and to avenge the wicked death of Scottish Queen Mary."

"How did the San Salvador blow up?" Bess asked.

"I do not know. We are all watching the English ships that are sailing near the land when suddenly El Draque he appears behind us." He frowned: "How can a man do that unless he has the Devil with him? We wait for them to come close and fight, but they keep sailing away and just shoot

94

their cannons at us, boom, boom. Many times we try to get them to come close so that we can fight like men, but each time they will not come.

"Then Juan Martinez de Recalde in the San Juan de Portugal cannot wait any longer and he attacks the English fleet by himself. We cheer him, he is so gallant. But the English do not accept his challenge. They just shoot at him with the guns. And the San Martin has to chase them away."

Diego closed his eyes. Whether from tiredness or in an attempt to recall the event, Bess couldn't tell. She waited patiently for Diego to continue.

"Then in the afternoon, when the shooting has stopped, Pedro de Valde's Nuestra Senora del Rosario, on our left, he hits another galleon. It is an accident. We are all watching anxiously when suddenly there is a great explosion and I am in the water. I do not know how it happens. Perhaps an English cannon ball hits our gunpowder store, perhaps one of our gunners is not very careful… I do not know… I am in the water, the ship is on fire. I call out but on board people are running about trying to stop the fire and no one hears me. In the sea, there are bodies and much wreckage. The ships sail past and I hold on to a piece of wood. I can still see our brave ship burning but the other ships they pull it away and I am alone in the sea with many dead bodies." He paused. "I hold on for many hours then I hear waves splashing. I swim in the dark and find myself on your England."

He lay there with his eyes closed. Bess pictured the event

he had described. Both fell silent, each occupied with their own thoughts.

Finally, Diego said in a flat voice: "Please, I am tired."

Bess wanted to ask more questions, anxious to know every item relating to this momentous event but one look at Diego's face told her the Spaniard was exhausted. She pulled on her wet shoes.

"Yes, sleep. Tomorrow is Sunday. I will come after church and bring food and clothes."

Eyes closed, Diego nodded. "Each time I say, why do you do this?"

Bess gazed down at him. She'd asked herself the same question a hundred times throughout the previous night and there was no sensible answer that she could give him; there was none that she could even find for herself.

8
Miracles Happen

Porthluney beach was deserted. Nothing new in that. It bordered the Caerhays estate, with no hamlet or cottage, indeed no building, other than the empty fisherman's hut, within sight. Next to the beach was a field, rarely used, in which sat the barn where Diego lay; farther on, above a distant copse, she could see the roof and chimneys of the manor house. Despite the nearness of the distant roofs, Bess was satisfied she'd not find a better, more private hiding place than here.

Leaving the cliff path, Bess glanced across at the rocks where she'd first heard Diego's whimper of pain and the soft sand they had staggered across to get to the barn. She eased her shoulder where the Spaniard's blow had struck and for a brief moment wondered what in God's name she was doing here, tending an enemy of the Queen's realm; and an ungrateful one at that.

Crossing the field once again, Bess quietly circled the barn, peering cautiously through cracks in the barn's wooden sides, determined not to be caught out a second time. Diego, eyes closed, was sprawled on a heap of straw. Satisfied, she crept round to the front, making just enough noise to warn him that someone was approaching.

"Diego?" she called softly.

No answer. She paused. Was he preparing to strike her

again? No, she would have heard him limping towards the barn's entrance if he was. Nevertheless, she slipped through the doorway fast and stood there with her back against the wall. Diego was still on his straw bed, his eyes now open, watching her.

He gave her a superior smile. "This time I do not attack you. But you think I might. That is good. It shows you are afraid. And so you should be. You should all be afraid of Spain in this miserable country of yours. We are invincible. And soon you will know how much. Until then be very afraid."

Bess bridled: "What have I to be afraid of?"

"Our might, of course. You will be slaves to our command."

"Never." She walked over to where he lay and angrily tossed a bundle down at the Spaniard's side, angry at his superior, sneering tone. "There's an old smock I found lying in our fish store, a sack you can use to cover yourself at night, some bread and fish, and a leathern bottle filled with ale. It's all I could manage," she said short temperedly. Why did he continue to rile her with his arrogance? The Armada would be defeated; then they would see who was the victor and who was the vanquished.

Diego unwrapped the bundle and wrinkled his nose. "Phwaw! The fish, it smells."

"It's not the fish, it's the sack. We use it to carry crabs in."

Diego gave a shrug. "It is still welcome. The night is

98

cold." He unwrapped the food and took hold of the leathern bottle.

"You've been fortunate," said Bess. "The weather's been mild this past week."

"Yes, I remember your terrible English weather: it rains when you expect the sun to shine, and the sun shines when you expect it to rain. And, sometimes, both at the same time."

Bess smiled despite her annoyance. "Something like that." She glanced at Diego's foot: it was weeping badly and there was a worrying smell of sickness about it.

Diego pulled the wooden stopper out of the flask and drank deeply. "Ugh! What is it?" he exclaimed wryly.

"Home brewed ale," Bess replied with some surprise. The Trevanions prided themselves on their home brewed ale; it was the best for miles around.

"It is sour."

Bess picked up the bottle and sniffed the contents. "That's not sour. Our beer is bitter, but that's considered good."

Diego took the bottle. "I am not accustomed to your drink." He tilted the bottle and took another mouthful, swallowed it quickly and pulled a face.

"Don't you drink ale in Spain?" Bess asked.

"We drink wine. Sometimes with water, but mostly just wine."

"Only the rich drink wine in England. Mostly we drink ale or spring water, even those who can afford something more." Then: "Are you rich?"

"Why do you ask?" Diego queried suspiciously.

"Just interested, that's all."

Diego screwed up his eyes as though in pain. When he opened them again, Bess noticed that they were dull and lacking in sparkle. She studied the Spaniard's face; it was flushed, the skin was dry and hot looking.

"No, we are not rich," he said. "Perhaps to a fisherman we are, but there are families in Seville much richer than the Olivarez."

"You're not eating. The fish is good."

"I do not doubt it, but I am thirsty. I will eat it in a moment."

He finished the ale. Bess took the bottle and refilled it from the stream. When she returned, Diego was picking listlessly at the food.

"You are right, the fish is good," he commented, making little attempt to do more than just taste it.

"My mother baked it. She cooks well. That was her profession before she married my father," Bess said proudly. "Is your mother a good cook?"

"I do not know; she has never tried. We are not peasants," he sneered. "We have servants for that kind of thing." Diego screwed up his eyes again. "My head, it is hurting."

Despite his curt dismissal of her mother, Elizabeth, as being a peasant, Bess reached out and touched the man's brow. It was hot: he was running a fever. The Spaniard recoiled sharply from her touch.

"What are you doing?" he hissed.

Thinking, why did she bother, the man was rude, arrogant and ungrateful. Nevertheless she tried answering as civilly as possible. "I was seeing whether you have a fever."

"Do not touch me." Diego raised his hand and felt his brow. "I feel nothing."

"You're very hot."

"The day is warm."

"No warmer than yesterday."

Diego felt his brow once more. "It is no more than a head pain." He settled back on the straw and closed his eyes. For almost five minutes neither of them spoke.

Finally Bess broke the silence: "Is the smock suitable?" she asked.

Diego opened his eyes. "Suitable?" he said, glancing at it, his lip curling. "It is a peasant's garment." Bess eyes flared angrily. Diego sighed, sat up and said wearily: "I do not know. Let us find out."

Bess helped him remove the tattered remnants of his old blouse and jerkin; she could feel the softness of what had once been fine silk and velvet. No wonder he'd been dismissive of the fisherman's smock. Luckily, the man's knee length breeches, scorched at the bottom where they fastened below the knee, were still serviceable, for she had no idea where she might get another pair. Made of soft leather, they must have helped protect his leg; his burns confined mainly to

101

his calf and foot where the breeches ended and where what were once his hose began. He slipped the smock over his head and became entangled in one of the arm holes.

Bess tried not to laugh. "Move your head to the right," she said. "You're trying to put it the through the wrong hole."

Diego's head reappeared. He was red-faced and it was plain to see it had been an effort. Slowly, his face lost all colour and turned a sickly grey. Swaying, he reached out to steady himself. "Everything is turning round," he said weakly.

Instantly, Bess regretted her amusement: "Put your head between your knees," she urged. "Lower, so that the blood runs to it. Now breathe in."

Slowly, the spasm passed. In a muffled voice, Diego said: "It is better. The turning has stopped."

Bess corrected him: "Spinning. When we feel giddy, we say our head is spinning."

Diego raised his head and Bess was shocked to see how pale he looked; his face, glistening with sweat. "It was the sudden action; trying on the smock," she said. "I have had it happen to me."

"When you wear a smock?" Diego asked hoarsely.

Bess smiled. "No. Standing or sitting up too quickly, after you've been lying still."

"Never before has this happened to me."

"Sit quiet for a moment."

The Spaniard was beginning to shiver. "I feel so cold.

Before I was hot."

"It will pass. The smock looks good. Like a Cornish fisherman," she joked.

"Two days ago, I would be insulted." He paused. "Now I am not so much."

More like ten minutes ago, Bess thought. "Good," she said. "The more Cornish you look, the better. People will take less notice; they'll just think you're a stranger from another village."

Diego thought about it. "Like when you first see me, on the beach?"

Bess nodded. "Yes, I did, didn't I?"

Diego suddenly emitted a sharp gasp. "What is that?" he whispered.

Bess turned to see what had attracted his attention. "What is what?"

"Something moved. A shadow, over there."

Daylight showed through a slight gap between planks, giving a narrow glimpse of the field outside. "There's nothing," she said.

"Yes, I see something move. Someone is out there." Diego's voice dropped to a hoarse whisper. "It is the soldiers. You have brought the soldiers."

"I brought no one. There's nothing there. I'll show you." She stood and moved towards the doorway. Diego watched her leave and saw her flit past the gaps in the planking as she circled the barn. "There's no one," she said, reappearing once more in the barn entrance.

"I see you go past. It is the same. A shadow."

"Perhaps a cloud passed across the sun," Bess said.

"No. It move too quick to be a cloud."

"I've been round the barn. There's nothing there," she told him.

Diego fell silent but continued to watch gaps in the barn's walls. "I must leave soon," he said, eventually. "It is too dangerous. For me, and for you. Already you are doing too much. If anyone discovers me, you will have danger."

"You're in no fit state to go anywhere, yet."

"Yes. I must go to Penryn. Soon. Now."

This was the second time he had mentioned his intended goal. It came as no surprise, she thought. Penryn was where he'd been brought up. Bess felt her heart miss a beat and, with somewhat of a shock, realised the feeling was similar to that once experienced only by the nearness of Robert. Yes, she admitted, she'd miss this Spaniard: but was that the same as wishing he'd stay? The longer he remained here, the greater the chance of his presence being detected. "You're not strong enough to travel," she said, her voice sounding more like a plea than a statement. "When the time comes, I'll get you there. Till then you must rest."

"How will you?"

"How will I get you there?" How, indeed. "You're asking me questions I can't answer at the moment. I don't know how, but I will." She almost added: If that's what you want.

Colour was rapidly coming back to Diego's cheeks as the fever returned. "Why, Penryn?" she asked. "Do you know someone there?"

Diego looked at her. "It is better if you do not know."

"If I was going to betray you, I would have done so by now," Bess retorted.

"It is not that. It is better if you do not know, then you cannot be accused."

"I'll have to know in the end."

"No, I must go alone."

"We'll talk about it again, when you're well."

Diego once more lapsed into silence, lying back and closing his eyes. Bess sat there gazing at his face, realising for the first time how handsome he was, his face tanned by the sun to a pale shade of olive-brown, his eyes dark, almost black, or would be if his face wasn't so wracked by pain. She shook her head. Concentrate, she told herself, on what you intend, not on how he looks. The chances against getting him to St Mawes and across the Fal estuary were immense, if not impossible. She should never have said she would try. She couldn't use Lilybeth, their fishing boat, she'd be forced to 'borrow' one - and 'borrowing', however one worded it, was stealing. And the alternative of skirting the estuary, journeying by road, the long way round via Truro, would be too gruelling - not for her, but for Diego. She glanced down at his leg: it would take days, weeks, for that to heal properly. Even then it would be too weak to support him on a ten-mile hike, for that's what 'journeying round' meant. On the other hand, he couldn't stay here much longer; sooner or later someone was sure to discover his presence. She was not sure that someone hadn't already done so. Her claim that there'd been no one outside had been made more to reassure Diego. For a brief moment, she thought she'd seen a flash of movement, herself.

Diego opened his eyes. Bess thought he'd fallen asleep, but it seemed he'd also been considering the problem. "If I have a horse, I can ride to Penryn." he said.

Where would she get a horse? "We don't own a horse. We have a mule in the village, but it's used every day to take the fish cart into Truro. Anyway, I doubt you could ride with that leg. It would rub against the saddle and the horse's flanks." She grinned. "You'd have to ride side-saddle, like a woman."

"Can I not hide with the fish and travel to Truro? There must be a Catholic priest there who will help me?"

"Most Jesuit priests have been imprisoned since the conflict, and you'd do well not to rely on all Catholics being willing to risk their necks to help a foreigner: most are confined to their homes and closely watched by neighbours. In any case, there wouldn't be room on the cart; it's not that large and every inch is crammed with baskets of fish. You'd not remain hidden for more than a minute."

"Could I not hide in one of the baskets?"

"No, you're too big."

The afternoon sun, streaming through the hole in the roof and cracks in the planking, made patterns on the dirt floor.

"There are horses at Trewartha Manor, less than two miles from where we live but there'd be no chance of me getting hold of one: the Squire has a stable lad who guards and grooms them." Once again they fell silent. "There are certain to be horses here, on this estate, at Caerhays," Bess said at last.

"Where are the stables?"

"I don't know. I know where they are at Trewartha but I've never visited Caerhays."

"Caerhays?"

"This is Caerhays, where we are now."

"The stables, they will be near the house?"

Bess nodded reluctantly.

"Which way is the house?"

"That way." Bess pointed. "About a half-mile inland." Recalling the trouble they'd had getting from the beach to this barn, there was little chance of him making it that far.

Diego looked thoughtful. But said no more about it. "So, where is your village?" he eventually asked.

"About two miles down the coast from here. Possibly less," said Bess.

"East or west?"

"West. To the east lie St Goran and Mevagissey.

"What is your village like?"

"It's a fishing village, some thirty cottages set around a

cove, a valley behind and steep hills either side." Bess tried to think of more to say. She'd never been asked to describe her village before; everyone knew it. You write a diary, she told herself: think about where you live. Then realised she'd not written a word since sighting the Armada. "There's not much to say about it," she said lamely, "We earn our living from the sea; it's peaceful; nothing happens - at least, nothing before the Armada came - we work hard; life is good; my family have always lived there and I can't imagine living anywhere else. I've a brother away in the militia, guarding Plymouth; and a younger one at home."

"Does the road to Penryn go through it?"

She knew Diego was asking such questions in order to plan the journey ahead. "No," she said. "There's no road to Penryn from there. You either have to go by way of Truro, which is a long way round, or travel to St Mawes and cross the river estuary by boat."

"Estuary?"

"River mouth," explained Bess. "Penryn is on the other side."

"Ah, yes, I remember. There is a castle there."

"Yes, St Mawes Castle is this side of the river; Pendennis Castle is on the other side. Together they guard the mouth of the Fal."

Diego wrinkled his brow. Bess could see that the fever was mounting. She could even feel the heat radiating from his body and found it slightly disturbing. "Why don't you try and sleep?" she suggested.

"In a little time. First, I must know where I am. It is terrible to be lost."

"I cannot stay much longer. They'll be expecting me home."

Diego nodded. "Is the road to St Mawes far from your village?"

"No, not far. You have to go inland about two miles - through St Veryan and out to Crugsillik; you join the road there. Or you can follow the coast round to Carne, cross the beach at Pendower and pick it up at Treworlas."

Diego smiled, painfully. "Such funny names."

"No more than those you mentioned yesterday."

Diego's face dropped. "I do not mean to offend," he said stiffly. "Forgive me."

Asking forgiveness of a peasant, Bess mused, that was progress indeed.

Diego shifted position gingerly, taking care to move his foot gently. Bess glanced down at the wound.

"I don't think we should bathe it any more. It doesn't seem to be doing any good. Perhaps we should keep it dry," she said.

Diego glanced at the burn but made no comment.

"Does it hurt?" she asked.

Diego nodded. "But my head it is hurting more. It is going boom boom boom, like a cannon." He closed his eyes for a moment, then opened them again. "Is there any more news of the Armada?"

"Our vicar told us this morning that it has been defeated but no one is certain whether to believe him."

"What is a vicar?"

"A Protestant priest."

"Ah, yes."

"Our vicar hates the Spanish and Catholics so much, any news he gives us is suspect."

Diego shrugged. "All priests are the same. They have no understanding: they are always right and everyone else is wrong." Bess's face showed her astonishment. Diego looked at her. "Do you think we do not have those kind of people in our country?" he commented.

"I've never thought about it. Until recently, that is. We rarely think about Spaniards as anything other than enemies. Individuals are never considered; we know nothing about them. You are the first foreigner I have ever spoken to."

Diego smiled. "Foreigner! I have not before thought myself to be a foreigner. But you are right: it is much the same in our country."

The sun's rays had reached his injured foot. He shifted position to move the leg into the shade, and looked at Bess: "What do you think is happening?"

Bess hesitated. "I think they are still fighting in the Channel: wooden ships take a lot of sinking. Rumour has it that the biggest cannonade the world has ever seen took place on Tuesday off Portland Bill. How many ships were sunk, no one knows, but sooner or later both sides must run out of powder and shot."

"We have twenty-five store ships full of gunpowder." The pride still hovered there but the remark was much less arrogantly stated.

"The wind has been blowing from the west for more than a week. At that rate they should be somewhere off Dover."

"That is near Calais?"

"Yes."

"That is where we are to join the Duke of Parma."

"So we've heard."

"They will meet and sail across the sea and land in England."

Bess didn't answer.

"He has a hundred thousand men. When they land, nothing will stop them."

"Then Drake will have to make sure they don't land."

"That is not possible."

"Miracles happen. Even Protestants have faith."

"Faith in what? The Holy Father has blessed our venture. You think Drake is more powerful than the Bishop of Rome?"

"The Pope is just another man; the same as Drake."

Diego crossed himself. "That is heresy. The Holy Father is God on earth."

"Let's not argue; we both have our beliefs."

"But it is important. You are wrong."

Bess rose from the ground. "I must go now. I will see you tomorrow. I go fishing in the morning but I'll come in the afternoon."

"Do not worry, I have a friend to keep me company." Diego searched in the dry straw and fetched out a small cage made of twigs bound together with straw. He opened a flap in the top and took out a dormouse. It lay in the palm of his hand, looking up at them with wide eyes, its furry tail curled around his little finger. "See? This is Ferdinand. He also lives here."

"Where did you find the cage?"

"I make it," Diego said proudly. "The wood is lying on the ground."

"They're hazel twigs; used to peg down the straw thatching in the roof," Bess explained.

"Now I use them to make Ferdinand a castle."

Bess smiled. "It's a dormouse. Some children keep them as pets; they're good company, very friendly."

"Yes, he is my friend." Diego looked up and stared at Bess closely. "Perhaps you are also a friend. But I am not sure."

Bess felt a sudden surge of pleasure. She smiled and made her way to the door. "I'll see you tomorrow. Look after Ferdinand."

"Goodbye."

"Not goodbye. We say 'keep well' or 'fare you well'. Goodbye is only used when we are going away for a long time."

Diego nodded. "Then keep well, and thank you for your help."

"Keep well," said Bess, and looked back at him and grinned. "The smock looks very fashionable."

But as Bess passed through the barn doorway, she failed to hear him repeat the whispered "Goodbye."

9

Trouble

If anything, Jep Trist's condition had worsened and Henry feared he might have caught the plague; but, as there had been no outbreak in that part of Cornwall for thirty years or more, it was difficult for him to be sure. Jep was not only suffering from severe stomach pains but was experiencing a high temperature that refused to go down; and, other than keeping him warm when he was shivering, cooling him down when he was sweating, and feeding him broth when he was not retching, there was little more that his wife, Kate, could do.

Henry was visiting him at this moment and it was with a certain uneasiness that Bess, Nicholas and Elizabeth sat in their kitchen awaiting his news.

"How is he?" asked Elizabeth anxiously, the moment her husband stepped through the door.

Henry shook rain out of his hair and hung up a wet looking cloak. "No better, but then he can't get much worse," he said. "Kate wouldn't let me near him and spoke to me out of the top window. She's with him day and night and looks tired to death, poor soul. Let's hope she doesn't go down with it as well. The children are staying with Will and Alice Trudgeon till it's done with one way or the other." Henry's chest rose as he took a deep intake of breath. He'd known Jep all his life. "'Tis a sad business, that's for sure."

"Will he get better?" asked Nicholas.

"If what we believe to be the case is true, then I doubt it," replied Henry. "Though it's been known, they say."

"Is there anything we can do?" asked Bess.

"No, Kate can just about manage, and we need to cut down the chance of it spreading."

"We can bake food and leave it outside on the step," Elizabeth suggested.

"Aye, there's no harm in that."

"Does this mean we'll be going into Truro again tomorrow?" Bess queried anxiously.

"No, Will Trudgeon is taking the cart in. He's taken Jep's sickness badly." Will Trudgeon ran the ale house where Jep had been a regular customer - too regular some thought.

Henry helped himself to cold rabbit that he and Nicholas had snared up on The Jacka and Elizabeth had roasted for their supper the previous evening. He paused, a rabbit leg halfway to his mouth.

"I can remember when he and Will both courted Kate at the same time: one, one day; the other, the next." He smiled. "The dance she led them. Till the day of the wedding, I don't think either of them was quite certain which one she'd marry."

Bess smiled. "I'd not expect my choice to stand for that."

"Then you've a lot to learn, daughter," said Elizabeth. "You'll be surprised what they'll stand for. Love is forever blind when it wants to be." She began clearing dishes from the table. "Come on, you can't sit here all day; time you were out in the bay and Nicholas was off to school."

"It's pouring with rain, woman. We can't go out in this."

"Well, you're not stopping here. A little drizzle never hurt anyone."

Bess peered out the window: it was coming down in bucketfuls. Henry's face dropped. About to argue the point, he thought better of it and sighed. "We'll mend pots until the weather breaks." Bess glanced at the flat grey sky; there seemed little chance of that awhile, the heavens were full of it.

Fortunately, within the hour the sky had cleared, the sun shone and rocks around the cove steamed in the warm humid air.

They stayed out in the bay until noon; then, on the way in, with a breeze filling the sail and Lilybeth rippling through the water, Henry said: "Old Gabby, at Polgrain, how is he? It must be him you visit: there's no one else over that way in need of left off clothing and stale bread."

Bess's mind raced. The suddenness of Henry's comment regarding the hermit had left her tongue-tied. She wanted neither to lie, nor tell her father the truth. "Gabby?" she replied. "Oh, he keeps himself to himself. If it weren't for the dog barking, no one would know he was there."

"Aye, that's true. Well, no one needs help more. You'll be the first to get near enough to speak with him for years. He's like a frightened deer, shying off at the first sign of

116

humans." Bess remained quiet. "If he needs anything more, let me know and we'll see what can be arranged."

Bess flushed. She had no wish to deceive her father: it was he who had jumped to this conclusion. But she still felt embarrassed about not telling him he was misled in what he was thinking.

"You know," her father continued, "there are people who think Gabby to be some kind of sorcerer. Not true: it's just that he prefers his own company." Henry reconsidered while adjusting the sail a mite. "And that's not even true: misguidedly, he believes he's destined to avoid his fellowmen - more's the pity - due to his reckless past."

Bess knew the story. Twenty or more years back and only a week into his marriage, Gabby, who thought himself a swordsman, fooling around with his new wife and pretending to lunge at her did so at the same time she stepped forward to embrace him. The sword passed straight through her heart, killing her on the spot.

Bess remained quiet. Her father made no further mention of the subject and, having unloaded the catch and eaten a midday meal, Bess set off once more for Caerhays, passing Polgrain and Gabby's barking dog and reflecting on her father's words and the hermit who lived in isolation there.

The barn was silent when she arrived. She stepped inside to find the straw empty. Arm raised, she whirled, expecting to feel the thud of a wooden stave.

"Diego?" she queried. The name hung in the air. Slowly

she lowered her arm, her eyes searching the shadows. The barn was deserted. Bess lowered the sack of food and walked over to the straw pile. The dormouse lay on the ground, dead; the remains of the broken cage lying next to it. She glanced round: tiny spots of blood dotted the dirt floor. Bess bent down and touched them: they were dry.

Outside, the wet grass showed tracks leading north. She paused, recalling their conversation of the previous day, trying to judge where Diego might have gone, knowing full well which direction, just hoping he hadn't risked everything through sheer impetuosity.

She ran across the field where the barn stood and climbed a stone hedge on the far side. Ahead, lay a copse. Above the tree's tops, the slate roofs of outbuildings belonging to the manor house showed; between the copse and the stone hedge, rippled a field of barley, ready for cutting. She searched for signs of flattened stalks where a body might have crawled, but could see nothing larger than a narrow run made by a rabbit or wildcat. Climbing down, she circled the barley field.

"Diego? It's me," she called.

Nothing stirred. Standing there, her eyes searching the landscape in vain, the copse appeared larger than she had first thought.

"Diego?" she called softly.

Through trees on the far side she could glimpse sunlight and stone built walls with slated roofs. A bramble clung to her skirt and dragged at the cloth. She bent down and released it.

"Diego?" she repeated, her voice raised slightly louder.

The name echoed through the small wood and, for a moment, Bess thought she heard an answering cry. Stealthily, she made her way forward, keeping an eye out for traps set among low growth and fallen leaves. The slate roofs ahead she knew would have attracted Diego's attention; the possibility of finding stables there, drawing him like a moth to a candle. She reached the far side of the copse. Fifty paces of rough grass separated her from a stone wall and it was obvious that she was looking at the windowless rear of buildings set round an inner yard. Let into the wall to her right, was an oak door. Bess studied the grass but once again could see no tracks.

She ran forward on tiptoe, pressed herself against the stonework and listened: sounds of someone working drifted out. She glanced down: a gap showed beneath the closed door. Lying full length on the grass, she squinted under the lower edge. Across a cobbled yard, two farm workers were mucking out a stall. Stables and a wall surrounded the yard on three sides, the fourth side fronted a sanded pathway; beyond that lay a well-tended lawn with yew trees that had been trimmed into various shapes. She wondered whether Diego had lain here, as she was doing, felt a cold nervousness at the thought and was about to get to her feet again when a foot stamped hard on the back of her neck, grinding her face into the ground.

"Steal the master's harness, would you?" a rough voice growled. "We'll see you hang for that."

Bess, her face flattened, found herself pinned firmly to the ground. Above, a latch turned and the door swung inwards. Out of the corner of one eye, she could see the two farmworkers turn to face them.

"Fetch the master, Will," cried the rough voice. "Tell 'im I caught the thief who'm been stealin' his harness."

"I've never stolen anything in my life," Bess retorted. She could hear whoever Will was, running up the sanded path towards the house.

"Hold your tongue, thief."

Bess's cheekbone was beginning to ache from the pressure; her neck felt as though it had been kicked by a mule. A few moments later, she heard Will return.

"The master says to hold her here. He'll be along directly."

"Oh, I'll do that, make no mistake," the voice growled.

Five minutes passed and Bess heard the sound of boots crunching on the path. They stopped a few feet from where she lay.

"Let her up."

Bess sat up, rubbing her neck. A tall bearded man, dressed in a silken shirt and velvet doublet, towered over her. Next to him stood a ginger-haired gamekeeper dressed in rough leather breeches that stank of poor tanning.

"Steal my harness, would you," hissed the tall man,

uncoiling a horsewhip. The gamekeeper grinned expectantly.

"No, sir, I would not. I've not stolen anything," cried Bess.

"My man here caught you at it."

"Begging your pardon, sir, that's not true. I was watching your men at work, from under the gate."

The man hesitated and turned to the gamekeeper. "You said she was the one who took the harness."

"She was here, sir, spying out the land. Come back to take the rest, of that I'm sure."

The man turned back to Bess. "So, you scoundrel, what were you doing spying if it wasn't to steal something?"

"I was curious to see what it was like. The house and grounds, I mean."

"You'll not believe that, sir," leered the gamekeeper.

"Don't tell me what to believe or you'll get a stripe across your own back," the man said and the gamekeeper lapsed into sulky silence. "Stand up. What's your name and where are you from?"

Bess rose to her feet. "Bess Trevanion, sir."

"'Tis true," cried a voice to the right of Bess. "She be Henry Trevanion's daughter from over at Porthloe."

Bess turned her head and recognised the farmworker who'd spoken as Will Horsewell, betrothed a year or more to Jane Lovell in the village. She nodded her thanks and turned back to face her captor. The man lowered his arm and said: "Do you know who I am?"

"Yes, sir. You're Sir Hugh Fitzwilliam. My father has pointed you out to me."

The hardness in the man's eyes lessened. "I know your father; he's a good man. Too good to deserve a daughter who steals another man's harness."

"I'm no thief and, with the greatest respect, sir, I'll have no one call me one," Bess replied angrily.

"Hold your tongue," snarled the gamekeeper. "You'll not talk so freely when the master lays his whip across your back."

Sir Hugh rounded on him. "I told you to keep quiet." He turned back to Bess. "What are you doing here?"

"Sir, I was doing no harm. Simply lying on the grass looking under the gate."

"Why would someone do that if it wasn't to commit a misdeed?"

Bess hesitated. "It was pure curiosity. Nothing more."

"Curiosity can kill a cat."

"If you please, sir," called Will Horsewell. "I'd like to say somethin'."

Sir Hugh nodded.

"She's a strange lass, for sure, but she's no thief. She spends her time, when she's not out fishin' with her father, watchin' things and writin' down words about 'em."

Bess stared at Will in surprise. She had no idea that her interest was that known outside of the family.

"What kind of words?"

"Readin' words," said Will.

Sir Hugh pondered the information. "Do you know anything about the harness that was stolen from here this morning?" he asked. Bess shook her head but guessed that it was Diego's doing. Sir Hugh's eyes bored into her. "If I find you've been lying to me I'll tan the hide off your back."

"I've not seen nor touched any harness, sir. I was out fishing with my father all morning and hadn't been here more than a few moments before I was jumped on by this man."

"Jeremiah did no more than his duty. That's what he's paid for."

"I'm not laying complaints against him, sir. It's just that he has uncommonly powerful feet."

Sir High's mouth twitched. "Aye, he has that. And his temper's no less potent. But, for all that, he's a sound man."

"I still think she was after stealin' something, sir," said Jeremiah, his voice still edged with malice.

"Perhaps. But somehow I think not."

"Thank you, sir," said Bess.

"You'll not thank me if I find you've been lying." He gazed pensively at Bess, then turned to Will. "Take her up to the kitchens, get her something to eat, and make sure she stays there. Saddle up a horse; I have a mind to speak with her father and find out more about this sickness in their village." He looked keenly at Bess and tapped his thigh with the whip. "I don't usually measure people wrongly. Let's hope I haven't done so this time."

Will took Bess by the arm and, with a gentle push, propelled her up the path towards the house.

Bess was surprised how big the building was; by far the biggest building she had ever seen, with enough rooms to house her whole village. Large, glassed, mullioned windows, set in granite walls, looked out on smooth lawns bounded by yew trees. Above the pillared porch, Sir Hugh's family crest was cut into the stone lintel. Below, either side of the entrance, carved granite beasts guarded the large oak door. One end of the building was covered in thick creeper, making it look like a wall of green leaves. High above the greenery, the gable end was wood-framed, similar to houses Bess had seen in Truro.

"'Tis a rare sight," said Will proudly. "They say the house is two hundred years old. That bit's new," he added, pointing up at the wooden framework. "Sir Hugh had that done two year ago, when one of the chimneys on the weather wall crumbled."

Bess gazed up, counting. "How many fireplaces do they have?" she asked in wonder. In more than a dozen different places, the roof sprouted clusters of chimneys on carved brick stacks.

"I don't know. I've only been in the kitchens. But you can see a huge fireplace in the hall when the main door's open where they burn logs bigger than a man in the winter. I know 'cause 'Arry and me have to cut 'em."

"Who's Harry?"

"'Arry's the man I was workin' with when Jeremiah caught you spyin' on us."

"I wasn't spying on you, Will. I was just looking."

"Were you goin' to write words about us?" Will asked, a touch of pride was laced with curiosity.

"Perhaps." Bess hadn't written anything for days now. Diego took up all her time.

They entered a courtyard at the rear of the house and passed through a stone flagged scullery. In the centre, a well stood open; above it, hung a wooden bucket suspended by a rope from a beam in the ceiling.

The kitchen was bigger than the Trevanion's whole cottage. Iron cooking pots hung on whitewashed walls. Next to an open fire with a spit, stood a giant brick oven. In the centre of the room was a long table at which a middle aged woman and two young girls, no more than twelve years of age, stood preparing food.

"The master says to give this lass somethin' to eat, and we're to stay here till he gets back," Will told her.

The woman glared at them, studied their feet and sniffed noisily. "Are your boots clean? We've just put down fresh straw."

Bess looked down. "They seem to be clean, mistress, but if you want, I'll take them off."

"If I wanted you to take them off, I'd say so." She indicated Will. "It's him I'm concerned with: I can smell muckraking on him." Will looked down at his soiled boots. "It doesn't matter," scolded the woman. "You're in now and it's too late to do anything about it." She pointed at a stool set by the table. "Sit there and don't move. You, Will Horsewell, stay where you are. Jane cut her a piece of cheese." One of the girls bobbed, hurried over to a cupboard and proceeded to cut a wedge from a large round of cheese. "Not the good side," shouted the woman. "Take it from the side that's going mouldy."

The cheese was hardly speckled at all and good tasting. With it, Bess was given a piece of barley bread and a cup of well water that was sparkling clear. Poor Will was offered nothing, despite pointed remarks on how good it all looked.

Sir Hugh strode into the kitchen an hour later. "Off with you. Your father tells me you're no thief." He stared at Bess, curiously. "He admits you're a mite strange and dreamy at times, for a fisher lass, but vouches that you'd not touch another man's property, and I take his word."

Bess rose from the table. "Thank you, sir."

"I'd like to see some of this writing you do."

"It's only for my own amusement. I think you'd find it rather dull and poorly executed."

"I'll be the judge of that. You speak well, there's no reason why you shouldn't write well. Your father says that it's about things you see and thoughts you have." Bess nodded. She'd never really thought much about what she did, but that seemed a fair description. "Paper's not cheap.

Where do you get it from?"

"I save the little I earn and use scraps that come to hand. Sometimes the Reverend Ffermer gives me a sheet."

"Come over, show me what you have written and I'll find a few sheets for you."

"Thank you, sir."

"Off with you, then."

Bess thanked the servants and nodded at Will.

"Jeremiah's waiting outside," said Sir Hugh. "He'll see you to the courtyard gate. You can cut through the copse and back the way you came."

Jeremiah glared at Bess when she joined him, then strode angrily ahead towards the stable block. Reaching the door in the courtyard wall, he turned, his voice hoarse with resentment. "Remember this and remember it well, fisher girl. I look after the grounds round here, not Sir Hugh. So keep off my land. Otherwise you'll find yourself with a mantrap round your ankle."

10
A Tiring Day

Bess was halfway through the wooded copse when she heard the plaintive cry - a soft call, full of pain and anguish, coming from the middle of a dense mass of ferns. Her heart missed a beat. She halted and glanced quickly round. With no sign of the gamekeeper following her, she switched her gaze to the courtyard door but it was too distant and obscured by trees for her to see whether it was open or closed. The call, repeated, drew her eyes back to the ferns, the sound little more than a hoarse whisper.

"Bess, I am here."

Keeping her voice low, she replied with a soft, "Diego?"

"Help me, Bess. Help me," he sobbed.

There was a heart-rending sense of hopelessness and despair in the cry. Mindless of any traps, Bess hoisted her skirt and bounded through the ferns. Diego was lying on the ground, sprawled against the trunk of a tree; clasped in his hand, the missing harness that had resulted in Bess meeting with so much trouble. The Spaniard's face, flushed bright red with fever, was turned towards her; eyes dull from exhaustion, his lips cracked and dry. She glanced down: caught around Diego's injured foot was a rabbit snare. Trying to pull it free, the leather thong had bitten into the raw flesh making it bleed and ooze puss. Any annoyance she'd felt at his having caused her to fall foul of Sir Hugh and Jeremiah quickly evaporated as she bent down, loosened the noose, and gently eased the snare away.

"I try to get free, but I am too tired," said Diego tearfully.

"It's off now," Bess said softly. "Come, I'll help you back to the barn."

"Then I see you through the trees." His hand grasped Bess's arm, his fingers digging into the flesh. "Help me get a horse, Bess." He held up the bridle and reins. "See? I have the harness. I can ride without a saddle."

"You can't ride; I've told you, you're too weak with fever," Bess told him gently. "You'd simply fall off."

Tears sprang into his eyes. "I must. I must," he choked.

"Let me help you back to the barn," she repeated. "I promise I'll get you to Penryn the moment you're well."

Frustratedly, Diego waved his hand in the air. "The stables, they are just over there."

"I know where the stables are, but I will not help you steal from Sir Hugh. We'll get to Penryn without that."

Petulance crept into his voice. "Why will you not help me? Why do you keep me a prisoner? You are cruel. My father he says all English people are cruel." His voice changed to a childish plea. "Please, Bess, help me. I am rich. I will send you much gold."

Inside, Bess felt her earlier annoyance turn to anger at the thought that she might be bought. "Go get your horse, then," she hissed. "But do not expect me to help. If you take it, you go alone." She dropped her voice to a whisper: "Steal a horse from Sir Hugh and you'll not stay free for more than a few moments. They've already found the harness is missing and are watching for you this very minute."

"How do they know it is me?" Diego asked frantically. "They do not know I am here. You have told them?"

"I told them nothing. I was looking for you and they caught me near the stables. Sir Hugh's gamekeeper jumped on me. They thought I'd taken the harness and was returning for the saddle. I had a hard task persuading them I knew nothing about it."

Diego's voice broke. "I am sorry. I do not mean to cause you trouble." He began to cry in soft stifled sobs. "Ferdinand is dead. I break his cage with my hand. Everyone I meet is hurt. I wish I had never come on this dreadful Armada. Better if the explosion had killed me like the others."

Bess felt his pleas tug at her heart. "Hush, someone will hear you," she said softly. "Come, leave the harness by the tree, the gamekeeper will find it when he comes looking to see what his snares have caught." Bess placed her arm round Diego's shoulders, half expecting him to draw away, but the Spaniard lay against her, quietly. "We'll get to Penryn. I'll find a way: trust me." Bess found her pulse racing at the feel of Diego's body pressed close to hers. Inside her head, an image of Robert, his face saddened by what he was seeing, reared up accusingly. Diego's hurt, thought Bess. It is sympathy, nothing more. Sympathy for another human being, nothing to do with whether he's friend or foe, nothing to do with romantic notions of love, the word 'love' springing into her thoughts without any bidding. She thrust it quickly aside: emotion was taking over her mind.

Diego's hand opened and the harness fell to the ground. Bess picked it up and lay it near the tree. "Come, I'll help you back to the barn."

***

It was late when Bess finally arrived home, supper long past. Getting Diego back to the barn had taken longer than she would have thought possible. The strain was such that there were times when she wondered whether they would ever reach it. Diego's hobbling was painfully slow, the day's effort had drained him of every last remaining ounce of strength. And by the time they reached the barn, Bess was as exhausted as the person she was supporting. Wearily, she removed Ferdinand's remains, made Diego as comfortable as possible, and hurried home.

Her father was sitting outside in the late evening sun, waiting for her. Bess had quite expected him to be angry at the trouble she'd caused, but other than mention that Sir Hugh had visited them, and that Bess's curiosity and writings could no longer be considered virtues if they entailed trespassing on other people's property, he hardly acknowledged the event.

Bess apologised, but her father said no more but sat, unmoving, for so long that Bess was forced to ask if he was feeling unwell.

"Nay, Bess, lass. Just tired and sad." He studied her searchingly.

"What is it?"

"Oh, nothing. I was just wondering what it must be like to be sixteen again and free from worldly worries."

Bess looked at him in some surprise. She'd never before considered her life to be free of care and her expression must have shown it for Henry smiled.

"Aye, I know. There was never a parent yet who understood their child. I probably felt the same at your age." He sighed. "Your mother's inside, best tell her you're home and get some supper."

"I've eaten at Sir Hugh's. He told the kitchen wenches to give me food while he paid you a visit."

Her father nodded, absently, then said: "Jep died this afternoon."

Bess was shocked. Although the news came as no real surprise, the announcement was unexpected and she didn't know what to say. Somehow, it was hard to imagine the village without Jep.

"Kate's laying him out now. She won't let any of the women help, which I suppose is as well, but it doesn't seem right, somehow. Forty years living with your neighbour, then no one to help carry out the final rites. It's as though we're all failing to pay him the respect he's due. The Reverend Ffermer's been down and the funeral's on Wednesday. The quicker he's buried now, the better." Henry wiped a hand across his face. "Walter Trengrove's making the box. This time tomorrow, he'll be nailed down tight and that's the last this world will see of Jep Trist."

"How's Mistress Trist?"

"Kate? So far she's not gone down with it but ask again on Friday. If she hasn't caught it by then she should be free, the children can go back and she can start building up her life again. What kind of life it will be with no man about the house is hard to say, but we'll see she doesn't want. If it hadn't been for her selflessness over the past days, half the village might have caught it by now."

"No one else is feeling sick?"

"Not so far." Henry touched the wooden door post. "Let's hope God spares us."

"Amen to that," Bess said gravely.

Her father's face cleared. "Still, there's little point in sitting here mooning. Tell me about Sir Hugh and the manor house. Is it as grand as ever?"

"Why? Have you been inside?"

"Aye, years ago, when Sir Hugh married. All the villagers sent members to wish the pair health and happiness. Richard Pyne and I went from here. Sir Hugh invited us into the big hall and gave us all wine. I remember because it's the only time I've ever tasted it."

"What's it like?"

"Wine or the big hall?"

Bess smiled. "Both."

"Well, wine is sweet, not honeysweet like mead, and tastes of berries. Can't say I was much taken with it as something to quench a thirst. Doesn't compare with good ale or cider."

"And the big hall? Will Horsewell says there's a fireplace there where they burn logs bigger than a man."

"Ah, I'd forgotten that Will works for Sir Hugh."

"He spoke up for me."

"Did he, now. I must remember to thank him for that."

"Well, what's it like?"

"What, the hall? Well there's no doubting that it's big: bigger than our entire cottage, with carved wood round the walls, just like St Veryan church, and the ceiling all covered in plaster roses…" Henry screwed up his eyes as he recalled the event. "Aye, I remember the fireplace: a huge great hearth, big enough to stand up in, with stone seats built inside and Sir Hugh's motto carved into the mantle. A fire was alight even then, and that was the middle of summer. 'Twas a glorious sight."

"What about the rest of the house?"

"We didn't see more. Just had our wine and left." Bess sat on the ground next to her father, imagining the wedding that had taken place in the big manor house before she was born. After a while, Henry asked: "What happened this afternoon? What were you doing on Sir Hugh's land?"

"Just looking. Suddenly his gamekeeper, Jeremiah, grabbed hold of me, sent Will off for Sir Hugh and accused me of stealing a harness."

"Jeremiah's not a man to trifle with. He bears a grudge for a long time."

"I did no harm. There's no reason for him to spite me."

"What are the kitchens like? Big, I'll be bound, and filled with servants."

"Huge," replied Bess. "There were three servants just to prepare supper." She proceeded to tell him about the cheese and what the woman in charge had said about taking it from the mouldy side.

Her father laughed. "That'd be Ann Trewennick. She's been with Sir Hugh since the wedding. Must be nigh on twenty years now. I'll allow she's a mite frightening, but her bark's worse than her bite."

"They were all kind, except for Jeremiah. Sir Hugh promised to provide me with paper."

"Aye, he showed great interest in a fisher lass writing - astonishment, even. Many fishermen can't even write their names. Said he'd like to read some of it."

Bess wasn't sure that this was a good idea. So far, only the family had heard her speak some of the words; no one had actually read them.

Henry rose to his feet and yawned. "Time we were all abed. It's been a tiring day." He glanced at Bess. "I expect that's true for both of us. There's another one tomorrow. The days seem to get heavier and heavier, lately."

Bess gazed at her father. Jep's death had touched him

deeply.

***

Lying in bed, Bess wondered where all this was leading. What would happen when she got Diego to Penryn? Would she ever get him there? What would happen if he were to die before then? She thrust that thought roughly aside. It was up to her to see that he didn't. Jep's death was making her mournful. If Diego's plan on finding himself washed ashore in England had been to get to Penryn port he must know someone who would take him off her hands.

The thought was unsettling. Did she want him taken off her hands? He was more to her than a mere bundle of washing to be passed on from one person to the next. But what other alternative was there? He'd entered her life and now she was unsure that she ever wanted him to leave. Is that what love was like? Love! She chided herself for thinking such thoughts. What she was doing was charity. Her reward would come in heaven.

11
Only If They Find Out

Porthloe was unusually quiet the following morning. Death was no stranger, the village having suffered outbreaks of disease a number of times in the past, from typhus to cholera; measles, diphtheria, chicken pox and smallpox all having taken their toll of both young and old during Bess's short life span alone; but never to her recollection the dreaded black death or plague.

But Jep's death was somehow different, she mused sadly. He'd been much loved for his befuddled thinking - often as a result of too much ale - and for his unexpected aptitudes. There were few children in the village who, at one time or another, hadn't received a toy boat, withy cradle or spinning top crafted by Jep's skilled hands.

Bess, though, would always remember him as dancing up and down on the cobbled hard at the harbour mouth, shouting, 'They be coming this time, for sure'. Was that only ten days ago, she asked herself? Ten days for a man, filled with life, to become sick, then die, soon to be buried and never to be seen again? If his passing was felt this deeply by the villagers, how much more must he be missed by Kate and their two children?

Nicholas came to the cottage door and sat on the low wall beside her. "What are you gazing at?" he asked curiously.

She opened her eyes, "Gazing? My eyes were closed."

It wasn't often he took the trouble to ask her what she was doing or what she might be thinking. As brother and sister, they were close but not that close. She looked at him trying to deduce what might have caused this sudden companionship. Boredom? Jep's death?

"Just thinking," she said.

Nicholas snorted, "More like daydreaming."

Bess smiled. "Aye, daydreaming. It seems, so they tell me, that I have a reputation for it, so I must fulfill expectations." She turned her head and looked at him. "Not exactly true: if you must know, I was thinking about Jep and Kate Trist."

Nicholas shrugged, reached down, plucked a grass stalk, stuck it in his mouth and chewed the end. "'Tis sad, but there's naught anyone can do to bring him back, they tell me."

"A manly approach," Bess said, "but true none the less. Poor Kate must make the best of it, as we all must."

He spat the grass stalk out and chose a fresh one. "Father says it's not always easy to think like that but it's God's purpose and we must try."

"Women are practical creatures, Nicholas. Don't fret yourself: with our help Kate Trist will manage." She closed her eyes once again, head thrown back, soaking in the warmth of the sun.

Nicholas sighed and said: "Men, women, love. I know nothing of such things."

Bess laughed. "And neither should you at your age."

"Next year I enter my teens. Isn't that the start of it all, they say?"

"Thirteen? I hope not."

"You're no more than three years older and you have feelings for Robert Williams."

Bess's eyes flicked open, her face flushed. The subject of much past teasing, she was surprised that he should take what sensibility she showed this seriously. The truth was, she hadn't thought of Robert for days. Not true, she told herself: she'd more than once experienced feelings of guilt. "What difference does it make to you what my sentiments are?" she said.

"None. Unless they're for the man in the barn."

Bess's heart missed a beat. "So it was you outside the other day," she said quietly.

Nicholas nodded. "So who is he? And why is it such a secret?"

Bess did not know whether to be angry or worried at this intrusion. "You followed me," she said.

"I was curious. You kept disappearing. So who is he?" he repeated.

"He's no one; just a man who's hurt and needs rest."

"Where's he from? He's not from round here, that I do know."

"From up country."

"Where up country?" Nicholas persisted.

"Nowhere special; just up country," Bess replied lamely.

"As soon as he's well he'll move on."

Nicholas frowned. "So, why is he hiding in that old barn? Why doesn't he stay in the village? Then we could help."

Bess thought furiously. "He's too ragged and unkempt for the village."

Nicholas laughed scornfully. "Too ragged for Will Trudgeon's ale house? I doubt that."

"He has no money."

"What is he, then? A wandering tinker?"

"No, just sick. He's hurt his leg and cannot walk. As soon as it's better, he'll be away."

"Vagrants have come through here before and you've not lifted a finger to help them," Nicholas said, his eyes on hers. "Why is this one different?"

"I found him on the beach at Porthluney. He was injured, unable to walk. The barn was the nearest place."

Nicholas's expression stated clearly that he didn't believe her. That she was being spare with her rendition. Porthluney was an isolated beach, far from anywhere. No one would travel that way without a reason.

Bess said: "It's true. I found him on the sands, among the rocks."

"When?"

"Last Friday."

"How did he get there, if he can't walk? There's no road nearer than two miles from Porthluney, and that's little more than a track."

"He was washed up by the sea. I'll answer no more questions." Bess stood up.

Nicholas grabbed her arm. "Shipwrecked?" he persisted, his eyes wide at the thought.

"No... Yes... His boat was smashed on the rocks."

"If he's been shipwrecked we must see what father says. He'll want to help a shipwrecked sailor," said Nicholas, all too innocently. Bess knew that look. "It's a tradition of the seas," Nicholas proclaimed.

"No," blurted Bess.

Nicholas gazed up at her. "So, why is it such a secret, Bess? If he was shipwrecked, we'd all like to help. If he's hurt then he needs grown-up care."

"He's getting that from me."

"Take me to see him."

"You keep away from him." Bess dropped her voice. "Keep away from him, do you hear? He's too ill to be worried."

"Why would I worry him?"

Bess didn't answer.

"Take me to him or father will know within the hour," stated Nicholas bluntly.

Bess glared at him in frustration. Nicholas quietly waited: victory was his and he knew it.

"If you see him and know what I say is true, will you then let him recover his strength in peace?" Bess breathed angrily.

Nicholas nodded.

"He can stay in the barn and you'll tell no one?" she pressed.

"If what you say is true, he can stay there until he rots for all I care."

"And you'll tell no one? Not even Francis Bosawen?"

Nicholas shrugged. "Why would I tell Francis?"

"Because you always do."

Bess tried to think. If Nicholas saw Diego, would it satisfy his curiosity and would that be the end of it? Probably: boys lost interest quickly. Diego's English was nigh on perfect. It had fooled her that first time.

Nicholas said: "Take me to see him. If you don't, I'll follow every time you leave the house."

Bess wavered. He was very capable of doing exactly that. "And you'll not say anything to anyone?" she asked.

"If it's as you say, why should I?"

***

"He's sick," breathed Nicholas. "Really sick." They stood watching Diego toss and turn on the straw. The Spaniard seemed totally unaware of their presence; his eyes, glazed, stared blindly up at the barn's straw thatching, his body reacting to the delirium gripping it.

"What's wrong with him?" Nicholas asked.

"His foot's badly burned," Bess said.

"There's more to it than that. He's dying from fever." Nicholas's eyes opened wide. "He's the one who brought plague to our village."

"It's the effects of his injury."

"He could be the one who caused Jep Trist to die."

"That's not so. Jep caught it in Truro," Bess argued softly.

"How do you know? If, as you say, he comes from up country, that's where the sickness comes from. He could have carried it to Truro with him."

"He never came through Truro and he never met Jep."

Nicholas was frantic: "How can you know what he did, where he went before you found him? Tell father, before we all die."

"No."

"He's dying of plague, sweating like a pig. That's why they call it the Great Sweat."

Bess hesitated. What if her brother was right? No, he couldn't be. Diego hadn't been near a plague source. Unless they had plague on the Armada. It was possible. Anything was possible. No, he would have gone down with the fever long before this. It was ten days since Diego had been in contact with those on board his Spanish ship. Jep had fallen sick and died almost straight away, from its first appearance. Unless Jep had carried it around with him without knowing and it took ten days to surface…

"I'm telling father," Nicholas said.

"No."

"Why not, for God's sake?"

"It's not plague. It isn't, I know it isn't." Bess gestured at the writhing figure. "Take a look at his injured foot. That's the cause."

"I'll not go near him," shivered Nicholas.

"It's a little late to be thinking that. You wanted to come. Well, now you're here. Anyway," she said, "I've been near him and you've been near me. If it is plague, it's too late to prevent it now."

Suddenly, Diego cried out. Bess's heart missed a beat as she heard the foreign tongue. "We need cold water to cool him down." Bess held out the leathern bottle. "Fetch me water from the stream."

"That wasn't English. Is he a foreigner?" Nicholas came closer and gingerly took the bottle from her. "Ugh! That foot!" He wrinkled his nose. "What happened to it?"

"I told you: it was burned in a fire. Now, fetch water and hurry."

Nicholas moved towards the door. Bess looked at the weeping foot. She could smell the poison: the flesh was raw, oozing white droplets. If the droplets turn yellow or green, she thought, she'd have no choice but to hand him over to a surgeon. Or cut his foot off herself, but she knew she would never have the nerve to do that. She tidied the straw pile as Nicholas returned, lifted her skirt and tore off a strip of petticoat - wondering how to explain even that when it came to her mother's enquiry when it came to the family's washday - soaked the strip in water and gently bathed Diego's face, wiping away the sweat.

"What about his foot?" whispered Nicholas.

"Leave it. It's best left dry."

"How do you know that?"

"I don't. It just seems better that way."

The cooling water lowered the body temperature. Diego's taut muscles relaxed and he stopped twisting and turning on the straw. Once he muttered a sentence in Spanish, Nicholas frowned, but said nothing. Then, as the fever passed its height, Diego opened his eyes, saw Bess and whispered her name.

Bess smiled down at him, and felt a sudden deep flood of affection flow through her body. Robert had moved her, but this man had her heart racing like no other. "Hush," she softly said to him. "Rest."

Diego gazed past her shoulder and spied Nicholas. His eyes opened wide and he struggled to sit up.

"Hush now. 'Tis my brother come to help."

Slowly Diego relaxed and sank back on the straw bed, his eyes fixed on Nicholas. "He will not tell?"

"No, he'll not tell. You're safe with us. Now sleep."

Diego nodded. "Water?"

"Yes." Bess held the bottle to his lips. Most of it was used, and Diego drained the rest. "We'll refill it and leave it here."

Diego nodded.

When Bess returned from the stream, Diego was sleeping while Nicholas stood watching him.

"He's a handsome man," her brother said quietly. "For a foreigner."

Bess glanced at him; it was too late to turn back now. "Aye, for a foreigner," she said.

"Who is he?"

"A Spaniard, washed up from the Armada."

"An enemy," breathed Nicholas, his eyes wide with astonishment. "They'll hang you, Bess."

"Only if they find out."

"How long do you think you can keep this secret?"

"Until he's well."

"You're mad."

She sighed. "Perhaps. But I'm committed now."

"And if I tell father?"

"Then I'll hang for sure. For once he knows, it'll only be a matter of time before the village notices that the Trevanion family is spending much of their time at Caerhays and stops to wonder why. No, this is my problem and mine alone."

"What about me?"

"You got yourself involved; do what you think fit. I can't stop you telling father, or anyone else for that matter. But there's no way I can plead my innocence."

"Yes, you can. You can say that you didn't know. I heard him: he speaks English."

"Aye, and perfect."

"There you are, then. You can say you thought he was a traveller from up country. How many people have we heard from outside of Cornwall that we would know where they come from?"

"I've given him my word. To help him reach sympathisers in Penryn, who'll smuggle him back to Spain."

"Bess, he's an enemy. Help get him back to his own country and most likely, one day, he'll be back to kill us."

"Look at him, Nicholas. If he ends up in an English gaol in that condition, he'll die for sure. Look at his foot; he'll be lucky to live let alone fight anyone again. No, my mind is set. You're the one who has to decide what to do."

12
Leave Him Be

"I'll finish these, Father," Bess said gently, lifting the last basket of fish on to the harbour wall. "You go on up to the house, take off that smock and pick up a clean shirt." Henry nodded solemnly. Women and children stayed home at times like these. Burying people was men's work.

Bess knew that Jep's funeral service would be highly moving: the Reverend Ffermer speaking the words with feeling, the wooden box lowered into the open grave, a final prayer said while handfuls of dirt were thrown down on the lid. The men would then walk back across the fields recounting Jep stories: the first two or three recounted in a sentimental vein, the telling gradually becoming more boisterous as one tale followed another. By the time they reached the village, every man would be crying with laughter. It would then seem only fitting to take up Will Trudgeon's offer of a pot of ale to send Jep off; a pot that would inevitably develop into two, then three. Bess could see it all clearly in her mind as she walked the cliff path to Caerhays.

A fresh wind was blowing in from the sea when she reached the barn. Inside the dilapidated structure she gazed down at the feverish form. Diego gazed unseeingly up at the barn roof, his eyes focussed on a mental picture only he could see. Occasional words, in what she assumed must be Castilian or Spanish, burst forth from cracked lips. His clothes were soaked in sweat and it was then she noticed the smell: the sickly odour was being caused by something other than sweat: yellowish-green, evil-smelling puss was oozing from the raw flesh. Should she wipe the matter away with a dry rag, wash the leg, or leave it as it was? The simple truth was, she didn't know.

Diego muttered and thrashed his arms about wildly. Suddenly the Spaniard's voice rose to a shout and he sat bolt upright, staring over Bess's shoulder. Instinctively, she turned her head to see what had so violently attracted his attention but the barn was empty. She pushed Diego gently back and smoothed his brow. The fever was running high, dangerously high, his body was a raging inferno and she didn't know what to do.

***

With a heavy heart, Bess walked up the hill towards their cottage as Nicholas, who'd obviously been waiting, came down to meet her. Raucous sounds from Jep's wake were ringing out from the alehouse behind her.

"They seem to be enjoying the send off," she said with a smile.

"Aye. How's your Spaniard?" young Nicholas asked, falling into step beside her.

Bess glanced round. "Hush! Do you want to get me hanged?"

"You'll do that without any help from me. How is he?"

"Worse. The fever has taken hold and he's rambling. And

149

his leg looks bad. I fear he might lose it. I cleaned it as best I could and left him to fight the fever; but the truth is, there's nothing more I can do. I'm no physician and I worry about leaving him. Should anyone happen to come by the barn, they'll hear his ravings and immediately know him for what he is."

"That's why I say hand him over, have done with it and good riddance."

Bess halted twenty paces from the wall of their cottage and dropped her voice: "If they imprison him, then at best he'll lose his leg, at worst he'll lose his life."

"So?"

"So, I intend seeing that he recovers."

"Why? So that he can kill innocent women and children again?"

Bess plucked at a wild flower growing from a crack in the stone hedge. "He's not like that."

"'He's not like that'," Nicholas mimicked. "You've known him but a few days; during that time he's been too sick with fever to do anything other than lie there on the straw, so how can you be sure what he's like? As soon as he recovers, he'll be back to killing and pillaging."

"You sound like the Reverend Ffermer," she said, plucking the petals off the flower stalk.

"And who's to say he's not right? A man with far more experience of life than you or I."

"And more bigotry than the rest of the parish put together."

"Tell the truth. What is this Spaniard to you?"

Bess shuffled the dropped petals around with her foot. What was Diego to her? She looked at her brother. "Frankly, I don't know. And that's the truth of it."

"And what of your feelings for Robert? Has this Spaniard taken his place?"

Bess sighed. The truth was, she'd hardly thought of Robert once since Diego had entered her life. Did that mean Robert had been no more than a village girl's fancy? "When I found him on the beach he was just someone needing help," she said. "Then, I found out who he was but it made no difference, nothing changed, he was still someone in need of help. Beyond that, I cannot think. I have tried summoning up enmity but nothing comes." Bess smiled ruefully. "He even tried to crack my skull - that was on the second day. I was angry, but for no more than a moment, and then only with the kind of anger I'd feel if I was involved in an argument with you or a friend - there one minute, gone the next."

Nicholas was shocked. "The man tried to hit you over the head?" he asked.

"He was far too weak to do me any harm. He hid behind the barn door and attacked me as I came in."

"And you say he's not a murderer? You'll nurse him well, Bess, and he'll kill you for your pains." Then, proudly: "If he'd tried to break my skull, I'd have stamped on him like I would a cockroach."

Bess studied her young brother: "Yes, I truly think you

151

would."

"He's an enemy, Bess," Nicholas stated bluntly. "That's what you do to enemies. Anyone who doesn't is a traitor."

"I'm no traitor," Bess responded angrily. "I feel nothing for any cause - English or Spanish, Protestant or Catholic."

"We're at war with them, Bess," Nicholas pleaded.

"That doesn't mean we have to look at everything from that one viewpoint."

"What other viewpoint is there? You and your precious Spaniard…" Nicholas paused and opened his eyes wide. "Precious! Is that it? He's rich?"

Bess turned on him angrily. "You know it's not. I've no motive other than to get him well."

Nicholas's eyes gleamed. "Is he rich, Bess?"

"I don't know. He's a noble person; you can tell by his clothes."

"What, those rags? That smock?" he derided.

"Rags they may be, but once they were fine silk and soft leather. And the smock, I gave him."

"Fine silk means he's rich, Bess. Rich! He could be worth a fortune." Nicholas's eyes gleamed with avarice. "Drake takes hostages and ransoms them all the time."

Bess shook her head. "And what would we do with a fortune?" she asked.

"Spend it, of course."

"On what? We're fisher folk. What need have we of anything we haven't already got?"

She could see Nicholas endeavouring to think of things.

"You see? Nothing."

"A new boat. And larger. A sword, a horse, a big house, servants, there are plenty of things." They started to move towards the cottage once again; the noise from the ale house behind them, continuing to ring out. "So, when are you seeing him again?"

"Tomorrow afternoon. When we get back from fishing."

"Let me come with you."

"No."

"Why not? I might be able to help."

"You'll scare him."

"Me? Scare him? I'm but just a twelve year old lad."

They stopped at the door. Bess lowered her voice. "You're a strange face and that could worry him. Especially now, while he's befuddled with fever."

"No more than just a few days ago, you were a strange face. I can look after him while you're out in the bay."

"You have school to attend."

"Only until noon."

Bess suspected that her brother might well be thinking of the Spaniard's value in terms of gold. "No, it's too dangerous," she said. "I don't want you involved. Leave him be. He's got enough problems just getting well."

***

The next day, Diego, his eyes glazed, was barely conscious, mumbling words that Bess didn't understand and that barely sounded like words at all. His wounds still smelled sickly and conjured up the stench of bad meat.

"I see him," rambled Diego, switching from Spanish to English. "I see him. He help me."

His face was bright scarlet. Bess knelt down beside him and wiped his brow. He must be referring to whoever he was trying to reach. The unknown Catholic well-wisher in Penryn, she thought. "Yes, you'll see him," she said. "Stop worrying. I'll get you there, somehow. As soon as you're better."

"He help me."

"Yes, he will help you. Now, save your strength." Bess stroked the man's head, calming his fever, trying to lull him to sleep.

"You not understand. He help me."

"I understand. Now sleep."

The worried frown left the Spaniard's face. Slowly, his features relaxed, his eyes closed, and his breathing assumed a rapid but regular rhythm. Bess studied him, taking in the soft beard that was beginning to replace the stubble. His black hair, longer than fashionable men wore it, was tangled and hung halfway over his ears, more like that of a country dweller or fisherman. Good, she thought, it would make him less conspicuous when they were ready to move. Though, God knows, there was little chance of that yet awhile. Bess's gaze moved down to the scorched breeches and raw flesh. There was no point in fooling herself, the leg was worse. If the wound didn't mend soon he would need to lose his leg. And how would she cope with that? She was no surgeon, indeed the very thought made her blood run cold. There would be no alternative then but to let the militia know; they had men who were skilled in such matters. But would they waste those skills on an enemy? Or would they simply leave him to lie in a filthy cell until the leg rotted and the poison finally killed him?

And what would they then say about her? There was little sympathy for Protestants who helped Catholics at the best of times; none at all for one who aided an enemy in time of war. She shook her head vigorously to rid it of niggling doubts. "You knew that when you embarked on this madness," she muttered aloud.

Diego stirred at the sound. Bess smiled and brushed the man's hair away from his closed eyes. Madness or not, it was too late to do anything about it now.

She picked up the leathern bottle, surprised to find that there was still water in it. The container felt cool to the touch, not warm as she would have expected. She took out the stopper and sniffed at the contents, then tilted it against her lips: the water tasted fresh, not flat. She looked at Diego. Could he have staggered to the stream? Somehow, she doubted it. But what other answer was there? No one else was likely to fetch and carry for a sick stranger; not with plague in the area.

I see him. I see him. He help me. The words flashed

through her head, causing her to rethink their meaning. This was no ramblings of a fevered mind; no reference to someone in Penryn, as she had first thought; this was something that had happened here, this very morning…

Bess strode angrily to the door.

***

She caught Nicholas emerging from the soil closet, clutching his emptied chamber pot. All evening he had stayed close to their parents, sensing her anger. Now, carrying out his toilet before retiring to bed, Bess had waylaid him outside the turf-hut at the bottom of the garden. She grasped his arm and swung him against the closet door.

"Leave go of me," he hissed.

"You went to the barn. Don't deny it, I know you did."

"I've been in the house all day."

"Don't lie. You went there this morning, while I was out in the bay."

"What if I did?" Nicholas snapped.

"I told you to stay away from there."

"I did no harm. In fact, the opposite. I fetched fresh water for the papist, then left."

"Did he see you?"

Nicholas rubbed his arm. "I don't know. I couldn't tell. His eyes were open but they looked right through me. He just stared… He's bad, Bess, really bad. He's going to die."

"He is not going to die."

"Hah! What do you know? If he's due to die he will and

156

there's naught you can do about it."

"He is not going to die."

"Why not? Because you say so? It'll take more than words to mend that leg. Have you smelt it? It's rotten. In two or three more days, the flesh will go green and fall away from the bone, Francis says. And when that happens nothing can stop it."

"You've told Francis?" Bess shrieked.

"Quiet. I haven't told anyone. Do you think I'm mad? Francis was talking about war in general, about soldiers, about when they're wounded."

Nicholas was right, what did she know of such matters? "Something will turn up," she responded lamely.

"Yes, the militia."

She turned away, despair flooding through her body. Sensing her distress, Nicholas took her hand. "Give it up, Bess. It's not too late."

"It is… At least it is for me." The words ended in a sob as she suddenly realised how much she would miss Diego when the time finally came for him to depart. She'd be desolated. "In a few days the fever will pass. Once that happens the leg will heal," she said stubbornly.

Nicholas said: "You'll not stop me seeing him."

Bess sighed. "Aye, I know that. I could never tell you what to do when your mind was set. But I still don't understand: why get yourself involved?"

"It's exciting."

"Exciting?"

"Yes, exciting. And there could be a reward at the end of it. Anyway, if it's any comfort, I don't think it'll be for long. Then you'll have to bury him."

Comfort? Comfort? How could he talk like that? It could be the greatest loss she'd ever know. It would be like tearing her heart out by the roots.

13
Country Medicine

"Stranger coming," murmured Will Pascoe.

The men glanced up from sorting the morning's catch to stare up the hill at the approaching cart. Bess shaded her eyes and spied the giant form of militiaman Will Bligh, seated alone behind a tired looking horse. Behind Will she could see soft sacks of what looked like flour and lumpy ones she guessed must be turnips, all due for the garrison at St Mawes Castle.

"Will!" called her father, dropping a live lobster into one basket and picking up a crab to drop into another. "What brings you to these parts? Not that you're not always welcome."

Will Bligh pulled the horse drawn cart to a halt and nodded his head in greeting to the fishermen. "We heard rumours of plague. My officer asked me to look into it on the way back from Tregoney. Well not so much asked, as told me. So, Henry, how fare you all at this worrisome time?"

Despite the greeting, Bess noticed that Will was keeping a safe distance between himself and the villagers. And she couldn't blame him for that.

"Thank him for his concern. Not the Black Death, tell him, but the next worse thing. Jep Trist, one of the villagers, caught the Great Sweat and died on Monday. We buried him the day before yesterday."

"Anyone else?"

"Not as yet, God willing. We think it's cleared, but ask again in a week. In the meantime all our fingers are crossed."

Will nodded and urged the horse forward a few paces, moving the cart fractionally closer. "Aye, you'll know by then. If it's any help, an aunt of mine, back in Dorset, used to say Cuckoo Pint was good for the plague. She called it Wake Robin, but it's all one and the same. Come to think of it, I've spied it growing back there, under a hedgerow." He pointed back the way he had come. "Green pointed leaves, broad at the stem, pointed at the top, some with black spots. She used to crush the leaves to bring out the juices, and give it to the sufferer to drink, then place the bruised leaves over any sores. It seemed to work; or did the last time she used it. Anyway, the sickness went and we assumed it was that we had to thank for it."

Henry nodded his thanks. "We'll remember that. Plague's a rarity here, away as we are from city life. With poor Jep, we didn't know what to do."

"Aye, it's not easy to work out what's right. Some of the old remedies are no more than witches' brew, but Aunt Polly was well-respected for her knowledge. She's gone now, God rest her soul, and she was no witch, that's for sure."

"We're grateful. Physicians in Truro won't travel out as far as this. Anyway, most just take your money and recommend broth and leeches."

Will nodded. "It appears to be under control, then, you

160

say. Good, I'll tell the captain that. Incidentally, more news has come through of the battle. It seems, on Saturday, Howard sent in fire ships off Calais and broke up the Spanish fleet, leaving Drake and the rest to pick off stragglers one by one. There's no notion of how many we've sunk but it's the first news of a victory. Perhaps with good fortune this is the beginning of the end."

There was an approving murmur from the rest of the men. "Aye, that's good news indeed. We'd not heard that," stated Henry in a satisfied voice.

Will said: "Aye, good news but I keep thinking of all those poor men dying. War's a terrifying business, Henry. I'll be glad when it's over and I can get back to Dorset where the only fighting we ever saw was between my aunt and uncle when he came home drunk from the alehouse." He smiled. "She used to make him drink a potion that made him sick as a dog. He swore he'd have her put in the ducking stool, but never did. So," he added, "I'll tell the captain there's naught to worry us yet awhile. With luck, he'll tell me to call again."

Henry smiled up at him: "Aye, we'd like that. You'll not stop and have supper with us?"

"No, I have to get back."

"I'll ride with Will to St Veryan," Bess said suddenly.

"If he'll allow," admonished Henry.

Bess reddened. She'd spoken on the spur of the moment. "I beg his pardon, I meant no forwardness. Will knows that."

161

"And none presumed," Will grinned. "The company's more than welcome." He offered Bess his hand. "You can sit on a flour sack in the back."

Bess climbed aboard as Will turned the cart, expertly backing and turning in the narrow lane until they faced the way he'd come.

"Will, did your aunt ever tell you a cure for burns?" Bess asked, halfway up the steep hill.

"Burns," mused Will. "Let me see, burns… Yes, she did. The thatching on one of the village cottages caught fire once and a young boy got scarred. Why? Who's been burned?" he asked, peering at her over his shoulder.

"Your aunt, what did she say?" asked Bess, sidestepping the question.

"What was it now?" Will mused. "Boiled ivy leaves are good. But the best cure, she used to say, is bruised St Peter's Wort leaves. Strange old woman: full of notions about herbs and such like. Had a cure for everything. They didn't all work, mind you, but most did." He paused, then added: "She never found a cure for her growing old age, though, more's the pity. I miss her sorely."

"What do you do with the leaves?"

"Lay them on the burns." He turned and glanced back at Bess again. "Why these questions about burns?" Seeing her serious expression, he pulled the cart to the side of the lane. "I saw no signs of a fire. Who's been burnt, Bess?"

Bess, about to say no one in particular, found herself

pouring out the whole story: finding Diego on the beach, helping him to the barn, washing his wound, trying to control the fever. It came out in a torrent. When it was over, she glanced at Will, aghast at what she'd said, but found only concern on his face.

"Bess, why have you told me this?" he asked after a while. "I could report you to my captain and you could find yourself in prison, even hanged."

"I'm well aware of that. And I don't know why. It came out before I could stop it. Ever since finding him, I've known I was doing wrong, but there was nothing I could do to stop myself."

"Wrong, Bess? Wrong? What's wrong with helping someone who is sick? No, I don't think it's wrong. Others might." He brushed a fly away. "Does Henry know?"

Bess shook her head. "I don't think so. At first, he wondered where I was going every afternoon, but then convinced himself that I was aiding an old hermit who lives in the valley. So will you report me?"

Will sighed. "Nay, Bess. They'd not understand. They'd just lock you up, or worse." He gazed up the empty lane. "I've a horror of killing," he said, his voice softening. "I used to sit for hours listening to my aunt tell me the virtues of medicine, but such fascination never came to anything. We never had the money for me to become a physician; nor even to be apprenticed to one. Nor ever shall have." He turned to face her, his face set firmly in decision. "If you'll allow, I maybe know enough medicine to help."

"All I ask is help to cure his sickness: he and I can make our own way from there. He knows of people in Penryn who'll help him back to Spain."

He nodded. "Aye, I've heard tell of Catholic sympathisers there, but I've also been told they're watched day and night."

"We'll cross that hurdle when we come to it. First, I must get him well."

"Do you know St Peter's Wort?"

"Little yellow flowers that grow in the woods, usually near a stream?"

"That's it. Slightly bigger than St John's Wort."

"There're some in Lamorran Woods," Bess murmured. "There could even be some in the valley at Polgrain."

"The plants will be full grown now and in flower, so you won't miss them. Pick fresh leaves, wash them in a stream, and pound them with a clean rock so the juices seep out. Make sure you wash them first; no good doing it after they're bruised, you'll just wash away the juices. Then, keeping them clean as possible, lay them over the burns. Don't wash the burn; water's bad for it. That's why it's weeping; it should have been kept dry from the beginning. Can you recognise borage?"

"Blue flowers? They're out now. I saw some down the lane."

"That's right. You know your herbs."

"Some. My mother picks borage; we have it with fish."

"Aye, they make a good vegetable; like dandelion leaves."

"We have those too."

"Give him borage to eat. It will help bring down the fever. Change the St Peter's Wort leaves as often as possible; at least every day. Meantime, I'll tell my captain that I couldn't pick up all the stores and will have to return for the rest on Saturday. It's certain he'll agree - he'll have no choice. I'll meet you where the road forks to Treviskey and we'll go and look at this Spaniard of yours."

Bess could feel a tightening in her throat. She swallowed, forcing back tears. The strain of tending Diego on her own, with no one to help her decide what was best, had been great. Too great for comfort. "What time of the day?" she asked chokingly.

Will ruffled her hair. "As soon after midday as possible. I'll be there at noon."

Bess climbed down. Will jerked the reins and the laden cart moved forward. "Best get back before the captain starts thinking that I've deserted with the rations."

"Aye, we wouldn't want that," said Bess.

"'Tis a good thing you're doing, Bess. Don't let the worry of it get you down."

***

The door was bolted fast. Despite rattling the latch and repeated calls, Henry was unable to rouse anyone. Back home at their cottage, he asked Elizabeth whether she'd had sight of Kate Trist on the previous day.

Elizabeth was busy sweeping out the kitchen. "No, I didn't have time," she said.

"Did anyone see her?"

"I don't know. You'll have to ask around. I expect Alice called, if only to tell her the children are well."

But when Henry asked Alice Trudgeon, he received a similar reply: busy serving in the tavern, and what with Will taking the fish cart into Truro since Jep's departure, she'd found no time, but intended visiting today, she told him.

Concerned, Henry went back to the Trist cottage and banged on the door. This time, when there was no reply, he put his shoulder against the wood and forced the bolt away from the door jamb. Up, on the floor above, Kate was lying on a straw-filled mattress, soaked in sweat and barely conscious. Weakly she waved him away. "Too late," she croaked. "Keep away or you'll spread it through the village."

"Nonsense, we've heard of a cure."

"There's no cure. There's naught but God's mercy."

"Let me help."

"Keep away. Why do you think I barred the door?"

"You can't shut us out like this."

"I can and I have."

Henry tried his best to comfort her but he knew deep inside himself that she was right. If Kate was to come through the fever then time alone would prove it so. He fixed the door and left, promising to return in the morning.

When he told Elizabeth the news, she was upset, blaming

herself for not having called on Kate the previous day.

"It wouldn't have made any difference," Henry said. "She went down with it on Wednesday evening. Anyway, it's as well you didn't: the fewer who have contact with her the better. But she's a brave soul; she knows from nursing Jep what it's all about."

"Yes, but…"

"Quiet, woman, you're fretting unnecessarily. Kate speaks good sense: we have to think of the whole village. Kate knows that, let's observe her wishes."

***

Over the coming days, Bess carried out Will Bligh's instructions to the letter, and by late Friday afternoon detected not only a drop in Diego's fever, but the fact that the leg had begun losing its bad smell and the burnt flesh was looking much drier.

So it was with a lighter heart that she set out on the Saturday to meet Will at the road fork and found him sitting cross-legged on the grass, leaning against a wheel, with the cart pulled into the shade.

He rose to his feet as she approached and glanced cautiously round to make sure no one was in sight. "How is he?" he asked.

"He seems a little better. The fever has lessened. I think the herbs are working."

Will smiled. "So, Aunt Polly knew what she was talking about, then?"

"It's early days, but it seems so."

"Where can we hide the cart? If the stores get stolen, the captain'll have the skin off my back."

"There's a copse down the lane. We can drive it in there, and hope no one hears the horse whinnying."

"We'll pile brushwood over," said Will, "and take him with us."

By the time they had finished, nothing but close searching inspection would detect the cart's presence. Giving the camouflage a final approving look, Bess took hold of the horse's halter and led the way with Will asking if anyone else had gone down with the Sweat.

"Jep's wife. She was well until Wednesday," Bess replied. "Now she's as poorly as Jep was before he passed away."

"The Sweat's a plague. When it strikes, it strikes fast."

Bess nodded. "The barn's across this next field," she said.

"Does he know I'm coming?"

"Diego? No, I wasn't sure he'd understand, so I thought it best not to say. When he sees you he'll be greatly startled, but I can explain... There's the barn."

"It looks a mite tumbled down."

"All the better. It means no one makes use of it."

Will nodded. "Aye, I suppose so."

"Best leave the horse here and go on foot: if he hears hooves he'll panic."

As they neared the entrance Bess called: "Diego?"

"Bess?" Diego's response had an edge of nervousness to

it: he'd heard two sets of footsteps.

"Yes." Bess stepped through the doorway, Will close on her heels. Diego lay on the straw bed, leaning against a post. Seeing Will, his face paled.

"He's a friend, Diego."

Diego pressed his body against the post, his eyes riveted on Will's huge form.

"This is Will Bligh," said Bess. "He's the one who told me how to lessen your fever."

"I'll wait outside," murmured Will. "Call when you want me."

"No!" Bess exclaimed. "He has to know who his friends are. You've risked more than anyone: as a soldier, you'd be hung for certain if you were caught." She turned to face the young Spaniard. "Diego, if it wasn't for Will, you'd be dead by now. When your fever was at its height and your leg was turning green, he showed me how to ease the pain."

"He is a soldier?"

"Yes, but a less than willing one. He hates war."

"How can he hate war if he is a soldier?"

Will spoke sharply: "I'm no lover of Spain. My only thought at the moment is to speed you on your way: the sooner you're gone, the safer it will be for Bess."

Bess watched as Diego endeavoured to absorb this. "I do not ask for your help," he said finally.

"Then think yourself fortunate we're giving it freely, for if Bess hadn't found you and I hadn't suggested a treatment,

169

as she's said, you'd be dead by now," Will told him brutally, "and we'd be digging your grave."

"There are too many people knowing about me. It is not safe."

"Two, that's all," said Will.

"Three. He was here. He give me food and bring me water."

Will looked startled. "Who's he talking of?"

"Nicholas," replied Bess quietly. "My brother."

"You didn't tell me he was involved," said Will.

"He followed me. Now he insists on coming here when I'm out fishing."

"Another peasant," said Diego.

Will reacted angrily: "Mind your tongue, Spaniard. If it wasn't for peasants like us, you'd be rotting in a cell or dead."

Bess smiled. "'Tis a joke, Will. Between Diego and me."

"Yes, it is an amusement," Diego muttered sullenly.

"Who else haven't you told me about?" asked Will.

"No one. It's just us three."

Will peered at them both then slowly relaxed. "Let me look at his leg."

Bess turned to Diego. "Will knows about these things. It was he who suggested the borage."

"Ugh! Disgusted!"

"Disgusting," corrected Bess.

"Disgusted, disgusting, it is awful."

"It's bringing your temperature down, and the crushed leaves will stop the rot in your leg," Will said sharply. Then, turning to Bess, asked her if Diego complained like this all the time.

Bess smiled. "Not all the time. Just most of it." She turned to Diego and said: "Let him look at your leg."

Reluctantly, Diego nodded. Will gently removed the bruised leaves and gave a sharp intake of breath on seeing the raw flesh. "If it's like this now, what the devil was it like when you found him?"

"Bad," said Bess. "Weeping badly. Then it began to smell."

"Well, it's not doing that now, thank God." He glanced at Diego. "You're lucky not to lose it, or worse."

"I would rather die than have only one leg," said Diego vehemently.

Will reached out a hand and felt Diego's forehead. Diego flinched. "Still hot and dry." He turned to Bess: "But you say it's down?"

"Yes, to what it was. Four days ago, it was raging."

"How do you feel?" Will asked Diego.

"Thirsty... tired... not strong," responded Diego. "But better."

"It'll be a good few days yet before you're better. I doubt whether you could even stand on that at the moment, let alone walk. Have you tried?"

"Yes. I fall down."

"I'm not surprised."

"What did Nicholas have to say?" asked Bess.

"Nicholas? What is Nicholas?" said Diego.

"My brother."

"Ah! Nicholas! He not say anything. Just fetch water and give me food. I eat; he watch. Then he goes. Say that he will come again tomorrow."

"We'll see about that," said Bess. Will glanced at her curiously, but Bess chose to ignore his questioning look. She'd deal with Nicholas.

Outside, standing by the horse, Will wanted to know whether she was not concerned that Nicholas might, thoughtlessly, tell someone. "He's a boy, Bess," he said. "Not a man. Boys talk to other boys."

Bess said: "No, he knows well what will happen if anyone should find out. In fact, it's he that keeps warning me I'll be hanged. No, it's the excitement that draws him here. The excitement of coming face to face with a Spaniard." She thought it best not to mention Nicholas's remarks on obtaining a ransom.

"Boys have friends," pursued Will. "And friends talk among themselves."

"He only found out a few days ago."

"Can't you stop him?"

"How?" Bess asked. "I've tried; he takes no notice."

"It could prove dangerous," warned Will.

"He knows that."

Will looked at her. "No, I mean for you."

Bess shook her head. "Nicholas won't tell anybody."

"No, but someone, a friend, a nosy neighbour, could always follow him."

"For that matter someone could follow me. As Nicholas did. The only way I can avoid that happening is to not come here at all."

"I suppose so. Warn him again; tell him to be careful."

"He already knows that," sighed Bess.

Will jerked his head at the barn. "I'll call and see him again, as soon as I can get away. Unfortunately, I can't promise when. My officer makes those kind of decisions."

Bess smiled and nodded her thanks. "Just you being here, whenever you can, is more than enough," she said.

"He's an ungrateful patient."

"It's not that. He comes from a different world, Will. He's used to ordering servants around, getting them to obey his every wish."

Will smiled. "Like peasants," he said.

"To him, we are."

Will nodded and climbed on the horse. "That doesn't mean he has to treat us as such, Bess."

***

Nicholas was right, Bess thought, lying awake in her cot. Why was she doing this? her brother had asked. Will, in turn, had called Diego an ungrateful patient. And, in many ways, it was true: he was. But that was what it was all about:

his needs, not her needs. Was that what love was? All about giving, not receiving?

She had no way of knowing. Her experience of such was limited. She'd been enamoured of Robert, but Diego occupied her thoughts in a totally different way. Robert had been a local prize to be won. With Diego she wanted to protect him from all the evils of the world, with no thought as to her own desires; bring him happiness with no thought to her own joy. So, was this love? she asked herself again. She supposed it was. But then how did he feel about her? What did he see when he looked at her? A sun-tanned girl smelling of fish? He must be used to ladies who dressed fashionably, with faces powdered and hair styled in the latest fashion.

She sighed. What did it matter? In a few days, he might be gone. All she knew was she had to do what she was doing even if he showed no such feelings in return.

14
A Dreadful Thing

Henry, in a state of shock, stared wide-eyed at Kate's body. Her death was no surprise; it was the nature of her end that he found distressing. Forced to break in the cottage door again, he had expected to find her dying, even dead - but never like this. He leaned against the bedchamber door, struggling to control his emotions. Not once in his memory had anyone in the village resorted to such a measure.

Slowly, he made his way down to the kitchen and searched for a knife. Found one, tested the sharpness with his thumb, climbed the ladder to the first floor once again and, taking great care not to touch the body, cut it down.

"Why?" he muttered.

No. Why was obvious. This way, no one could nurse her; no one could disregard her wishes when she was unconscious, or be with her when she died. This way, no one would have to lay her out; no one would have to attend her funeral. This way, she'd be thrown into an unconsecrated grave, separated from the village and the villagers by her action, so no one might carry it on to the next household.

He gazed at the sprawled form of a woman he had grown up with; a person he and the rest of the village had known for more than thirty years. Or had they? Had any of them given true consideration to the woman they had once known as Kate Pascoe and later as Kate Trist? Had they ever thought of her as an individual, as anyone other than the wife of Jep? Had he, Henry Trevanion, or any of them, come to that - other than possibly Jep himself - realised the strength of character residing in that body? Or the depth of love for her fellow men? A depth so great, she would rather damn her soul for all eternity than spread among them the suffering she and her husband had been forced to endure these past days. No, none of them had really known Kate for what she was.

So, what was he to do? He knew one thing, there was no way he was going to allow Kate to have her name written in the parish records as a suicide. The shame on her children would be undeserved. He'd handle this matter himself. The answer was to tell no one, keep out neighbours, and keep away the Reverend Ffermer who, if he knew the truth, would certainly refuse her a Christian burial alongside her husband.

Henry moved to the window and peered out. The Trist cottage stood on a bend in the lane, separated from neighbours' views, its front door unseen by the rest of the village. No one had seen him arrive, and he'd make sure no one saw him leave. He went back down to the kitchen, searching for tinder.

***

On Sunday, the Reverend Ffermer said prayers for poor Kate Trist who, lying ill in her bed, had burned to death. No one seemed to know how the fire had started; the cottage's thatched roof and upper floor had been badly damaged and only a timely warning from Henry Trevanion, followed by prompt action from the rest of the villagers, had saved the building from being totally demolished. It was a great shock to all, announced their vicar solemnly, and she would be buried next to her husband on the coming Wednesday.

The one blessing, he said, was that the fire had almost certainly killed off the Great Sweat that had infected the Trist household, and the villagers could now relax.

Listening to him, Henry wondered whether that was true. He certainly hoped so. If the vicar said it was, it must be. Who was he to argue medical matters with a man of letters?

The sadness of Mistress Trist's death was even more marked, the vicar continued, when contrasted with God's glorious, wonderful news that the Armada was finally being defeated as he spoke.

"Drake was almost sunk last Monday," he shouted, his voice echoing round the vaulted ceiling. "But God reached out His protecting arm and saved The Revenge, even though it had been holed in forty different places. The battle raged throughout the day and many papists have been despatched to hell, chased there by fine English round shot, fired by brave English seamen. Now the enemy is reaping its just desserts. With the Armada foundering on sandbanks off the coast of Holland, it is naught but a matter of time before the last Spanish hell-ship is sunk, and the last devil-spawned Spaniard is killed. Glory be to God."

Where their vicar managed to obtain his news, they were never quite sure, but he was invariably right and this occasion was to prove no exception, as Will Trudgeon found out on the Monday, when he took the catch into Truro. Already folk were talking of Drake and Howard having won the final battle. What had happened to Parma and the army waiting in France to invade, no one knew. Some said it had been unready when the Armada arrived off Dunkirk, others said that Parma had fled fearing that he'd be destroyed like the Duke of Medina. Whichever was true, the result was relief from a threat that had hung over their heads for more than a year.

Henry agreed that the news was splendid, but tried to warn against feelings of complacency. "The Armada's large," he said. "The biggest fleet the world has ever known, and it'll take a devil of a lot of sinking. I don't doubt that victory is within our grasp, but rumours, like rivers, have a way of growing in size the farther they get from their source. We'd do well not to think that it's all over until Howard and Drake return and say it is."

"But the news bears out what the vicar told us on Sunday," argued Will.

"Aye, it does. And it might well be true. Let's hope it is. But our vicar's not infallible, nor for that matter are the citizens of Truro. If everybody ended up saying, 'Well, that's it', and the Spanish fleet was saved at the last minute, then what?"

"Well, I believe it," said Will crossly.

"And we'll all pray that you're right, Will," said Henry. "But remember, it wouldn't be the first time that news coming out of Truro was proved false."

If the war is over, thought Bess, listening to their talk, where does that leave Diego? Will he still be classed as an enemy? Or can he now be free to walk abroad in relative safety? Even able to return to Spain without too much hindrance? Instead of inspiring her, the thought was upsetting. Wasn't that what she wanted, she asked herself? The reason behind all her nursing him back to health? Yes, but now it was that much closer, any joy she might feel - indeed, should feel - was sadly lacking. The truth was, she would be loath to see him depart. Loath? Sad? No, she would be devastated.

**

"Tell me about Spain," said Bess.

Diego was feeling muzzy and light-headed; his limbs ached with fatigue. Though why this should be, he was at a loss to understand; he had done little other than lie on this bed of straw for the greater part of two weeks. He shifted, easing his damaged leg into a more comfortable position.

"Spain? It is very beautiful." He thought quietly for a moment. "England is very green, but our grass is more dry, from the sun. The green of our trees is dark, much darker than in England, but the sky is blue. We have grey skies only in winter, when it rains. Not like England where it rains one minute and the sky is blue the next so that you do not know whether it is winter or summer.

"Our family, we live in a city," he continued. "Seville. It is very old. The Romans lived there many hundreds of years ago. Now, it is the most important city in that part of - how do you call it? South? Southern? - Spain. That is why my father chose to live there. Seville is one day ride from Cadiz. Cadiz is also very old. Your Drake sailed into the harbour there last year and set fire to all the ships. Did you know that?"

Bess nodded. "Yes, we heard about it. One of the men from a neighbouring village sailed there with Drake." There was no doubt about it, she thought, listening to him describe his home, Diego was a handsome youth with his deep brown almost black eyes and slightly olive skin. Her heart gave a lurch.

"The man is a devil," Diego was saying, his voice soft, no longer constantly stirred by anger. When he was reminiscing like this she could listen to it all day. "Cadiz is very beautiful. The harbour is big. Across the opening? Entrance? Is that the right word? Is a long, thin land." He drew a line in the air with his finger parallel to the ground. "This land keeps the waves from coming into the harbour and the sea inside is very calm. It is the most beautiful harbour in all of Spain."

"What are your cities like?"

"Cadiz and Seville are bigger than Penryn or Truro, I remember that. Much bigger. I expect they are bigger than Plymouth. With white houses and with narrow streets made of round stones."

"Paving or cobbles. We have those in some of the streets in Truro."

"Ah, yes, I remember… The houses in Spain are much different to English houses. Spanish houses are made of stone with roofs made of red tiles. In between the houses, we have many courtyards with fine fountains, and everywhere there are lemon and orange trees. In the spring, the trees are covered in flowers, and in the summer we pick the fruit and eat it. You do not have orange trees in England?"

"Not that I know of. I've never tasted lemons or oranges. I've seen them; seamen bring them back from Spain and sell them on the quaysides, but I've never tasted them."

"You have never tasted oranges?" exclaimed Diego in astonishment.

Bess laughed. "We can't afford such luxuries."

"You must come and visit me in Seville. I will pick oranges and lemons for you every day. We will drink wine and I will show you grapes growing on vines. We make wine from grapes. Did you know that?"

"Yes, Richard Pyne, one of the villagers once sailed with Hawkins. They landed in Spain and saw vines there growing on land cut into the hillsides."

"Yes, that is right. They are called vineyards."

Bess smiled. "It all sounds very exciting."

"No, it is not exciting. It is very beautiful and very happy."

"By exciting, I mean different to England."

"Yes, it is different to England… very different."

He lapsed into silence. Bess studied his face: sadness showed alongside the fatigue. Yet, for all that, he was still a very handsome man. And very different from Robert Williams. But then that was to be expected. She found it difficult to imagine Robert talking about Cornwall with the same enthusiasm that Diego had used to describe Spain. In fact, she doubted whether he ever thought about such things. Perhaps he would if he was far away and separated from home; perhaps distance made the heart grow more fond of things as well as of people. Was she fond of Robert? She had once thought so. More than fond. Now she was no longer certain. Diego seemed to have taken over her affections in a way she would never have thought possible.

"So, what will you do when the war is over? When you get back to Spain?"

Diego had been gazing dreamily into space. He looked at Bess, as though he was surprised that she was still there. He'd been thinking of the aged servant, Roberto, who had once been his tutor, wondering if he was still shutting all the grills and windows at night. He smiled: Roberto had a thing about the night air. Strange, he could picture Roberto more clearly than anyone in the household, including his father and his brother. Anyone, that is, except his mother.

"I am sorry, I do not hear what you say."

"I said, what will you do, back in Spain, when you get home?"

"What I always do." What did he do? He couldn't think of anything important enough to tell her. "Help my father on the estate." He'd never done a day's work in the vineyards or the wine cellars in his life. "Manage the house when he is away." Roberto did that. "Look after the merchant business." Philip did that, or the warehouse managers. "Help my mother." She had Dona Juana de Jerez as her constant companion. He suddenly realised that there was hardly any need for him to be there at all: everything was done by somebody else.

"It sounds a very busy life."

Diego felt guilty. Why was that? He had never felt guilty about his life before. What did these people know about his kind? Work was all they lived for. Without work they would die. Was that true of his life? If his father and brother did not work, would the Olivarez family starve? Perhaps they would, he thought with some surprise.

"There must be a lot to do. Your father must miss you."

Did they miss him? He missed them. He missed them with a pain so intense that it tore at his heart.

How he longed to smell the sweet scent of jasmine drifting up from the courtyard, hear the soft buzz of cicadas, even to have Roberto call him El Senorito instead of Senor would be wonderfully welcome.

"Yes," he said, hoarsely. "There is much for me to do."

**

Perched upon one foot, easing the damaged one, Diego stood

at the barn door, clutching the wooden frame. The moon appeared, filtering through cloud, giving just enough light to show the surrounding landscape. The slate-grey sea was smooth, flat, calm. The clouds parted and, for a moment, a channel of silver stretched to the horizon. South, all the way to Spain.

Was the moon shining over Seville? he asked himself. It was hard to believe that this was the same moon. In Spain it looked much larger and it would scatter silvery light over the whole countryside. Even a new moon seemed to have more light at home than a full moon here.

Home. The word conjured up pictures of the broad valley across which their house faced. Bess, with her questions, had stirred up emotions he had not realised existed. He flexed his leg. He did not normally react this way: the fever must have depressed him more than he realised. He must get away from here before he became smothered by their concern.

A night owl screeched. Something rustled in the nearby grass. Diego hopped painfully back to the pile of straw and carefully lowered himself down on to it, the effort bringing out a prickling sweat. Bess and her giant soldier-who-wasn't-a-soldier friend were right: he was still too weak to move more than a few paces. How long must he stay here? Two more days? A week?

God protect him, it must be no more than a week, he would go mad. Yet, from the moment he woke, lying here waiting for them to appear, he could not stop gazing at the barn doorway, hoping that each tiny sound heralded their approach. What had become of him? Dependent upon a group of peasants? And enemy ones at that. Philip would have a seizure. And his father? Diego's mind went blank: for the life of him, he couldn't imagine what his father would think. Presumably, he had views on such matters? Consorting with the enemy. No, that wasn't true. It was Bess and Will who were doing the consorting, who were the traitors, he was merely the receiver of their actions.

He sighed. War was a dreadful thing. No one back home would ever understand what he and the rest of the Armada had gone through. To them, war was something glamorous that happened miles away in a foreign land. Parents proudly sent off their sons, who in turn went joyfully, telling themselves they were brave and bold, that this was an adventure to be enjoyed by the fortunate few. And, on their return, what great moments could they relate? That they had seen men blown to pieces in front of their eyes? Run through with swords? Blood flowing like water? In years to come would such terrible memories become softened with time? Made acceptable? Or would they always be a nightmare from which they would waken, screaming? Just as importantly, what would historians make of it all, a hundred years from now?

The trappings of pomp and ceremony attending the Armada's departure: the flag waving, the drums, the trumpets, the cheering crowds, the flower-strewn water, what had it all come to? Here he was, isolated in an alien land, seeking refuge in a derelict barn, reliant upon the charity of local fisher people.

The rest of the massive fleet, he knew not where. It was obvious they had not landed and conquered this country as intended. He was even uncertain now whether they ever would; a thought that would not have entered his mind two weeks ago.

His mother had had more sense. While everyone was busy congratulating him on being granted a berth on the San Salvador, envying him the privilege, she had foreseen the reality, the horror, the pain, and pleaded with him to remain at home. Was she still weeping? Still dreading hearing bad news? Had Philip returned to tell her of the reported disaster aboard the stricken San Salvador? Her son, Diego, missing, presumed dead? Would such news be the end of her? Probably. She'd take to her bed and prepare herself for her Maker. How on earth could he have been so selfish? How could any of them have been so cruel? He, his brother, his father: they were merchants, not soldiers. None of them had thought past the excitement. They had treated it like a fiesta, something to break the monotony of their daily routine.

It must be a very busy life. He sighed. Bess had suddenly made him realise just how frivolous his life really was.

She had also made him realise how much he would miss this Cornish fisher lass when he got home - if he ever got home. And, if he did, he would owe it all to her. She had sacrificed everything to help him. A wave of affection suddenly swept over him. No one had ever shown him such solicitude. Not his father, his brother, not even his mother. His face softened. Well, perhaps his mother. But mothers always showed affection for their sons. What Bess was showing was different; what she felt went beyond that. Far beyond. Suddenly it dawned that she might even be feeling love for him and the thought was like a lightning bolt. More importantly, he suddenly felt that what she might be feeling for him, he might also to a large degree be feeling for her. How could his feelings for her have changed in so short a time? But deep down he knew they had. She had saved his life; without her help he would probably be dead. Was that love? He was inexperienced in such matters. But he felt something. He longed for her to come, was happy when she was here with him, and sad when she left. Was that mere affection for what she'd done? Or was that the beginnings of love? And if so, how could that be? He was rich, she was poor, a mere fisherman's daughter. Yet he had a feeling it was so. A feeling that was growing steadily, day by day.

15
The Road to St Mawes

Diego's face was flushed. Whether through anger or a worsening of the fever, Bess couldn't readily distinguish. Either way she was concerned. She reached out a hand to feel his brow, he knocked it away and pointed his finger accusingly at Will. "I ask, did he send the man?" There was an element of fear in the voice. No, not fear, Bess realised, but panic.

"What man?" Will asked, frowning.

"The man who is here this morning."

Will took a step forward. "I sent no one. Who was he, Diego?"

Diego stared up at the giant. "He come here and find me."

Will glanced at Bess. "Nicholas?"

She shook her head. Nicholas was a twelve-year-old boy; no one would mistake him for a man. "No, anyway he knows Nicholas. No one other than us three knows he's here." A worrying thought entered her head. She turned to Diego. "His appearance. Describe him?"

Diego's eyes flashed angrily. "Appearance? Describe? I do not know these words."

"What did he look like?"

"He look very cruel and fierce and carry a long stick. He wears clothes that smell and he has a red beard. I never see a red beard before."

"Jeremiah," breathed Bess.

"Who's Jeremiah?" asked Will.

"Sir Hugh's gamekeeper. Sir Hugh Fitzwilliam owns the land this barn stands on, and the whole estate for miles around. Jeremiah's a brutish man, the last person I'd choose to know about this."

"I tell him I have fever and he go."

Will said: "Tell us what happened, Diego."

"I tell you," Diego shouted.

"All of it, from the very beginning."

"I hear this man coming and I think that it is Bess and you, so I do not hide. He come in, see me and ask what am I doing here. I tell him I am sick and have bad fever."

"Did he see your leg?" asked Will.

"I do not think so. No, the straw hide it. Why do you ask?"

"Then what did he do?"

"He come toward me with his stick, I think he is going to beat me. But when I say I have fever he stop and go away."

"He must have heard about the Great Sweat and Jep's death," said Bess in a low voice.

Will nodded: "Aye, and wasn't taking any chances," he muttered.

"Why do you whisper?" Diego queried crossly.

"We're not whispering; just speaking in a low voice," Will told him. "And I advise you to do the same. Did he say anything else?"

"Yes, he tell me he go and fetch dog. If I am not gone before he return he will make dog attack me."

"Do you think he realises that you're foreign - a Spaniard?" asked Bess.

"I do not know."

Will shook his head. "Diego's English is passable. You've said so yourself. No, if this Jeremiah thought he was a Spaniard he'd fetch the militia, not a dog."

Thoughts tumbled through Bess's head. To have all this end through a chance visit by an uncouth gamekeeper was too much... Her voice caught in a sob. "I must move him," she said. "Before Jeremiah gets back."

"Aye, the question is where."

"No, Will. You've done enough. You go, I'll do it."

"Let's not fall out about it," Will said. "Go, fetch the horse while I look at his leg."

"You have a horse?" Diego asked excitedly.

Bess reached the doorway and quickly stepped back into the barn's shadows. "Too late, Jeremiah's coming," she whispered.

"By himself?"

"With a dog."

"Has he seen you?"

"I don't think so."

Will dropped his voice. "Get behind the door. Is the dog loose?"

"No, on a rope."

"When he comes in grab the rope and tie the dog fast before it realises what's happening," Will said.

Bess looked quickly round trying to assess where and how.

Will said: "I'll deal with the man; Diego, you stay there on the straw and don't move." He moved to stand on the other side of the doorway. They could hear the dog panting. The sound drew nearer and a shadow fell across the threshold.

"Still here?" said Jeremiah. "I warned you." The dog came through the doorway, bristling at Diego lying on the straw. "Get him," snarled Jeremiah.

Bess stepped out from beside the door opening and grabbed the rope, holding it fast, as Jeremiah let go. The dog leaped forward and the rope tightened round its neck throwing the animal off balance. Bess hung on, digging in her heels. At the same time, Will grabbed hold of Jeremiah, lifted him off his feet and threw him against the wall. Bess, looping the rope tight round a post, heard a wooden side panel snap as the man's head cracked against it. Teeth bared, the dog snarled and snapped, confused by the sudden appearance of not one but two foes from different directions.

Bess kicked out and felt her shoe connect. The dog yelped. The rope held and tightened round its neck once again. The dog floundered, fell on its back, struggled back on its feet and leapt forward again, snarling and choking, straining against the rope, its forelegs scratching at thin air, its hind legs scrabbling on the dirt floor. At the far side of the barn, Jeremiah lay inert, his head at a strange angle. Will, his face pale, stepped back and leant against the wall, staring down at the fallen gamekeeper.

"Is he all right?" asked Bess. The twisted neck gave its own answer.

"I dare not look," said Will.

"Poof!" said Diego. "The man is evil. He deserve to die."

"Shut up!" snapped Will.

"Perhaps he's just stunned," said Bess. She stepped cautiously forward. The dog leapt at her, spraying spittle. Jeremiah's eyes were open, gazing blankly into space. Bess bent down and touched his neck, feeling for a pulse. She reached inside the man's shirt and searched for a heartbeat. There was none. She glanced at Will; the giant was leaning back against the wall, his head thrown back, his eyes closed tight.

"It was no one's fault, Will," Bess said softly.

Will opened his eyes. "He's dead, then?"

Bess hesitated. "Yes," she said at last.

"God in Heaven," Will muttered. "What have I done?" He moved away, the dog leapt again, straining to attack him. Will circled the animal, keeping it between himself and the body on the floor. When the length of the barn separated him from Jeremiah's body, he sank down on his haunches and stared hopelessly at Bess.

"What are we to do?" she asked.

Will made no answer.

"Will, it was no one's fault."

"Aye, it was," he whispered. "It was mine."

"No, if anyone's, it was mine, for bringing you into this."

Will stayed silent, horror clearly etched across his face.

"Will," Bess insisted. "We have to come to a decision. What do we do?"

Will looked up and slowly forced himself to focus his mind. "What we set out to do, I suppose," he said, shakily. "Move Diego out of here. It's even more vital now." He nodded at the body and swallowed. "He'll be missed, they'll come searching and when they find him a manhunt will start."

"We must bury him," said Bess.

"I've taken his life, I'll not add to that by burying him in unholy ground. Leave him where he is."

"If we do, Will, they'll find him," cried Bess.

"Aye, they'll find him. Eventually. There's naught we can do about that."

"Not eventually, Will. They'll hear the dog and find him before nightfall."

Bess could see him thinking what they might do with the dog. "No," she said. "Not that."

Will shuddered, then nodded. "Aye, enough is enough, don't concern yourself. Anyway, with luck we'll be away before then."

***

Bess trotted the horse over from where they'd hidden it in a neighbouring field. "Here," she called. Will came to the barn opening with Diego cradled in his arms and lifted him up as though he were no more than a bag of feathers.

"Stick your leg out straight; that way it won't rub against the horse's coat," he said. "No, don't try sitting astride; sit sideways."

"Am I to ride like a woman?" asked Diego. "I can ride without such help."

"You'll do as you are told," snapped Will. "You may well be able to ride a horse astride with two good legs, but not with that wound." Will turned to Bess. "Get up behind him and grip him firmly round the waist, that way he'll not fall."

"There is no need," said Diego. "I have been riding horses since I was a child."

"Not without a saddle, you haven't. And not with a wounded leg. You fall and you'll open up the wound again and ruin any chance of us getting you clear," replied Will tightly. "Now get up behind him, Bess, and let's not waste any more time."

Bess gathered her skirt, swung herself up, and gripped Diego tight, surprised at the keen pleasure it gave her, a sense of desire rising inside her that she understood only too well. She pushed it away. This was no time to think of such things.

Will took the halter and began trotting the horse across the meadow. They'd passed below the hill and had crossed the stream in the valley bottom before Will finally slackened speed.

"No sign of anyone," said Bess, glancing over her shoulder. She could still make out the faint sound of barking. With luck, anyone hearing it would think it was Gabby the hermit's dog.

"Praise be to God for that," puffed Will. He glanced up at them: "I'm out of sorts for this kind of thing. Sentry duty does little for soundness of wind, that's for sure." They walked on in silence, both thinking of what had happened back at the barn, and where they might hide Diego.

The cart was as they'd left it. Will tethered the horse to a branch and dropped to the ground. "Let me catch my breath and I'll lift you down," he said to Diego.

Bess slid off the horse and patted the animal gratefully. "What do we do, now?" she asked quietly.

Will rose to his feet and began clearing brushwood away from the cart. "I'll take him into St Mawes. He can hide in the cart."

"And when you get there?"

"There's an empty cottage, not far from the castle. I noticed it by chance the other day. He can hide there."

"What if the person who lives there decides to return?"

"It's half derelict. No one could live in it."

"Except perhaps a Spaniard," said Diego.

"Except a Spaniard who has little choice in the matter," said Will heatedly. "Except a Spaniard who by rights should be handed over to the authorities, and would have been some two weeks ago if some well-thinking person hadn't taken pity on him. Except a Spaniard who's an ungrateful wretch and would have died but for that same person's attentions."

Diego's face was flushed crimson. "Yes, I am sorry. I should not be angry. Bess has done everything for me and I am - what you say? - full of thank you."

"Now, let's have no more nonsense," Will said softly. "The day has taken its toll of us." He held up his arms. "Right, down you come." The Spaniard slid unwillingly into Will's arms. "There, that wasn't so bad, was it?"

Diego gave a reluctant nod. "No… for a Spaniard," he said. "Not so bad."

Will's lips twitched. "Aye, for a Spaniard."

Bess, about to smile at the exchange, quickly straightened her face. "What next?" she asked.

"We'll make an opening between the sacks so that he can lie down, then pile them around him. When we get to St Mawes, I'll carry him into the cottage and go on to the castle. I won't be able to get him anything to eat before tomorrow…"

"Food!" cried Bess. "I left it behind in the barn."

"There's nothing we can do about that now: we're not going back for it. He'll just have to manage. The sacks on the cart contain flour and raw turnips. He's welcome to taste one of those." Will looked at her. "Bess, I can't leave the castle when I like, I'm subject to duty. Nor will I be able to get away for any length of time, which means only one thing: you'll either have to come to St Mawes or Diego will have to make his own way from there. And I don't think he can."

"I've already thought of that. I'll come to St Mawes, though I've no idea how I'm going to manage it."

"There is no need," said Diego softly. "You have done enough. I can find my own way."

"That's not what I mean. I mean, I have no idea, as yet, how I'm to get you across the Fal estuary, not how I'm to get to St Mawes. But get you across, I will."

"So, how did you think you were going to do it, when you started out on all this?" asked Will.

"The truth is, I never thought that far ahead."

"Well, you're going to have to think about it now. First, you have to find an excuse to visit St Mawes for a day or two, maybe three. If you can't find an excuse that holds water, you'll just have to do it anyway and try explaining your action when you get back. One thing is certain, he can't make the journey alone. And if I were to be absent for that length of time, I'd be posted as a deserter and every man in the castle would be out looking for me."

"I know that," replied Bess. "Anyway, you've done more than enough. It's up to me, now."

Diego took in a deep sighing breath. "I do not understand. Why do you both risk your lives like this?"

"I've no idea," sighed Will. "We must be mad."

Five minutes of moving sacks around and a space was

made where Diego would be hidden from view; then, with Will's help, Diego crawled into the space. Will climbed back down. "You move the last sack into position while I back the horse into the shafts."

Bess nodded and grasped hold of the sack and looked at Diego. Tears formed in her eyes. Monday! Suddenly, the two days before she would see Diego again seemed like an age. Anything could happen to him and she'd never know. She thrust the thought angrily aside. "You'll be all right," she said.

Diego gazed back at her and a wave of emotion suddenly surged through his body. He leaned forward, pulled her to him and kissed her full on the lips. "Forgive me," he said, his voice broken by the intensity of his feelings. "Do not desert me, Bess," he whispered. "Come to me in St Mawes. I need you."

Her pulse racing, Bess blushed and nodded, her heart, despite the tears, singing with joy, "Apologies are not warranted." Then: "Can you breathe?" she asked. She couldn't. She felt she would never be able to breathe normally again.

"Of course he can," snorted Will, coming up behind her.

"Yes, I am well," said Diego.

Will helped move the final sack into place. "See you in St Mawes," called Bess with a catch in her throat.

"Yes, I will see you in St Mawes," called Diego. "Bess…" he started to say, then halted, lost for the right words.

Bess reached out her hand, gripped his and squeezed it hard. So much to say but this wasn't the time. She turned to Will: "Today's Saturday. I'll leave it a day and come on Monday., whether I've arranged matters or not. It'll be late afternoon before I get there. It's a three hour walk."

"If I can get into Tregoney, I'll be able to meet you on the road. The same place as today? Or at Treworlas?"

"Your captain must have a mighty deep purse."

"I keep telling him I have to go back and collect things we've paid for but the merchants have run out of. He just curses the merchants."

"And if he finds out?"

"How? He never leaves the castle."

"You'd better go," Bess said.

Will nodded. "God be with you."

Bess reached out and took hold of Will's hand. "God be with both of us." Then: "Will…" She paused. Best not to mention the subject of Jeremiah further. Will was the kind of person who might dwell on it and be plagued by remorse. "Till Monday, then. But not Treworlas; somebody might see me loitering there. I'll start walking. Meet me on the road to St Mawes."

***

Will slowed the cart down as the horse pulling it reached the fork in the road that led down to St Mawes castle, his eyes searching in each direction - down the hill towards the harbour, towards the castle, back the way they had come.

All was quiet, no one on any of the roads. Ahead, the sea sparkled in the sunlight, shining like polished blue steel. The view always enthralled him. He might be a Dorset man but he could still see beauty in this Cornish scene. But now he had other things to worry about. He flicked the reins and urged the horse on.

The derelict cottage lay near the top of the hill. "Nearly there," he said in a low voice. "Stay hidden," he warned without turning his head.

Behind him, Diego murmured something in a muffled voice. What it was, Will couldn't hear but assumed the Spaniard had understood the need for caution.

"Nothing is approaching and I'm about to turn in behind the cottage. Don't show your head," he warned as he heard Diego move. "Not until we are safely out of sight."

Safely? he thought. There was nought safe about this. The castle was less than half a mile away. Few militiamen came up this way: other than the occasional horse drawn cart, traffic was non-existent; most movement was from the castle to the harbour and back again. Nevertheless, he was a fool to get caught up in all this. Hiding the horse behind the cottage wouldn't stop the animal whinnying.

He pulled the cart to a halt. "Don't speak," he said, keeping his voice low. "Voices can carry." He climbed up into the cart and began moving the sacks.

Diego looked at the cottage. The back of the house was worse than the front. The straw thatching had rotted; the window was just a hole in the stone wall and open to wind and rain; the door hung crookedly by a single, rusted iron hinge.

"It doesn't look much," Will said defensively, "but it's all I can find."

"It is only for two nights," Diego said. "The windows have no glass. Let us hope it does not rain."

"It's a farm worker's cottage. Farm workers, like fishermen, can't afford glass. They have wooden shutters to keep out the weather, but unfortunately these have long gone. Either rotted or taken for firewood," Will said, anxious to be moving before someone came by and heard the horse neighing. He opened the back door: it gave a loud squawk that set his heart racing.

Inside, the rotted straw gave off a sour smell. Diego looked for access to the upper floor but saw just a hole in what was left of the ceiling. "Where is the staircase?" he asked.

Will smiled. "This is not a rich man's mansion. Cottages don't have staircases. If you want to go up to the bed chamber you climb a ladder."

Diego looked around: one room on the ground floor, one room above, a broken ladder lying in the corner. And that was all. This was the first time he had ever been in a peasant's hovel. Did people really live like this?

Suddenly, he was struck by how much he had and how little someone like Bess had, and how much she must have struggled to find enough food and rough garments out of their meagre supplies in order to feed and clothe him. "No matter," he said. "I thank you. It will do fine."

Will looked at him. "It's not good, but it'll have to suffice. I'll try and bring food later."

Diego smiled ruefully. "Do not worry. It is more than good."

***

Will came by foot as the sun was setting. The lane was quiet. It was payday: anyone with sixpence in their pocket to spare, would be on their way from the castle to the inn, just off the harbour, by way of the lane that ran along the shoreline. Proving this was so, he heard raucous laughter drifting up the hill from the tavern below.

Inside the cottage, the ground floor room was empty. Will looked round, his heart in his throat: had Diego risked going outside? Then saw the ladder had been put in place and guessed that, somehow, the Spaniard had managed to climb to the room above. He mounted the ladder, wondering whether it would hold his weight. It did. Upstairs, Diego was asleep. Treading softly, not to wake him, Will placed the cloth wrapped food near his head and stood there gazing down at the Spaniard, his eyes taking in the injured leg below the fisherman's smock. The light was going as dusk fell but there was enough to see that the leg was healing. No lover of Spain, Spaniards or anything Spanish, he nonetheless felt a glow of satisfaction. His knowledge of medicine, though scanty, had saved a man's life.

Meanwhile, the Spaniard would have to make do with what little food he'd brought, for he'd not be able to call again until Monday. And then, hopefully, Bess would be with him.

Quietly he climbed back down the ladder again.

***

Diego woke to find dawn breaking; the sun about to rise, the sky aglow with a pearly light that foretold a fine day. He lay there thinking. Bess, would she come? He hoped she would. Hoped? No, he suddenly realised he would be devastated if she didn't. No one had ever shown him such solicitude, such tender loving care. Not even his mother. Transcending all fear of retribution, patriotic pride, national prejudice, Bess had nursed and cared for him. Was this, he once again asked himself, what love was all about? The giving of oneself? Regardless? Monday seemed so far away…

16
The Derelict Cottage

It was Monday at long last and Bess had reached Trewithian before she heard the wheel-creak and shod hooves of an approaching cart. To her relief Will came into view. He pulled up and Bess climbed up to sit beside him.

"How is he?" she asked, settling herself on the seat.

"Well enough. I haven't had an opportunity to see him since Saturday evening. And then he was asleep. But the leg seems to be healing at last and there's no sign of any fever. I expect at the moment he's chaffing at the bit, eager for your arrival. Have you brought victuals?"

Bess held up a sack. "Some bread and baked fish."

"Thank the Lord for that. Enough for two, I hope. I'd not hope to keep feeding the both of you without raising someone's suspicion."

Bess smiled. "No, we wouldn't want to do that. The truth is, you've reached your mountainous size already, Will, but we've still a way to go."

"Aye, that's true enough.."

Bess turned and looked at the stores stacked in the back. "Despite your claim on Saturday, Will, I couldn't see your captain letting you out again this soon. There's me quite expecting I'd have to walk the full distance, then ask for you at the castle in order to find out where this cottage is you've found us."

Will chuckled. "I hid three sacks. Then told him the merchant had run short and said to return on Monday. As I'd already spent his money he could do little other than abuse the merchant for being a money grubbing thief, and me for being a Devon dolt. I told him Dorchester is in Dorset. It didn't make much difference - he still thinks I'm a dolt."

Bess smiled. "Well, with luck you won't have to lie again. Is Diego fit enough to move, do you think?"

"His leg's still raw; the new skin that's forming is pulling at the wound, but it would be foolish to stretch our luck further so, yes, he has to be moved. How did you get away?"

Bess hesitated, but there was no point in leaving Will in the dark. "I left a message scratched on a slate in the food cupboard." Short and terse it had said: 'Gone to St Mawes. There is something I have to do. Be back in two days'. Bess just hoped that it wasn't too terse.

"What will they think, do you suppose?"

"I've no notion. I've never done anything like this before."

Will glanced sideways at her. "Has anything happened about the poor gamekeeper?"

"Aye, they found him."

"When?"

"We're not sure. It's my belief they found him Saturday evening. Anyway, news filtered back to our village that he'd presumably been killed by a poacher and Sir Hugh has posted a reward of ten gold pieces. So everybody's busy looking for someone to arrest."

Will shook his head. "Bad news."

They rode in silence for a while. "I'm sore distressed about the gamekeeper," Will said eventually. "I've prayed for his soul and my forgiveness every night. One time I worried about having to kill Spaniards, now my first turns out to be an Englishman."

"It was an accident, Will. It couldn't be helped."

Will grunted and lapsed back into silence.

"The problem," Bess said after a while, "will be getting hold of a boat. I hate the idea of stealing one, but I see no alternative."

"Try looking on it as borrowing."

"Stealing, borrowing without the owner's permission, it's all one and the same; just words to ease the conscience," Bess told him.

Will's regard for boats was that of a landsman - they were objects built to be used, nothing more. Whereas, to a seafaring man they were as personal and precious as a home. "There are boats on the harbour wall," he said, "that never seem to leave dry land; they stay there for days. With luck, the owner will never know it's been away."

Will also didn't know fishermen. The vast majority would go and see if their boat was safe at sunrise and again at sunset, even though it was beached.

She nodded. "Aye, if that's the way it has to be, so be it."

"Dusk tomorrow evening will be the best time; men's

eyes are tired from a day's work and the fading light will make it difficult for them to see clearly."

"Not possible," said Bess. "We need an incoming tide. Low tide is at midnight; it'll be on the ebb until then and could drag us out to sea. And going with the noonday tide in broad daylight, will be far too dangerous. We'll sail over in the early hours, while it's still dark. With the wind behind us and the tide in our favour, it'll not take more than an hour."

"And if there's no wind?" asked Will.

"Then it'll be a hard row and will take more like two. Whichever way, we'll be there before dawn."

Will nodded. Bess was surprised at his lack of seafaring knowledge; even a countryman must be aware of winds and tides.

"Anyone else gone down with the Great Sweat?" Will asked.

"Not yet. Jep and his wife are the only two so far. Father says if no one else gets it, we can thank Jep's wife, Kate, for saving us. She wouldn't let anyone near Jep, save herself; kept everyone at arms length while she nursed him; then wouldn't let anyone in the house when she suffered the same."

"Brave of her. There's not many who'd act like that. So who takes the fish into Truro?"

"Will Trudgeon, the alehouse keeper. I think he feels he's doing something for Jep who was a great friend as well as a regular customer. Kate's taken in the Trist children and the extra money from taking the fish cart must be more than welcome. She also minds the alehouse while Will's gone. Running an alehouse in a small fishing village can't be very profitable."

"Aye, I suppose so, though I never saw a poor inn keeper yet." The horse jogged monotonously on. "It seems the Armada has been defeated," Will remarked, "and the war's all but ended. Least, that's the rumour. But I don't think it can be considered over that easy. Easy in terms of politics maybe, but not so easy in terms of hatred and fighting."

"Have you told Diego?"

Will shook his head. "He'd not believe it. Though he might if we said the Spaniards had won."

"Father says to stay alert, such news can easily prove false, and it wouldn't be the first time."

"That's true."

"My first thought was that Diego would now be out of danger and could make his way home in peace, but war doesn't appear to end as finally as that."

"It'll be months, if not years, before relations are back to normal. If ever."

"Ever's a long time, Will." They fell silent. Bess wondered what her parents would say when her mother opened the food cupboard and read her message. More important, what would the daughter find to say to her parents when it was all over and she returned?

"Coming into St Just," announced Will.

Bess nodded. Two more miles. A feeling of excitement began to build inside her. "Whereabouts is the cottage?"

"At the top of the hill, where the road forks down to the castle."

As far as Bess could recall, it was open country at that point. "Any other dwellings around it?"

"No, it stands on its own; that's why I chose it. There's another, down the hill, towards the village, but nothing more until you reach a side lane that cuts down to the harbour. As long as you're quiet, no one will know you're there. You'll have to keep watch for travellers, though: the road runs near the house."

"How near?"

"About twenty paces."

Bess gazed at him in alarm. "Twenty paces?"

"As long as you make no noise, you'll be safe. The road's not used much; just the odd cart on its way to Tregoney or the ferry at Tolvarne. St Mawes is a sleepy place, the road leading to it is never that busy. Most people needing to do business in a town, travel to Penryn by water."

The broad vista of the Fal came into sight. Bess gazed across the open stretch of water to the distant outlines of Pendennis Castle where afternoon sun glinted off cannons guarding the Fal estuary. To the right of Pendennis Point, lower and huddled along the shoreline, Bess could see the grey stonework of Arwenack Manor and the splatter of houses that was the tiny fishing village of Falmouth, its facing foreshore in late shadow. Bess thought: we could be over there tomorrow night, or by the early hours of the following morning.

As though reading her mind, Will said: "Have you been there, before?"

She shook her head. "Never. I've been to St Mawes, but never across the water to Penryn or Falmouth."

"So, will Diego remember his way around? It's been what, five years? Things change."

"We'll manage."

The cart rounded a bend. "There it is," said Will.

The cottage stood on high ground, just off the road. Below it lay St Mawes village, with cottages along the water's edge basking in the afternoon sunshine. By the look of the weeds and saplings growing close to its walls, Will told her, the cottage was built of cob - Bess knew full well how that could crumble - and had remained unoccupied for years. Two holes gaped in the thatched roof and ferns grew out of the sides of a crumbling chimney stack. Tiny windows, their wooden shutters either rotted or taken by someone, stared blindly out at the surrounding weeds. Bess tried not to show her misgivings: the barn had been a palace compared to this. But then, she told herself, they were looking to stay here for no more than two days, not a lifetime.

"It's more comfortable inside," said Will, sensing her dismay. "We cleared debris from the ground floor, and the upstairs floor boards stop most of the rain." He pulled the horse up and glanced round, listening for anyone approaching. "There's a track leading round to a door at the back," he said. "We'll pull the cart in there."

Bess nodded. As the cart lurched round to the back of the cottage, Diego appeared, limping badly. At least he was now using his injured leg, Bess thought. She glanced over her shoulder, the road was hidden by the undergrowth.

"Bess…!"

"Tell him to keep his voice down," muttered Will. "I'll follow you in."

"…You came. I think you might change your mind when I am gone."

Bess jumped down, walked over and grasped Diego's arm in greeting, all the time wanting to feel him wrap his arms around her. Remembering the kiss he had given her, she had a distinctly warm feeling that Diego, but for Will's presence, would have done so again. She eased back and looked at his face. There was a softer look in his eyes. Gone was much of the arrogance of previous days. No longer was he looking at her as an underling, a servant, someone of no consequence. "No, I haven't changed my mind," she said. The knot in her stomach began to unwind. "Will said not to make too much noise."

"I am so happy to see you, I forget. I think Monday will never come. Now you are here."

"I'm pleased to see you, too," Bess said shyly. "Lets go in; Will's tethering the horse."

"Yes, come into my house." He took her hand. "It is not very beautiful, but it is better than an English prison. Tomorrow we go to Penryn?"

"First we have to spy out the land, and get hold of a boat."

"Yes, we must spy out everything."

Diego was like a young boy excited at the thought of going on a much-looked-forward-to journey. Will came through the doorway, ducking his head below the frame. Embarrassed, Bess disentangled her hand. "Well, what do you think?" Will asked.

Bess looked round. The stone floor slabs had long been removed - more likely there had never been any - but the bare earth was dry and covered with a layer of dust and straw from loose, blown in thatching. Above their heads - low enough to make Will walk with his head bent - oak beams supported the upper floor boards. No stairs joined the two floors; then Bess saw the ladder, its rungs broken in two places, still offered access. "Looks as though it's been deserted a long time, but it's dry," she said and glanced through the window space. Once again the nearness of the road gave her concern. "And secluded, if you're quiet and don't show your head," she added.

"Aye, noise is the biggest hazard. On a still day, voices can be heard from the road quite easily. You'll have to talk in whispers."

"Unfortunately, I have no food to offer," said Diego, glancing at the sack Bess was carrying.

"No matter. I have some."

"That is fortunate."

Bess laughed.

"Keep your voices down," scolded Will.

"Sorry. How's the leg?"

Diego lifted it stiffly. "It is much better. I do not have the leaves on it any more. Will says to let the air mend it." Bess glanced at the wound. Webs of new skin puckered flesh round the edge of the burn. "Sometimes it…" Diego faltered and made a scratching motion with his right hand.

"Itches?"

"Itches. Yes, that is right. It itches."

"Good. It's a sign that the wound is mending."

Bess turned to Will. "What are you going to do?"

"I have to get back to the castle. Tomorrow, I'll bring more food. In the meantime, get as much rest as possible. When will you go and look at the boats in the harbour?"

"In the morning. They'll notice a stranger, but with the extra militia and others up at the castle now, they'll hopefully not take too much notice."

Will nodded and walked to the door. "Don't forget, talk only in whispers," he warned.

Like lovers, Bess thought. They both nodded vigorously.

***

Henry stared at Nicholas. "She's done what?" he croaked.

For the life of him, Nicholas couldn't think how it had

got so out of hand. He'd tried to make light of it, only to find himself being questioned in such a way that he immediately became muddled, saying first one thing, then another. From there it was only a matter of time before the whole story was out. So far he had avoided telling his father that Diego was a Spaniard, but it was obvious that Henry had no intention of letting the matter rest.

"So, who is this man?" Henry demanded.

"A stranger. I don't know who. You'll have to ask Bess."

"So what's this man to our Bess, then? How did she become involved?"

"I don't know."

Henry frowned, recalling the direction Bess had taken each day. "Is this anything to do with Jeremiah, over at St Michael Caerhays?" he asked suddenly. "Is that where the man was hiding?"

Nicholas, startled by his father's insight, plainly showed his agitation. "I don't know," he said.

Henry ignored the denial. "Why would Bess get herself involved with some poacher or vagrant?" he pressed, more to himself than to Nicholas. "You realise that Sir Hugh has a manhunt organised, looking for whoever killed his gamekeeper?" He grasped hold of Nicholas and shook him. "For God's sake, boy, tell me what all this is about."

"Bess hasn't killed anyone."

"I'm not saying she has. We all know Bess wouldn't hurt a fly. But it's obvious by your expression that she's involved."

214

He took hold of Nicholas's arm and dragged him away from the cottage and out of Elizabeth's hearing. "Once and for all, tell me what's going on."

"Jeremiah was killed by Will Bligh."

Henry was confused. "Will Bligh? What, Will Bligh from St Mawes?"

"Yes."

Henry threw his hands up. "How did he become mixed up in this?"

Reluctantly, Nicholas found himself telling his father about the man hiding in the barn. How Bess had nursed him and Will had provided the medical knowledge. Of Jeremiah's discovery and the actions which had led to his death.

"If it was an accident, then we should tell Sir Hugh so. Running away and hiding will solve nothing."

Nicholas swallowed. "Bess couldn't do that; neither could Will."

"Why on earth not?"

"Because the man in the barn was a Spaniard," blurted Nicholas. "From the Armada, a survivor from a ship that blew up. Bess found him washed up on the beach at Porthluney, hid him and has nursed him when it seemed he would die from his injuries."

Henry stared at Nicholas, dumbfounded.

"A Spaniard! That explains Jeremiah's remark," he said, at last. "A few hours before, Jeremiah had told Sir Hugh that a foreigner was hiding in the barn. That's how they knew where to look. By 'foreigner' Sir Hugh thought he meant from up country, but Jeremiah said no, he thought he was from another country altogether. Don't ask me how he knew, by the man's accent I suppose; or why he didn't inform the authorities, but he didn't. Like a good servant, he told his master. Sir Hugh thought he'd got it wrong and told him to get the man off his land…"

"His name's Diego de Olivarez," said Nicholas. "He's the son of a rich merchant, come to see the Armada battling to conquer us; he's not a soldier. He was on the ship that blew up, that first day of battle, off Plymouth. Bess is trying to get him to Penryn, to papist sympathisers the Spaniard knows, who will help smuggle him back to Spain. I tried to talk her out of it, Father, but she wouldn't listen. Said it was her duty to keep him out of prison where he would surely die. And he did nearly die, his wound was terrible."

Henry was shocked. "Sir Hugh's alerting the garrisons at St Mawes and Truro. So far they think they're looking for a murdering poacher. If this gets out, they'll lock Bess up as a traitor or worse," he said.

"I told her that. It didn't make any difference. She said it was her duty as a Christian to save him. He was no soldier or sailor, Father. Just a man, not much older than Bess, who was attracted by the spectacle of it all."

Henry ignored him. "You'd think Will Bligh would have more sense. He's a militiaman, for God's sake."

"Bess said you knew what Will Bligh thinks of war: he

216

told you."

"Having views is one thing, acting on them is different."

"Not to Bess and Will."

"Aye, not to Bess and Will… So, where are they?"

"St Mawes, but I don't know where."

"Don't worry, I'll find them. Keep your mother safe and for God's sake don't tell her one word of this. Nor tell anyone else."

17
Set Fair

Bess woke at dawn with Diego's arms wound tightly round her. His eyes were closed, his breathing steady, and she gathered he was still asleep. Lying in his arms on the bare floorboards, she glanced out through the shutterless window. The sun, breaking the horizon, was sending shafts of light lancing through the bedchamber. She smiled: if one could call this poor, dilapidated room such. She couldn't even imagine how different it must be to the luxury of Diego's own bedchamber back in Seville.

Back home, her father would be getting ready to start another day's work, alone for the first time since Thomas had been called to the militia and Bess had taken on her brother's workload. Henry would find it hard pulling in the net by himself; even harder would be the questioning looks from other fishermen. Her father was a proud man and Bess was left to wonder what reason he would give for her absence. He wasn't a man to bother with lies; either he would say nothing, or tell the truth and be damned to everyone.

She sighed. Before, he had always sided with her in everything she did, however young or scatterbrained it might be. But this was no youthful exploit; this time she could well be accused of aiding the enemy in time of war. And yet, from a sea ablaze with the hatred and fury of battle, had come tender love and compassion.

She glanced fondly at Diego. He didn't look much like an enemy. In fact, dressed in a faded smock, his black curly hair tumbling over his forehead, he looked much like any other sun tanned Cornish fisher lad with Celtic blood flowing through his veins. It was only when he spoke that the foreignness became apparent. Watching him sleep, she felt nought but extreme tenderness wash through her and wished he could stay with her forever. So, why was she helping him leave? She would miss him, terribly. At the same time, deep down inside, she knew he could never remain. Was that what love was all about? Giving everything? Taking nothing?

Diego stirred, opened one eye, saw her and smiled. "It is early?" he asked softly.

"Dawn," Bess whispered.

"Mmm, that is very early."

"Not to a fisherman. Except for Sundays, we're always up at this hour."

"Ah, Sundays. Sundays in Spain, the bells ring, the sun shines and everyone goes to mass."

"It's no different, here."

"Except for the sun."

Bess smiled. "Yes, except - just occasionally - for the sun."

"The last time I go to church, before we sail, everyone is praying for victory. When we see England, we think it will be easy. It looks so... so..."

"Vulnerable?"

"I do not know that word."

"Quiet? Peaceful?"

"Yes, so quiet; so peaceful." He sighed. "But we are wrong." He looked at Bess. "The invincible Armada. Now it is not so invincible."

Bess hesitated. "They're saying that it's defeated," she said. "Those ships that haven't been sunk are now foundering off the Scottish coast."

Diego closed his eyes, digesting the news. Then said softly: "One hundred and thirty ships, thirty thousand men, how is it possible? But it must be true; I feel it here," He placed his hand over his heart, then moved the hand to place it over hers.

Bess felt a lump rise in her throat, a lump that was a mixture of desire at his nearness and sadness at their approaching parting. Her acknowledgement of this was becoming more certain with every passing hour, even while her body's desires grew ever more pronounced. She sat up, took hold of his hand and placed a kiss on the palm. Lying here like this would only lead to other things, she told herself. There were things she must do. She eased herself away and stood up. "If we are to get to Penryn, I must see about the means."

"Yes, how you say? Spy out the land." He looked up at her. "You will find a boat?"

"Yes, I'll find one," she said with more confidence than she felt. "You'll be sailing for Spain before the end of the week."

"Come with me, Bess."

The suddenness of the request took her by surprise. She looked down at him to see if he was joking. He seemed to be sincere. "And how would your family accept their rich son bringing home a fisher girl? An enemy fisher girl at that?"

"I do not care. Come with me."

"You say that now but reality would very soon put the situation in a different light."

"No, it would not, Bess. Once it would have, yes, but not now."

She stood up. A fleeting image of her father's angry face, on hearing that she had run off with a Spaniard, flashed before her eyes. "We'll talk of such things later," she said and bent to softly kiss his lips. "At the moment I am more concerned with finding us a boat."

***

The village had already wakened when she reached the harbour. Fishermen busy loading up lobster pots and nets and launching their boats down the slipway, with some of the early risers now already well out in the creek towards St Anthony's light. She hung around, watching men carry out familiar tasks that, at this moment, she should be helping her father with. One or two glanced curiously at her, but no one asked what her business was, and within half an hour the last of them had departed to harvest pots and search the sea for fish shoals, leaving her to stand alone on a deserted quay.

She glanced round: two boats lay nearby in the water,

tied to rings in the harbour wall, both vessels too large for her to handle alone. But on the near side of the harbour stood a lone fishing boat with furled sail, similar in size to the boat her father owned. Dragged up on the slipway, it lay angled on its side. Bess strolled over and glanced at it from the corner of her eye, pretending to watch the departing fleet make its way across a placid Falmouth Bay. A pair of oars lay in the bottom of the beached boat; across the transom was lettered the name, Mary Ann.

The hull was in the process of being scraped, one half still encrusted with barnacles and a coating of dried green slime. If St Mawes was anything like Porthloe, Bess knew the boat would remain here for the rest of the day, its owner out in the bay sharing a catch with a neighbour. Further scraping would restart only on the owner's return. And with more than half a day's work still to be carried out, Bess calculated that there was little chance of it being finished by sunset: which meant it would still be here that night.

"Did you find a boat?" whispered Diego, the moment she entered the cottage.

Bess nodded. "A boat called Mary Ann, laid up by the quay."

"Mary Ann, that is a good name. It has the name of Our Lady and an English name as well." He repeated it: "Mary Ann. It will be, how you say, good fortune."

"I doubt the owner will think so when he finds it gone."

"You will bring it back."

Bess nodded. "Yes, I'll bring it back." But she couldn't resist giving a guilty sigh. Taking something that didn't belong to her didn't make its eventual return any more acceptable. Diego asked if anything was wrong. Bess smiled. "No, nothing's wrong," she said.

"Mary Ann," mused Diego "It is a name I will remember forever."

Bess felt that she was unlikely to forget it, either.

"So, what are we going to do?" asked Diego eagerly.

"Let's not talk about it until Will comes."

Diego's face dropped. Bess explained: "I haven't finished working out how we are to do this, yet." The truth was she hadn't worked anything out.

"Can I not help?"

"First, I must try and think through the journey so there are no mistakes. A slip up at this stage and all we've worked for will be undone. We'll talk about it, the three of us, when Will comes."

Diego frowned sulkily. Bess sat on the floor, grabbed hold of his hand and, pulling him down to sit beside her, leaned back against the cottage wall endeavouring to picture the estuary and the opposite shoreline. Never having visited Penryn or Falmouth, it was difficult to imagine what they might encounter. She expected it to be much like St Mawes, with a jetty and houses built alongside the water, for that was certainly how it appeared from a distance.

"Why is Will not a physician?" Diego asked suddenly.

"He knows many things."

"Will is poor," said Bess. "He can't afford to become a doctor. Where would he get the money to study?"

Diego flicked his hand. "I am foolish. I do not think of such things."

"It's different for you," said Bess. "You can become anything you want: an officer, a magistrate, a merchant, a landowner."

"I will join my father, of course. That is what he wants me to do."

"And you? Is that what you want?"

Diego frowned then raised his eyebrows. "I have not thought about it. It is decided."

They fell silent. After a moment, Diego said: "Bess, what is it that you want to be?"

"Me? I already am."

Diego looked at her, perplexed. "I do not understand."

"I already am a woman. In our community women marry and have children. At the moment I'm also a fisherwoman, but that's only until my brother returns." Marriage made her think guiltily of Robert Williams. Somehow, it was no longer so desirable. What was truly desirable was out of her reach.

"Now I ask you the question: Is this what you want?"

"Yes, of course."

"To marry?"

Bess didn't answer.

"Do you not want to be a writer?"

Bess laughed. "People can earn money being a writer?"

"Of course. Someone has to write books. They do not write themselves."

"That's for learned men. And certainly not for women. I write for amusement. I am a fisherwoman, first; a writer for my own amusement, second."

Diego shrugged. "It is a waste."

"It is not a waste. If I enjoy doing it, that's enough."

***

Will came at noon. He had managed to collect a little food and they ate hungrily. Afterwards, Bess told him of the boat lying on the quay.

"Did the men speak to you?" he asked suddenly.

"Only to say that it was a good morning. Why?"

"The garrison's been alerted that the man who killed the gamekeeper over at St Michael Caerhays was a foreigner; some say a Spaniard."

"How can that be?" blurted Diego loudly.

"Keep your voice down."

"When did you hear this?" asked Bess concernedly.

"Yesterday, when I got back to the castle. A messenger from Sir Hugh Fitzwilliam came in and spoke to the captain. The captain then spoke to the garrison. The reward has gone up to twenty gold pieces and everyone has been alerted, including the fishermen of St Mawes. Our captain has also alerted Pendennis Castle in Falmouth."

"The last I heard, they thought it was a poacher."

"I don't know how it's happened but it has, and everyone's on the look out for an enemy agent, a spy. So far, no one's thought he might be from the Armada. That's too far fetched."

"It is dangerous," whispered Diego. "We will be caught."

"Not if we're careful," said Bess.

"The sooner it's over and done with now the better," Will said. "I think you should drop Diego off in Penryn tonight and sail straight back. With luck you could have the boat back in St Mawes by the morning and no one would be any the wiser. Can you get this boat into the water by yourselves?"

"Yes. I think this as well, Bess," Diego said. "In Falmouth, I can find my way to where I want to go."

"We'll see," said Bess.

"What about the boat?" repeated Will.

"Yes, we can manage," Bess said. "We'll need three lengths of round timber, all near enough the same thickness, to use as rollers. Getting the boat launched will be no problem; it's the far side that worries me: I'm not sure of the best place to land."

"Keep well to the right of Pendennis Castle: battlements surround a large area of the headland and they'll be well patrolled."

"It'll be dark when we sail past there. No, it's landing that worries me. If I land in Penryn or Falmouth, fishermen there will see the boat; some may even know the owner and come looking for him. And if I leave it abandoned on a beach it will be even more noticeable."

"I would land as near to where you're heading as possible; it will be less tiring for Diego; his leg's still not strong. The best thing will be to tie the boat up among others; there's no better place to conceal an apple than in a barrel of the same."

"Can we not hide the name?" asked Diego.

"We could hang a sack over the transom," said Bess. "It won't stop someone lifting it up, but it'll prevent casual observers reading it by chance."

"Is the boat recognisable without the name?" asked Will.

"No, there are dozens like it around this part of Cornwall."

"Then I would just tie it up and cover the transom. I still think it better if you drop Diego off and sail back before first light."

"I said, we'll see." She turned to Diego. "So, tell us who are we looking for when we get there?"

"A servant. Her name is Jane Mordaunt. She is old. She look after me when I am young."

"Is she a Catholic?"

"Of course."

"Then she'll be watched closely by the authorities. All Catholics are."

"I do not think so. She is not what we call a good Catholic. She marry a Protestant, so my father he is forced to tell her she must leave us. But each year she write me a letter when a ship is sailing from Penryn to Spain."

227

"Where does she live?"

"She and her husband are servants of Sir John Killigrew at a house they call Arwenack Manor."

Will stared at him. "Dear God!"

"You have heard of him?" Diego asked, in a pleased voice.

"What is it?" asked Bess.

"Sir John Killigrew is captain of Pendennis Castle. The most powerful man in this part of Cornwall. He's the one my captain has warned about a Spaniard on the loose. Arwenack Manor, where he lives, is the most handsome house in the area, some say in Cornwall. I've heard them talking of it at the garrison. Upwards of fifty people, they say, and more than thirty servants live there. It'll be like walking into a lion's den."

Bess thought quickly. "It might have advantages: no one will expect an enemy on the run to call there, and if there are as many around as you say, no one will notice two more. Where is this manor?"

"You can't miss it," said Will. "It's built on the edge of Falmouth, out towards the castle, facing the water."

Bess nodded: "I noticed it when we arrived and looked across the estuary," she admitted. Indeed it would have been difficult not to notice such a building. "If Jane Mordaunt is not a good Catholic and was dismissed by your father," she asked Diego, "what makes you so certain she will help you escape?"

"She is a very good nursemaid and she love me very much. Every letter she writes about the happy time we have together when I am a boy and she is my nursemaid. She is not a bad woman, but my father he is very strict. He is sorry she marry a Protestant, he like her also, and my mother, she like her, but she cannot stay in our house. It is very sad. I cry, she cry, we all cry. I know she will help me."

All three fell silent. Eventually, Will gave a slight shrug. "It seems we have little choice," he said.

"No," Bess agreed.

"But I wish you'd told us earlier," said Will.

"I do not tell you because I do not want to get you into trouble. If they catch you helping me, and find that you take me to see a Catholic, it might be bad for you. It will also be bad for Jane Mordaunt."

"I don't follow that argument," said Will.

Bess shrugged. "It would have made no difference," she said. "I would still do what I am doing."

Will sighed. "That's what I thought."

"Let's hope there's a ship leaving Penryn soon."

"I hear there are plenty anchored there. Turks, Moors, French, a couple of Dutchmen," Will said. "One of them is sure to be sailing south."

"Well, let's hope Jane Mordaunt knows somebody on board, otherwise we're back to trusting strangers."

"Yes, let us hope so," said Diego fervently.

"Amen to that," added Will.

Bess glanced out: the sky was a clear blue, the breeze gentle. Perhaps a little too gentle. Leaves on the trees were hardly moving.

"At least, the weather's set fair," said Will, noticing her glance.

Bess knew Cornish summers better than Will. Mists drifting in off the sea were common in this kind of weather. "Aye, it's set fair," she said.

18
"God Help Us All"

It was mid-afternoon by the time Henry reached St Mawes. He moored Lilybeth in the tiny harbour and stormed up to the castle, demanding to see Will Bligh. The giant Dorset man came to the gate, nodding at the guard who had summoned him, motioning to Henry to say nothing until they'd left the castle precincts. Not that Henry needed such telling.

Together, they walked back towards the harbour, seeking privacy for what both knew would be a difficult conversation. Will was the first to break the silence: "So, how much do you know?" he asked quietly.

"That's the devil of it, and the part that hurts most. Nothing. What little I've gleaned comes from Nicholas, not from Bess. Every day, out fishing, close as two people can get, and I know more of what goes on in my neighbours' houses than I do in my own."

Will halted by a rocky outcrop, glanced quickly round, then indicated that they should sit. "You know she loves you all deeply," he said.

"And this is how she shows it?"

"Yes, this is how she shows it: by keeping you out of it, by protecting you, by making certain you can't be accused of involvement."

"A better way would be for her to not become part of such action in the first place."

"A better way for others, maybe, but not for her."

"Yet she told her brother."

"Is that what he says?" asked Will. Henry nodded. "It's not so. He followed her and found out for himself. After that there was no keeping him out of it. He threatened to tell you if she forbade him."

Henry said, bitterly: "She told you."

"That was in desperation. The man was about to die. She discovered I knew something of medicine. I just supplied knowledge that enabled her to save a friend's life."

Henry turned on him, angrily. "Friend? The man's a Spaniard, for God's sake. Will, you're a militiaman. The man's an enemy of our Queen and her realm."

Will looked round carefully and lowered his voice. "Hush! Anger is making you lack caution. Aye, I'm a militiaman, but one pressed into it and acting against his principles. I gave what little knowledge I have freely in order to save another man's life. I'd have done the same whether he be a Spaniard, Chinaman or African."

"Where are they, Will?"

"Safe for the moment."

"Where?"

"Hiding."

"You'll not tell me?"

"No. For your own sake. And I'll not tell Bess you're here, either."

"I'll find her. I know she intends going to Penryn. And for

232

that she'll need a boat."

"Go home, Henry. Let her complete this on her own. It's her mission. Let her return to Porthloe with the task accomplished. Then forget it ever happened."

"You think we can forget?"

"Yes, I think you can forget and forgive. You have to, for Bess's sake."

Henry stared out across the harbour to St Anthony's Head. "So, what's this Spaniard like?" he asked eventually.

"Like you imagine any Spaniard to be: arrogant, untrusting - though that's not quite true any more - bombastic, full of himself. Rich, spoiled."

Henry looked at him. "Yes, that's how I imagine them. And how does Bess see him?"

Will thought carefully. "I'm not sure. But she doesn't see him in that light. She possibly sees him as the first real friend she's ever had." Will paused. "She might even be in love with him..."

"What the devil does that mean?"

"Or thinks she is."

"I'll find her and bring her to her senses. I'll search St Mawes; follow you when you leave the castle; search the whole of Penryn."

"Following me will do no good: my part is done."

"Are they still here? Or across the water?"

"Go home, Henry. Go home. Sail back the way you came."

"Not till I find my daughter and take her with me. Does she know the militia are looking for a Spaniard?"

"She didn't. She does now."

"She realises this is treason."

"She knows the realm thinks so."

"And that the penalty for that is hanging?"

"I told her that. She said, only if they're caught."

"God help us all."

"Aye, amen to that," Will said. "Spaniards and Englishmen alike."

***

Time is never easy to judge with no timepiece or hourglass to refer to, and especially in the dark with no sun to mark the passage of the hours. To Bess, the Trevanion's normal day began at dawn and ended at sunset; during which time the family worked until their tasks were finished and ate when they were hungry, all carried out in daylight hours. In winter they retired to their beds early; candles were lit when necessary but never wastefully. It was the same for all fisher folk: noting the exact hour had no place in their world. Now, though, with the tide due to turn at midnight, it was essential that they launch the Mary Ann and row round the headland in slack water, and then be able to take advantage of the incoming tide to help them cross the estuary. To start too early would entail them rowing against the ebb. Between them, Bess and Diego devised various methods of judging first one hour, then two, then three.

Finally, agreeing that it must now be midnight, they left the cottage and made their way down to the granite stone quay. Their progress was slow; Diego still found walking difficult. But at least Will had been able to provide him with footwear, if somewhat overlarge. Over her shoulder, Bess carried three lengths of wood, straight larch poles, lifted by Will from a collapsed farm fencing, each measuring three inches in diameter and three or four feet in length.

The village was in darkness: the only lights, a dim candle-glow issuing from one of the castle windows, plus the warning flicker of the lighted beacon at St Anthony Head. Stealthily, they approached the quayside. Reaching it, Bess breathed a heartfelt sigh of relief: the Mary Ann was still there. She felt around in the darkness and found the oars still inside; her hands moved up the mast and touched the furled sail.

"Is this the Mary Ann?" asked Diego in a low voice. Bess whispered back that it was. "It is very small," he said.

"She'll feel big enough when we try moving her." Bess strained her eyes; blackness wrapped itself around them like a thick cloak. It was impossible for her to see whether the slipway was blocked or not; even the water had lost its luminosity.

"The night is dark," whispered Diego.

"Good. That's what we want. Stay here, by the boat. I'll make sure nothing is in the way." Bess felt her way down to the water's edge and back to the Mary Ann. "All clear," she whispered. "Now, listen. We have to lift the back and slide a length of wood under, roll the boat astern by lifting the prow, slide another one under the stern, and keep doing that until she's in the water."

"With only three pieces of wood?"

"Three is enough. Each time, we take the roller from the front and move it to the back." Bess placed the logs on the quayside where she could find them in the dark. "The rollers are here; don't trip over them. Let's see how heavy she is." Exerting their full strength, they lifted the Mary Ann's stern.

"I must stop," gasped Diego.

"Rest while I position the rollers."

A moment later: "I am rested now."

"Right. This time when we lift, I'll slide the wood under with my foot. Ready? Lift…" They both heaved. "Now the same at the bow… Right…"

"I must rest," Diego gasped.

"Yes, rest." She could hear him breathing heavily.

Soon he said: "I am ready."

"Now we place a length amidships," Bess told him. "I'll lift the bow a fraction, if necessary." They did this. "Now we roll the boat gently towards the water; as it rolls off the length in front, pick up the wooden roller and place it under the stern, while I hold the prow steady. Do you understand?"

"Yes."

Slowly the boat lurched backwards down the slipway and, with a slight splash, into the water.

"It is there," exclaimed Diego in a voice that rasped from the effort..

"Are you all right?" asked Bess.

"Yes, I am well."

"Get in and sit in the stern."

Bess pushed the Mary Ann out into the creek and clambered over the side as it glided into the inky blackness. Sitting amidships, she took the sack she'd carried food from home in and tore it in half, then reached forward and tapped Diego on the arm. "Under the seat are a pair of oars, wrap this around one of the shafts where it fits into the rowlock. I'll do the same with the other one."

"I do not understand."

"No matter, I'll do it."

"No, I want to help. I am not an invalid."

"No one has said you are. Take the tiller and watch we don't drift against the quayside." Bess wrapped the oars so that they would make no sound when she came to row. As far as she could judge, the boat had hardly drifted one way or the other. "Perfect," she said. "Slack water. By the time we reach the point it will have turned."

She could feel the excitement radiating out from Diego in waves.

"Leave the tiller. I'll steer with the oars. Just make sure I keep heading in the right direction."

"I try, but it is very dark. I cannot see."

"Watch the light in the castle. Keep it to your right and

judge from that."

"I understand."

Bess fitted the muffled oars and wriggled them backwards and forwards in their housings; they made hardly a sound. Then, dipping the blades into the water, she rowed the Mary Ann slowly out of the harbour entrance. There were a few craft anchored in deeper water, but most were tied to the quay. They passed close to a large ship lying at anchor in the blackness. Bess gave an occasional glance over her shoulder to check their progress but in the main left their course to Diego's whispered 'more right' and 'more left'. The light from within the castle was now hidden by battlements. Bess made her way cautiously along the shoreline, judging how far they were out by the sound of waves breaking on rocks.

"The sky, it is getting light," whispered Diego.

Bess glanced at the coastline. She could see a faint outline of the castle on their right and the black shape of St Anthony Head on their left. "The moon is coming up," she whispered back.

"The soldiers. They will see us."

"It won't shine through: there's a mist hanging over the sky. But it will help us see the shape of the coast."

Bess tipped her face: what little wind blew faintly on her right cheek. She wondered whether it would increase as they left the shelter of St Anthony Head and moved out into the estuary. If not, it would be a hard row. The water was as flat as a millpond, hardly a ripple disturbed the surface, and the waves breaking on the shore sounded lazy and sluggish.

"We are passing the castle," whispered Diego.

"Farther out and we'll raise the sail."

A hundred yards or more and Bess shipped the oars. "Take the tiller. What little there is in the way of a breeze is blowing from the south so we may as well take advantage of it." Standing on the seat, she reached up to the yardarm and lowered the triangular sail. Darkness was no handicap; she'd carried out the task a thousand times on their own boat and could perform the action blindfold.

"We are not going very fast," said Diego.

"We're probably moving faster than when I was rowing. It's just that you can't feel it, sailing with the wind behind you."

"I can see the land."

Bess looked round: the coastline was visible as a black shape against the dark sky. "It won't get much lighter than this; the mist is too thick."

"But it is better, is it not? We can see which way we must go."

Bess adjusted the angle of the sail. "Steer a little to port… to your left."

Diego was offended. "I know that port is left."

"We're heading straight towards Falmouth," said Bess. "That's good."

"How can you know?"

"By the shape of the headland at Pendennis Point."

"Where is that?"

"To your left. You can just make out the castle against the sky."

"Ah, yes, I see it."

Bess sniffed the air; it was getting damper and colder, She knew what that meant. It was the one thing she'd feared might happen.

"The castle has gone," Diego exclaimed suddenly. "There is only darkness."

"It's a sea mist drifting in with the tide." She used the phrase knowingly. A fog bank was more scary than sea mist. Bess tried to keep any anxiety out of her voice. "Keep heading for the same landmark. With luck we'll stay ahead of it." They were running at an angle to the drift; sooner or later the fog bank, for that's what she now knew it to be, would catch up with them. She wished she could see the speed at which they were moving, she could then judge whether they would make more progress with her rowing. She moved aft, next to Diego, and tried to listen to the wake. There was a slight ripple, she doubted that rowing would give them that much more headway and decided to save her energy.

"A little more to port. The tide is making us drift," she said.

Ten minutes passed and Diego said: "The blackness is getting nearer."

Bess didn't answer, knowing that it would be only a

matter of minutes before they were wrapped inside it. They must then trust that the wind stayed the same and they kept heading in the right direction.

The clamminess of the fog reached out and gripped them. Suddenly, they were blanketed by swirling darkness. Shivers of raw cold ran down their backs. The spar dripped with moisture and the sail soaked up the wetness like a flannel. Neither spoke, recognising the fact that there was little they could do but trust that the fog bank was small and would soon drift past.

"Keep the tiller exact," warned Bess. "Try not to move it even an inch." Easier to say than to do, she thought. With luck, the calm water would allow them to maintain a straight course. Diego kept very still and said nothing; he was a landsman and the incident was disquieting. Bess, no less disturbed, had been caught in sea mists and fogs before, but that was always with her father, and in waters with which they were familiar.

"Perhaps we should row," said Diego at last.

"It will be too difficult to keep the boat straight. If one arm pulls harder than the other, we'll just go round in circles. Don't worry, it'll pass. My father and I are out in mists like this all the time," she lied.

"It is very alarming. It is also very cold and wet."

"All part of the English summer," she joked. Diego did not answer. Bess suspected that he had experienced more than his fill of English summers. Then, as suddenly as it had wrapped itself around them, the fog unfolded, forming a wall of blackness drifting ahead.

"I can see the castle," cried Diego.

"Hush, voices travel across water," Bess cautioned in alarm.

"I am sorry, but I am so happy to see the land again."

Landmarks ahead of them were hidden by the fog bank; Bess tried to judge from the position of Pendennis whether they had drifted off course. The castle was still on their port beam but seemed to be nearer.

"More to starboard," she said. "A little more… that's it. Keep her like that."

"Why do sailors call ships she," asked Diego.

"This is a she: she's called the Mary Ann."

"Yes, but even if it was called by a man's name you would still call it she."

"I've no idea why: they're always she and always will be… That must be the village of Falmouth ahead of us."

"Where?"

"Straight ahead. There's nothing to see, the village is small and in darkness. Follow the skyline. In that part where it dips down to the right of the castle."

"Yes, I see."

"Closer in, we'll row along the shore."

"How long have we been on the water?" asked Diego.

"Over an hour. Probably nearer two."

"Then we must be very near."

"Yes," Bess said uncertainly.

"What is the matter?"

"The castle has disappeared. There's another fog bank drifting in."

"How near are we to the land?"

"Half a mile. Quarter. Could be less."

Once more fog swirled round the Mary Ann, curtaining them off from the rest of the world, the dank air and dripping wetness saturating their clothes. Bess could hear Diego's teeth chattering and it wasn't long before her own followed suit. Time stood still. She had no way of knowing whether they were drifting landwards or floating becalmed. For one frightening moment, she had a mental picture of them drifting up the Fal, then slowly down again and out to sea.

She was about to say anything that came into her head, just to break the silence, when the ripple of waves sounded. She peered ahead into the blackness but could distinguish nothing. Suddenly, the prow bumped against something in the water and a strange voice mumbled. Out of the swirling darkness a boat grated along their port side. They held their breaths as it scraped slowly past and faded astern. Then another boat bumped them and their prow thumped something solid.

Bess gripped Diego's arm, felt for his face and placed a warning finger against his lips. Creeping to the bow, she reached into the darkness and her hand met a wooden post, slimy with weed. Drifting slowly past, she warded off another, then another, finally holding one tight to halt their drift. Gripping the wet post, she walked the boat forward, reached Diego sitting in the stern and whispered: "We've hit a jetty."

Diego stood up, his mouth disturbingly near hers. "Where are we?" he whispered.

"I don't know. I think it must be Falmouth. There are boats all around us. At least one has a man aboard, sleeping," she whispered.

"What shall we do?"

"Wait until first light lets us see where we are, then move quietly away before he wakens."

"How long to dawn?"

"Two hours; maybe less."

Bess tied the Mary Ann to a post, and they huddled in the bottom of the boat. Although they kept hearing bumps, they heard no more voices. Diego moved closer to Bess to keep warm. He was shivering with cold. She wrapped her arms round him and pulled him close, their bodies tight against each other.

***

Just before dawn the fog lifted, leaving a faint mist clinging to the water. At the first sign of light, Bess reluctantly eased herself away from Diego and sat up. There was a jetty and a very large house, but no sign of the village. Gradually the sky lightened but still the mists swirled around, hiding the houses then revealing them in misty form. In a boat moored farther along, Bess could vaguely see a huddled figure.

"We ought to try moving up river," she whispered, indicating the sleeping man. "Before he decides to wake."

Diego nodded. The mist was drifting to and fro - one moment, thick, the next, wispy. Quietly, they furled the sail, replaced the muffled oars and edged their way up stream.

"Is this the way to Falmouth?" Diego asked softly.

"It must be. The other way, there's nothing other than that big house and the castle."

"Stop!" hissed Diego.

Bess dug the oars deep into the water and glanced over her shoulder. Ahead in the hazy light was a second quay. Behind it, fishermen's cottages receded up a hillside. In the foreground was moored a huddle of small craft.

Falmouth. Not much larger, now they were close and in the middle of swirling mists, than Porthloe, Bess thought.

"We are here?" breathed Diego.

"Aye, we're here," Bess echoed.

19
Jane Mordaunt

It was still early, the mist was beginning to lift and Bess could see that Falmouth might be a fishing village, but it was larger than she'd first thought. Careful not to isolate their boat in any way and make it stand out from the rest of the craft tied alongside the stone quay, Bess eyed the village's slow awakening. Fishermen were now beginning to arrive for a day's toil. From the quayside, she glanced at the Mary Ann. Except for the two pieces of torn sacking she'd hung over the stern, it looked much like the dozens of others moored there. Falmouth might be larger than Porthloe but it was still smaller than the more important Penryn: no more than a village tacked on to the adjoining town. So, would any of the fishermen notice that a strange craft had joined their fleet? She hoped not. Looking round, Bess vaguely recalled her father saying that even this place had grown with the enlargement and manning of Pendennis Castle. Now, with the threat of an impending invasion, and the nearness of Penryn, it was bustling, with strangers here far less likely to be stared at than at home.

She glanced up river. Further along the shoreline, a number of foreign ships, anchored offshore, awaited their turn to come alongside the harbour walls of Penryn; while crews of those already tied to bollards, were already loading and unloading stores, or ashore at the chandleries surrounding the harbour. "Your Mistress Mordaunt should have no trouble searching out a ship sailing south," Bess said softly. "Penryn looks to be a busy port."

"Should we not go and look for her?" asked Diego in an equally low voice.

She could sense the eagerness in his voice. Meanwhile all she was feeling was desolation. "It's early. She'll be busy with her work. Best wait until the household she serves have all breakfasted," Bess answered. That's if she still works there, she mused silently, and if she still wants to become involved. People change their minds. Nursemaid Mordaunt had known Diego when he was small and there was no war between their nations. What she and Diego would do if she now considered herself to be no longer involved with the Olivarez family, Bess dared not think.

Narrow alleyways linked the quay where they stood to a street that ran parallel to the shoreline and up a slight gradient. "There must be nearly fifty houses here and I've seen at least half a dozen taverns," Bess said, glancing round.

"There is not half that number when we live here," said Diego. "Soon Falmouth will be bigger than Penryn."

Bess shook her head. "Penryn will always be the larger of the two. The merchants' offices and warehouses are there, so that's where the ships' captains will head."

"That may be so, but I know merchants," said Diego. "There is more room to build their fine homes in Falmouth. One day they will live here and Penryn will be where they

247

work."

"You're probably right," agreed Bess. "In time, everything changes." More's the pity, she thought.

Leaving Falmouth, along the estuary's south-western bank, they found Arwenack Manor with little trouble. The largest, the most imposing residence between the fishing village and the castle, it would have been difficult for anyone to miss it. Together, they stood in the lane running alongside the water and gazed at the house.

"It's the same large manor house we saw first light this morning," Bess whispered. "There's the jetty, I recognise the boats."

"We could have stayed here," Diego murmured. "We had already arrived."

"And have the boatman waking to wonder where we'd come from?" asked Bess.

"But is it not a good sign? We are lost in mist and still we arrive at the place we seek."

"It's strange, I'll allow you that."

"It is more than strange," said Diego. "It is God's work."

"Let's hope so."

The manor house was built round three side of a central quadrangle. A square tower with an arched gateway faced the water, dominating the main entrance. On the north corner stood a round tower, looking out towards the village of Falmouth. To the south, a high wall enclosed a garden and orchard.

Diego pointed to a side lane: "That must go to the kitchens."

Bess nodded. If Jane Mordaunt was still employed here, then that's where she would most likely be, in the kitchen region.

"What are you two varmints up to?" A boatman, who had been hidden from view, was standing up in one of the moored craft, his head peering over the side of the jetty.

"We're seeking a Mistress Mordaunt," Bess called to him. Probably the same man who'd been asleep while she and Diego had lain curled together; a man whose job was to watch over the jetty at night. If so, he'd been useless as a guard. "We've been led to believe that she might work here."

The man spat into the water. "Aye, she works here." He hoisted himself up onto the landing stage. "So, who wants her?"

"We've a message, from someone who knew her five years back."

The boatman advanced towards them. He was dirty and unkempt, and smelled of unwashed clothing and body odour. "And who may that be?" he asked.

"I'm not at liberty to say: it's personal," Bess said sharply.

"From one of her papist friends, I'll be bound."

Bess feigned surprise. "Surely not. I was told she'd married a Protestant."

"Aye, she did - more fool him - but that don't mean she

ain't still a papist." The man studied her with piggy eyes; switched his gaze to Diego, then back again to Bess. "Wait here. I'll tell her she's wanted," he muttered.

They watched him trudge down the side lane and disappear round the back. Five minutes later, he reappeared. "She'll be out in a while," he said, and walked back to the landing stage. Bess and Diego stood waiting, while the boatman continued to stare at them from the jetty.

"He does not like us," whispered Diego nervously. "Do you think he suspects?"

"I don't know. He's surly, right enough. When Jane Mordaunt appears, leave the talking to me. Don't say or do anything until we're sure it's safe."

Diego nodded.

"Is this her?" Bess asked.

"Yes," breathed Diego.

A short plump woman wearing a black serge skirt, linen bodice and starched cap, was approaching, wiping her hands on a rag. Her brown hair was streaked with grey, her mouth set in a tight line. Eyes switching suspiciously from side to side, she looked first at Bess, then at Diego. "You want me?" she asked bluntly.

Now that she was near, Bess saw her eyes had a softness that belied the grim set of her mouth. Diego kept very still and Bess could sense him holding his breath. "Mistress Mordaunt?" she asked.

"That's who I was told you were asking for."

"We need to be certain." Bess glanced at the boatman. The man hadn't taken his eyes off them. "It's confidential." Jane Mordaunt frowned and Bess thought perhaps she might not have understood the word. "Secret. Can the boatman hear?"

"Not if you keep your voice low."

Bess studied the woman, trying to assess her loyalty to the Olivarez family. After all, the woman had been dismissed by them five years back, and might still harbour ill feelings. Bess sighed and asked herself what other course they had. It was too late for doubts. "The message is from Diego de Olivarez," she said. "Does that name mean anything to you?"

"Diego?" The woman's face went white and for a moment Bess thought she was about to faint. "What is the message?"

"Don't move. The boatman is still watching us," Bess cautioned. "Diego is here."

"Where?" breathed Jane.

"Standing next to you."

For a brief moment Bess thought she might have been too abrupt. Jane Mordaunt turned her head and stared at Diego for a full minute. Slowly recognition dawned and her eyes filled with tears. "Diego," she sobbed.

Bess felt a lump rise in her throat. "Careful," she warned. "We've come a long way and we've no intention of giving ourselves away at this late stage."

"Jane," Diego whispered.

Bess had visions of them falling into each other's arms. "The boatman's watching," she cautioned frantically. "Is there anywhere we can talk?"

Jane pulled herself together and indicated the walled orchard. "Round by the gardens. He won't be able to see us there."

They strolled up the lane and turned a corner. Immediately, Diego and Jane embraced. Bess leaned against the wall and turned her head away. The boatman had left the jetty and was loping up the lane towards them. Soon as he saw Bess looking at him, he halted, turned and strolled slowly back.

"The boatman's trying to spy on us," Bess whispered.

"Diego, Diego, Diego." Jane was sobbing and laughing at the same time.

"Please," pleaded Bess. "If you value Diego's life."

Jane released Diego. "You're right. But if you only knew how I've longed for this moment. There hasn't been a day that's passed without me thinking of him."

Bess said: "Let's walk towards the castle; the boatman will find it difficult then to follow without us seeing him."

"He's a wicked man. He hates me."

"Why?" asked Bess.

"No matter. It goes back a long way, to when I first arrived here. It's not important. My Diego, he is important."

"You have not changed," said Diego as they walked. "You are as I remember you. The same."

"Ah, I wish that were so." She touched her hair. "More

grey, older, frailer, but at heart still the same Jane Mordaunt who sat you on her knee. But you… you have grown. You are a man." She looked him up and down and for the first time noticed his limp. "What happened?"

"It is better," replied Diego soothingly.

"He was washed ashore from the Armada," Bess explained. She gazed fixedly at Jane. "We need help to get him back to Spain."

"The Armada? Are they taking children to fight their wars now?"

Diego was hurt. "I am a man, Jane. And I did not go to fight: I went to see our victory. But, sadly, it did not happen."

Jane patted his arm and turned to Bess. "First," she said, "tell me how you've become involved? Are you a catholic?"

Starting with the discovery of Diego on the beach, ending with their landing that morning in Falmouth, Bess outlined the affair to date. When she'd finished, Jane Mordaunt looked at her and Bess could tell that she saw through her feelings for Diego and understood them; there was a tenderness in the eyes that was slowly being replaced by a hardness of purpose and a determination to protect her former ward at any cost. And Bess understood that. Though different to her own ambitions, they were similar in meaning. Bess gave the woman an acknowledging nod and saw her visibly relax.

"So how can I help?" Jane Mordaunt said.

Bess was surprised at the immediacy of the reaction. She had expected Jane to become flustered, say she was just a servant, a woman, how could she be expected to do anything worthwhile?

"Before you tell me, the first thing is food," Jane said. "You must both be hungry." Bess had given no thought to eating: now, suddenly, she felt ravenous. Both she and Diego nodded vigorously. "I thought so," Jane said. "Then we can talk about getting Diego away." She turned to Bess. "What about you? What are you going to do?"

Bess had tried not to think of their parting, even though this must be the final result - regardless of what Diego had said about her sailing to Spain with him. "I don't know," she said. "Make my way home. But first I'd like to be sure that Diego is safely on his way. Or, at least, that there is a ship that will take him."

Diego shook his head. "We are still talking about such things," he said firmly. "It is not decided. I want Bess to come with me."

Jane looked at him and frowned but made no comment, and Bess could see that she was anxious to take charge and eager for Bess to leave them. "Are they looking for two people or one?" she asked.

"As far as we know, only one," Bess said.

"Good. So two together, is not going to arouse suspicion?"

"Why do you ask?"

"I just want to know how safe it is for you to stay. Safe for Diego, I mean. Let's walk back and I'll fetch you both something to eat. Then this afternoon, on the waterfront, I'll find out which ships are sailing where. You'd best keep out of sight. After dark, I'll slip you into the house and you can hide there for the night."

"What about your husband?"

She hesitated. "Matthew? He's on guard duty up at the castle and will not be back till Monday. The master makes the men take turns. There a week, home a week, and worked to death wherever they are."

"If you dislike it so much, why not leave?" said Bess.

"Because there's nowhere else to go. Around here, you either work for the Killigrews or you starve. There're other kinds of work in Penryn, but I don't favour that. Servants don't find positions easily," she said and turned to Diego. "How I long for the old days…"

"Are you a good Catholic still?" he asked.

They had reached the house once more. Jane paused. "I was once, not so much any more."

"But you'll still help Diego?" Bess asked, her face showing concern.

"Don't worry yourself about that. But not because I'm a Catholic. But for the same reason you do." She turned and opened a back service door. "Wait here, I'll get you some food."

***

There were boats and large ships everywhere. There was also a strong military presence. It had been years since Henry was last in Penryn. The town was much like Truro in size, possibly larger and certainly busier, with grey stone buildings, busy wharfs, merchants, militia, fishermen, housewives and sailors, all milling around. The main difference lay in the number of foreign seamen speaking languages that were unknown to him.

The St Mawes boat that Bess and the Spaniard had used was unlikely to have been dragged up on dry land, he thought. It was more likely to be tied to a mooring where Bess could easily get at it. Why he was searching for a boat, rather than for Bess, he had no idea; he simply knew that finding the stolen Mary Ann appeared a sensible starting point. She needed to return to the Roseland peninsular as soon as possible and for that she needed a boat. Back in St Mawes, hearing of the missing Mary Ann had been a sliver of good fortune that he hoped wouldn't end up proving a false lead.

Two militiamen standing nearby were studying him hard. Did he look like a Spaniard? Henry didn't think so. Perhaps they just sensed that he was a stranger. One turned his back and muttered something to the other who walked over and tapped Henry on the arm with his pikestaff.

Henry stood his ground: "Yes, friend? What can I do for you?"

Hearing the Cornish accent, the man relaxed. "You live in these parts?" he asked.

"No, here on business. I'm from Porthloe, across the water in Roseland."

"Where the Spaniard escaped from."

"Where the Spaniard was hiding," Henry corrected. "Not difficult to escape from as no one had him in custody. Hiding in a barn just along the coast, we hear. Though, in truth, we've seen neither hide nor hair of him."

"We?"

"The village where I live. To be honest, I think the news has been exaggerated out of all proportion. For a start, no one truly knows that he is Spanish. Could just be from up North or a Welshman. Lots of people have unfamiliar accents. I've been sitting here listening to them all, just a moment ago. Foreign speaking doesn't necessarily mean the man you seek is Spanish. He could just as easily be a Moor or a Maltese."

The militiaman grunted. "Whoever, whatever, there's a reward of twenty gold pieces out for him. Not that we'd see a single piece if we found him: our captain would stick it in his own purse."

"Aye that's the way of the world. There's those that do, and there's those that make others do it for them."

The second militiaman approached. "What business?" he said.

Henry looked at him. "What business?"

"That's what I asked. What business has a fisherman, other than catching fish?"

"Fishermen buy boats. Not often, I admit; but if they can't build them themselves, then they must needs buy them from those that can. Mine's old, needs replacing and that's why I've sailed her here, looking to see what's going second-hand." The two militiamen were fast beginning to lose interest. Henry pressed on, hoping to bore them into a hasty retreat. "A boat has to be made right as well as look right. You have to inspect the planking, make sure there's no worm." The men started to move away; Henry followed them. "Then there's the keel: a good keel has to be well formed and not skimped." He raised his voice as the men reached an alley. "If you know of a good boat, I'm on the quay for the rest of the day…" They disappeared round the corner.

Slowly Henry relaxed and continued his search for the Mary Ann. Determined to find it before the situation got any worse.

20
Tragedy Strikes

Bess and Diego spent the rest of the day lying in long grass growing on top of a disused quarry. From here they were hidden from prying eyes and could see the roofs of Arwenack Manor spread below. The river estuary lay directly in front, the sea to the south; to their left, on a nearby hill, sat the blackened ring of the beacon fire that had warned Penryn and Falmouth of the Armada's approaching might.

The surrounding air was pleasantly warm and filled with the soft hum of insects; they'd eaten their fill of the food supplied by Jane Mordaunt and were now lazing in the afternoon sun, taking comfort from each other's presence, with Bess only too aware they must soon part, desperate not to mention the fact.

Towards the end of the day they watched the sun go down. Arwenack Manor and the village of Falmouth already in shadow; across the river mouth, the tiny hamlet of Nankersey golden from the sun's setting rays.

Cornwall at peace, Bess thought. She retied the bow in the front of her bodice and smoothed down her rucked up skirt, her heartbeat still raised, her body still tingling from the ardency and urgency of their lovemaking.

"England is beautiful," said Diego drowsily. Adding: "When it is not raining." He paused. "I do not know this before; I think it is grey and dull. But it is also very peaceful.

Which I do not expect."

"Mmm…" Just what she was thinking, Bess agreed, lying back with her eyes closed.

"Wars are very bad, I know that now. Whether you are a Catholic or a Protestant is not important. Is that what you think?"

"Mmm…"

He sighed. "But, unfortunately, it is not what we think in Spain. To us, God is everywhere, but only if you are a Catholic. Perhaps we are wrong and you are right; it is how we live that matters. But vicars and priests will never agree. Both think they are right."

"Mmm…"

"Bess Trevanion, she is a fool."

"Mmm!"

"There," said Diego crossly. "Now I know you do not listen."

Bess smiled. "On the contrary, I agree: Bess Trevanion is a fool."

"Yes, only a fool would help an enemy escape. Only a fool would know of such danger and not be afraid."

Bess swallowed. She reached out and took Diego's hand. "Aye," she said, huskily. She would miss Diego; miss him so much it hurt like a dagger thrust through her heart. Was this love? she asked herself. It was certainly deeper, more passionate than anything she had ever felt for Robert Williams. She turned her head: Diego was staring out to sea.

Could he see way beyond the horizon, to Spain, to his home, his family? To a world she could never hope to know? Aye, she thought, Bess Trevanion is a fool. Bess Trevanion is also afraid: afraid to think of a future alone with no Diego at her side.

***

The soldier bent down and lifted the pieces of sacking. In the darkening gloom, Henry could just see the name Mary Ann painted on the transom and watched the soldier's lips forming the words as he slowly spelled them out to himself. He probably couldn't read, but was simply remembering the shapes of the letters shown them by the officer in charge and counting how many there were. Satisfied, he turned and raised his voice in an echoing shout. Henry backed into the darkened doorway as men came running, summoned out of a nearby alley.

"The stolen boat," the soldier shouted. "It's here. The one the officer told us to keep an eye out for."

From the middle of the group, a sergeant stepped forward and read the name for himself: "Mary Ann," he muttered. He turned, taking charge, issuing orders on what to do. "You," he said to one man, "back to the castle. Report the finding to the captain." To two others: "You two stay here and keep your eyes open. Arrest anyone who goes near it. The rest, spread out and search the area."

"How will we know this Spaniard when we see 'im, Sergeant?" one of them asked.

"You'll know 'im 'cause 'e's a Spaniard. 'N' Spaniards ain't the same as us. That's 'ow you'll know 'im."

The men moved off. The sergeant stared at the boat. Henry, trapped by the militia's sudden appearance, huddled down in the doorway, hoping he'd not be spotted. Thirty yards along from where he squatted, the two soldiers left on watch did the same. It was too late for Henry to shift from where he was; they'd see him the moment he moved. The sergeant passed something to the two watchers and left to disappear after his men, or more likely to the nearest tavern, Henry surmised.

Darkness began to fall. Rush lights, outside one of the waterfront inns, shone yellow. The question Henry asked was: did he stay here and wait for Bess to return, or should he try and move away under cover of darkness and continue his search? He considered the alternatives: looking for his daughter was more important than watching a boat. He'd wait until the two watchers relaxed, then slip away in the blackness of the night and continue scouring Penryn.

***

Hand in hand, they walked down the hill and came out in a turnip field behind Arwenack Manor. Darkness was now almost complete, the jetty deserted, the boatman curled up asleep and out of sight or, Bess guessed, drinking himself into a stupor in the nearest tavern.

The kitchen door opened as soon as they tapped on it. Jane ushered them into a dark passage and quickly closed and bolted the door behind them. "The servants are all abed," she whispered. "Only the master's up, talking with someone. It'll not be long before they follow." The candle she was holding flickered, sending shadows scampering across the walls. "Stay close. I'll lead the way."

She took them up one passage and down another until Bess was quite lost. They climbed a narrow staircase that creaked under their weight, and up a ladder that led into the loft where she set the candle down on a box.

"This is my room; we're safe here," she whispered. Bess looked round at the wood plank walls. "No one can hear," Jane assured her. "Those are store rooms, either side." The room was bare: just one cot, a chair, a chest, a stool, and the box the candle was stood on. There was no window to show the gathering darkness and no second bed.

"It's not like the old days, but it's better than some have," Jane said defensively.

"Where does Matthew sleep?" Bess asked.

"Aye, I thought you'd ask that. I lied: Matthew left me a year ago. I don't know where he is or where he went. All I know is, he couldn't stand being bullied a moment longer for having married a papist." She spat the word. "'Tis done now. There's no good crying about it."

Diego reached out and took her hand. "It will not always be like this," he said.

Jane snatched her hand away. "While you two have been idling in the sun," she said sharply, "I've been searching.

263

There's a Moorish ship leaving Penryn, Monday, bound for Tangier and calling at Oporto on the way. I know the captain. He's carried letters from me to you in the past. I've promised that should he call in at Cadiz and wait a day or so, your father will make the extra journey worth his while."

"What is today?" Diego asked.

"Wednesday. Tomorrow's Thursday."

"Where will I stay until Monday?"

"On board. It will be safer."

Diego nodded. "We will go there tomorrow."

"No. Tonight. They're waiting for us, now."

"Tonight?" said Bess in surprise. So soon? Her heart sank.

"It is best. All the time you wander around loose, there's a chance that someone will recognise you for what you are. The same goes for you staying here."

For what you are, thought Bess and wondered what that was other than two persons in love.

"Can Bess not stay with me until we sail?" asked Diego.

"No. That's impossible." Jane glanced at Bess. "The space is too tiny; there's room only for one."

"It would not be possible, anyway," said Bess softly, desperately trying to hide any sign of her true feelings. "I must get home; my parents need me; they'll be wondering where I've got to."

Once again, at the quarry top, Diego had tried to persuade her to go with him. Once again Bess had said that it was

264

impossible. But that didn't stop him trying again.

"It is possible," Diego persisted.

"No. You have your world, I have mine."

Jane Mordaunt gave a soft sigh of relief and took Bess's hand. "It passes," she said, knowingly, and stroked the back of her wrist. "Believe me, whatever you're feeling, Bess, it passes."

A choked emotion welled up in Bess's throat. She turned away to hide her face in shadow. Knowing that Diego couldn't stay, that he had to go, didn't make their parting any easier.

"Then we will see Bess safely back to the Mary Ann," said Diego.

"There's no time."

"Then we must make time. I will not leave like this. I will see Bess to her boat, then we will go aboard this ship you have found."

"It's not necessary," said Bess. "Jane is right."

"It is necessary," replied Diego firmly. "The Mary Ann is moored in Falmouth harbour. Falmouth is on the way to Penryn from here, is it not? So, we will go there first."

***

Jane Mordaunt led Bess and Diego through dingy streets lit with the occasional torch, hugging deeply cast shadows as they went. A soft drizzle had moved in off the sea, making the cobbles wet and slippery. A snatch of song, followed by a burst of laughter, issued from a tavern on their left. The door was flung wide and a man staggered out to collapse in the street. They remained motionless, willing him to get to his feet and move away. The man slowly pulled himself up and wobbled drunkenly into a side alley to urinate.

Jane took hold of their hands. "Let's get away from here before someone sees us. The boat, where did you leave it?"

"Tied up near the quay," Bess whispered.

Jane turned into a narrow passage between two houses. Ahead, they could see faint reflections on water. "The quay's just ahead. Say your farewells here," she said.

"No," replied Diego. "We will see Bess safe, to the Mary Ann."

Bess felt Jane bridle. "There's no need," Bess told him. "I can find it from here."

"We will go with you. Then we will go and find my ship."

Jane's voice rose to a frenzied whisper. "This is senseless. We're taking unnecessary risks."

Diego was firm. "We are three people out having enjoyment with each other, are we not? If you say, two persons is not as dangerous as one person, then three persons must be better. We will say goodbye in the right way, in the right place. After everything Bess has done, it is a small thing for us to do."

"Let's not argue about it. Diego is right, they're looking for one Spaniard, not two women and a man." Bess shrugged her shoulders. They had said their goodbyes in the most telling way possible, that afternoon, in the field above the quarry. Now, hidden in the darkness of the alley leading to the quay, Bess said quietly, "But, if you prefer, I'm quite willing to say farewell here and go on alone."

"There is no argument," persisted Diego. "We go to the Mary Ann. There we will say goodbye. Then Jane and I will go and find this ship." He moved resolutely forward.

At the end of the passage, they halted. Bess peered out, trying to identify the Mary Ann in the darkness. The moorings had changed since the morning. If the Mary Ann was still there it must now have different craft tied up alongside. Had someone discovered it to be stolen and removed it? Had the owner arrived from St Mawes to sail it back?

"I cannot see which one it is. The boats have either been shifted," she whispered. "Or new ones have been added."

"What does that mean," asked Jane anxiously. "Someone has taken it?"

"I don't know. It's probably still there, mixed up with the others, but I cannot see."

"You will have to hide and wait until daylight, then search properly." Jane tugged at Diego's sleeve. "Come, we must go."

Diego ignored her. "It is that one," he said, keeping his voice low. "I can see the sack hanging over the stern."

"It's too dark to see clearly. You're imagining it."

"I have very good eyes at night. I see very good in the dark."

"You must have, if you can see sacking in this light,"

Bess whispered. "Which one do you say it is?"

"The one, two, three from that end. I recognise the shape."

"All fishing boats in this part of Cornwall look alike."

"It is the Mary Ann, I know it is," Diego persisted. "The quay, it is deserted, why should we not go and look?"

"I want to be sure it's safe first," said Bess. "Stay here while I make certain; if it's the Mary Ann I'll come back and we'll say our goodbyes."

***

"What was that?" whispered the militiaman, hiding in the shadow of the doorway.

"What was what?" replied his partner in a low soft voice.

"I thought I heard people talking. Low, like whispers"

"Lovers."

The militiaman shuffled nervously. "Something moved over by that passage."

"Can't be the Spaniard, if there was more than one."

"He could have found sympathisers. Pass me the pistol the sergeant left."

The second militiaman shivered. "I'm not touching that thing."

"Pass it to me and shut up," the first one hissed.

***

Bess moved towards the line of boats, hugging a warehouse wall, sliding cautiously from one shadow to the next. Water lapped the quay with a soft slapping sound. The third boat from the end certainly looked like the Mary Ann. A rat ran across the cobbles in front of her. She moved forward once more and saw the sacking as a dark smudge, exactly where they had left it. She moved closer, straining her eyes.

"Hold fast, Spaniard, and don't say a word. Move and we'll kill you."

Two figures emerged from the blackness of a nearby doorway. Bess turned at speed: her foot slipped on wet cobbles and her ankle twisted under her. She reached out to steady herself. A blinding flash and something thudded into her left side, knocking her to her knees. Then the ground seemed to give way and she was tumbling over the side of the quay. Her hand grasped a rope, her back hit a spar, and she was lying in the bottom of a boat with two pieces of sacking fallen across her face. She reached up to snatch them away, but her left arm wouldn't respond. The sacking fell away of its own accord. M...a...r...Mary Ann. The letters glowed faintly in the darkness, just two inches from her nose.

She forced her right hand to move across her chest. Her shoulder and left arm were slippery, the fluid warm. Water should be cold. Her left leg felt numb. Had she broken it in the fall? Diego! What would he do now? How would he get home? Diego! She must get up: they hadn't said goodbye. Pain started to lance through her body. The boat seemed to spin. Everything went black, blacker than the surrounding darkness, as Bess fainted.

The two soldiers climbed into the boat. The pistol and their pikes discarded on the quayside. They peered down, shocked by the outcome.

"Is he dead?" asked one.

"It's a woman!"

"A woman!" he cried and peered closer. "Looks as though it's blown half her side away. The bodice and skirt are black with blood."

"I didn't know it was going to go off like that."

A patrol came running from the direction of the main street. It halted at the open end of an alley, its members trying to judge whether it was safe to approach. A voice called: "What happened?"

The second militiaman stood up in the boat. "We thought it was the Spaniard..."

"Where is he now?"

"...but it was a woman. She's here, lying in the boat, unconscious."

Seeing that it was safe, the patrol came forward at a run.

"We heard the pistol shot and knew something was up," one of them said.

"She was searching among the boats. We warned her, shouted for her to stop. Then Tom shot her."

"I didn't mean to. It just went off."

"Where'd you get the pistol?"

"The sergeant left it. Primed and loaded."

"Just as well."

"How do you mean?"

"Well ask yourself: what's she doing here? A sympathiser,

I'll be bound, looking for the Spaniard. Must be. She found the right boat. What else could she be?"

"Aye, that's true."

"Young or old?"

"Not much more than a wench."

"Can we get a torch?"

"Leave her till the sergeant gets here."

"Has anyone gone for him?"

"I'd've thought he'd hear. It made a devil of a noise."

"Deafened me, it did. There was a big flash and a bang."

"Here comes someone now."

A figure approached at the run. They could hear his heavy breathing.

"Aye, that's the sergeant, all right," the first militiaman said. "I can smell the ale from here."

21
El Cabah

The sound of the pistol exploding stunned Diego and Jane. Both stood rooted to the spot, unable to believe their ears.

"My God, she's been shot," hissed Jane in horror.

Her words failed to register. "Shot?" whispered Diego.

"Quickly," Jane whispered. "Run before they see us."

"They? Who is they? There is no one here."

"Soldiers," mouthed Jane urgently.

As a confused Diego peered out from the alleyway, two men emerged from the blackness of the doorway where they had been hiding and moved cautiously towards the boat. "Bess is shot? They have shot Bess?" Diego repeated in a frantic whisper.

"Hush! They will hear you."

The two soldiers clambered into the boat. Jane pulled at Diego's sleeve. "Quickly, we must run. While they are occupied."

Diego retreated backwards into the alley with Jane tugging at his arm. He turned, resisting the pull. "Wait! Stop! We must help."

But Jane was concerned only with Diego. "We can do nothing," she whispered frantically. "The soldiers have her. Save yourself: it's what she would want, what she's been helping you to do these past weeks."

Diego shook his arm free. "No, we stay. We see if we can

help."

From the direction of Penryn came shouts and the sound of running feet. "Patrols," Jane squeaked in fear. "Heading for the quay. They'll be here any second."

Diego continued to resist her pleas. "Why are the people in the tavern not running out to see?" he asked. "They must hear the pistol shot?"

"With that rowdiness? I doubt that they'd hear the last trumpet."

"What do you think has happened?"

"I don't know. She's obviously not the Spaniard they're seeking. And they didn't see us, so the chances are they probably think she's someone who happened to stumble on a patrol and the patrol panicked."

"I do not think she has been shot. I think the noise of the pistol frightens her and she fall. That is what I think. That is why we must stay."

They watched as a sergeant came running and heard him order the men to leave the woman where she was and carry on searching for the Spaniard. "She's not going anywhere," he said callously. "Not with a lead ball in her side and that amount of blood. A cart from the castle can come and pick her up later."

Slowly the patrol and the two militiamen involved dispersed and Diego and Jane found themselves alone. "There, I told you so. They think that she's just someone who got accidentally caught by a patrol. Nothing we can do," Jane said. "We must get you aboard that merchant ship. The whole place is seething with troops."

"No. If Bess is hurt, we must help her. We will look and see what has happened."

"This is foolishness."

"Foolish or not. That is what we will do."

Diego stepped out from the shelter of the alley and moved cautiously towards the Mary Ann with Jane reluctantly following him. Reaching it, he grasped the mooring rope, pulled the craft close to the quayside wall and carefully lowered himself into it, wincing as his injured foot slipped on the wet planks. The boat rocked wildly and he spread his arms to maintain a balance. "I cannot see anything," he whispered. "It is too dark." Suddenly, his foot nudged something lying in the bottom of the boat. "Bess?" he whispered. "Is that you?" When no answer came he bent down, felt around, and gathered her to him. "Bess!" he whispered. "Yes, she is wounded," he called loudly. "She is bleeding."

"Hush! Someone will hear."

Diego could feel warm blood flowing over his arm. "We must get help."

"Help! For God's sake, we cannot help her, Diego."

He dropped his voice. "We will take her with us to the Moorish ship you have found. They will be able to help."

"How are we going to do that?" Jane's voice was frantic with worry. "Carry her for more than half a mile? You with your wounded leg, and me an old woman?"

"We will row the boat to Penryn."

"This is insane," Jane whispered.

Diego was insistent, his voice authoritative. "Do not question my orders, Jane. This is what we will do. I have decided. It is dark. I will stay with her in the boat at Penryn while you go aboard the ship and get help."

***

The drizzle had stopped. Dimly the tall masts of ships began to show against the night sky where clouds, beginning to break, allowed a watery moon to peep through one moment only to disappear the next. Having dropped Jane Mordaunt off at wharf steps leading up to the empty, silent, quay above and tied the Mary Ann up alongside, Diego sat in the bottom of the boat gently cradling Bess's unconscious form, waiting for a seaman from the Moorish ship to come and carry her aboard, and cursing their slowness roundly in his native tongue. Blood was soaking through his smock in a considerable quantity and help was vital. Bess stirred in his arms and her eyes slowly opened..

"Diego?" she whispered

"Hush!" he said. "Help is coming."

"Leave me. You should be aboard the ship."

"Jane has gone for help. Do not worry."

"I worry for you."

"I am safe. We will get you well, and then I will sail for Spain." But Bess had fainted once more. Diego held her and prayed.

Minutes later, out of the surrounding darkness, a voice whispered, "Diego?"

"Jane?" He strained his eyes and saw a black shape moving along the quay above his head. A Moor suddenly appeared out of the blackness, his face as dark as the surrounding night. Standing on steps behind him was Jane.

"Yes, it's me," she said, keeping her voice low.

Without a word being spoken, the Moor stepped into the boat, gently picked Bess up, climbed out with her body cradled in his arms, and disappeared up the steps.

Diego and Jane followed, Diego limping, Jane holding his arm hurrying him along, across the quay, past warehouses, to a ship tied up alongside, then up a gangplank that joined the ship's deck to the quay. The moon broke through the cloud base casting deep shadows, sharpening the scene with an unearthly blue-white light.

On deck a man stepped forward and whispered in Spanish "Welcome aboard the El Cabah, Senor. I am the captain. My name is Rashide." He spoke to the Moor carrying Bess in what Diego assumed was Arabic. The moor turned and Captain Rashide indicated for them to follow. "A cabin has been prepared, Senor."

The cabin, in the high castle at the rear of the ship, was small, measuring no more than six feet by six feet. It was already lit by a lantern and the Moor laid Bess down on a built-in bunk. "We are a merchant ship, Senor," the captain said apologetically. "It may be small but it is my first officer's cabin, he has given it up for your pleasure."

Diego nodded. "I must thank him. It is more than adequate."

The captain nodded to the Moor who touched his forehead with both hands in a salaam and left them. "So I now have two passengers," Captain Rashide said to Jane in heavily accented English.

"But only one who is going to Spain," she replied quickly.

"At the moment," said Diego. "But if two go I shall sleep on the floor and you will receive two payments."

The captain nodded. Jane looked less pleased and for a moment appeared ready to argue the point.

"What about the fishing boat?" the captain asked.

"I'll move it back where it was," said Jane.

"My men can do that."

"I may be old but I work in a kitchen and I still have my strength. No, I have rowed boats before and I know where it was moored," said Jane. "It will be best if it is found in the same place. They will then think that it's not moved from where it was and the girl has either recovered or been rescued by relatives. We don't want them prying into ships tied up in Penryn."

The captain nodded. "You are lucky, Senor," he said to Diego. "You have women who think of everything. Meanwhile we must see what we can do for the one who is wounded."

Tired and dispirited, Henry made his way back to the Mary Ann. He had searched Penryn and Falmouth most of the night without success. Now dawn was breaking. Approaching the quay where the boat was moored, he saw a handcart with a militiaman standing alongside, peering down at it and scratching his head. The hessian pieces no longer hung over the transom and the bottom of the boat was covered in a dark stain that hadn't been there before.

The militiaman glanced up. "You know anything about this, fisherman?" he asked.

"Know anything of what?" asked Henry and felt his heart pounding. To him the stain looked suspiciously like blood.

"A body that walks. Here one minute, gone the next."

A body? "I'm a fisherman not a riddle solver," Henry said shakily.

"A body here last night but no sign of it now. I get sent down from the Castle to collect it and there's nothing to collect but a puddle of dried blood."

"Whose body?" asked Henry, fearing the worst.

"A woman. Shot by a militiaman in error while passing, some say. Aiding the Spaniard, say others."

"Alive?"

"The woman or the Spaniard?"

"The woman, of course. I have no care for the Spaniard."

"Alive, I suppose. The dead don't walk. Someone must have carried her off to care for her, otherwise she'd still be here. As for the Spaniard, we're still looking for him with every hope we'll find the bastard and spare no mercy on the blackguard when we do."

***

Henry stood outside St Mawes Castle. Having been up all night searching the Penryn and Falmouth docksides and having sailed back here during the dawn hours to see Will Bligh, he was in no mood for the Dorset man's prevarication. Will came to the castle gate and the two walked in silence away from the fortress till there was no chance of their being overheard.

"Tell me, Will," said Henry, tight with anger, "where she is. I've no interest in the Spaniard escaping back to Spain or not. Only in saving my daughter. I've seen the Mary Ann they stole, tied up in Falmouth, and it has a large bloodstain in the bottom that wasn't there the previous day. A militiaman tells me that a woman was shot in error and fell into the boat, badly wounded. During the night it seems she was taken somewhere by somebody: probably to treat her wound, and that was all he knew. Sent down at daybreak to collect her, he found her gone.

"Now, I've no time for pretences and sob stories about helping fellowmen, I just want to find my daughter. So where is she, Will? Who did she and the Spaniard go to meet in Falmouth?"

Will picked a blade of grass and sighed. "Believe me, Henry, I had no wish to do but what I thought was right. But if Bess is suffering wounds, of course you must find her. Look for a Jane Mordaunt, a Catholic woman, servant in Arwenack Manor, Sir John Killigrew's house."

Henry looked at him. "Dear God! They couldn't have chosen a more dangerous liaison," he said.

"Aye, but that's where they were headed. If anybody knows where Bess is, then Jane Mordaunt will be able to provide the answer. But mind, her allegiance will be towards Spain and Diego, not Bess." Will slipped the blade of grass between his lips and gazed out over the water at St Anthony's Head.

"I'm well aware of that," said Henry bitterly. "It seems a rich Spaniard has more support at this time than a wounded English fisher girl."

"An unfair statement, Henry. He'd have had the same support from Bess and myself if he'd been poor."

"Knowing that," Henry said angrily, "doesn't help me find my daughter, Will."

***

Bess lay in the bunk; her side had been bandaged; luckily the lead ball had passed clean through and out the other side, tearing a hole in her side and causing a great deal of blood to be lost. Diego sat on the bunk and held her hand. "Come with me to Spain, Bess," he said.

"I cannot."

"How will you get home? You are wounded."

"I'll find a way."

"You have done so much. I can make you safe and happy. Bess, I love you."

"Yes, and I love you, but I cannot leave my parents. I am English: it would kill them. Not only that, I am a fisher lass. Your way of life is not something that I could take to."

"We would have our love."

"And I have no doubt that it would be a great love. But I would always be a stranger in your land, in your house, and to your family. Our love will not suddenly disappear, my sweet, it will survive even though we are apart. But my coming with you would always mean that I am happy only when you are near, never when I am alone or among strangers. At least let me remember everything in the comfort of my family and those who I know. I shall not forget you."

Diego sighed. "Sailing for home, will be a sad parting."

"Yes, it will. But not a tragic one. Don't let's make it any sadder."

Diego nodded. "I will ask Jane to help you."

Bess smiled weakly. In her opinion Jane Mordaunt would do everything in her power to get her home to Porthloe in order to prevent Diego taking her to Spain. And Bess couldn't blame her for that. She was once his wet nurse; Diego was once her baby.

"Yes," she said, "I am sure Jane will help."

22
Sweet Sorrow

The Mary Ann was gone, probably taken by the militia and hopefully given back to its rightful owner. Passing along the quay, reaching Arwenack Manor, Henry stood gazing up at the building. The size of the building and knowing who owned it, causing him to hesitate. He shook his head, angered at the indecision: Bess hadn't faltered, he told himself, no matter who the lord in residence was. The main entrance was clearly at the front; the servants' quarters, sited round the side. Purposefully, he strode up to the kitchen door and thumped loudly on it with his fist. The door was opened by a kitchen maid. "I wish to speak with a Mistress Mordaunt," Henry said. Seeing the tense look on his face, the girl bobbed and closed the door, to be reopened moments later by a grey haired woman with steely eyes.

"You want me? I'm Jane Mordaunt," she said, studying his face and clothes. "What can I do for you?"

"You can tell me where I can find my daughter, Bess Trevanion," Henry told her, his voice raised in anger.

Jane stepped outside and shut the door quickly behind her. "Let's not talk here," she said. The steely look had gone to be quickly replaced by concern laced with wariness. Beckoning, she led the way to the orchard where Bess and Diego had first made their presence known, and turned to face Henry.

"I could say that perhaps you should have done a better job looking out for her, three weeks back, then you wouldn't need to ask such a question. She would be home with you."

"You could, Mistress. And you'd be right. But recriminations will not help either my daughter or your Spaniard."

"True."

Henry noticed there was no denial of involvement. "So where are they?" he asked. "I have no wish to endanger your Spaniard. I only want my daughter. I hear she has been wounded and that makes my concern even more urgent."

Jane looked at him. "She is being looked after and you've no need to be afraid for her: she'll recover."

Henry breathed a sigh of relief. "She's here?"

"Do you think I would be that stupid?"

"So, where is she?"

She looked at him. "How do I know that once having taken your daughter safely away, you won't inform the authorities of Diego's whereabouts and claim the reward I'm told is being offered?"

"For twenty gold pieces? Do you think I would put my daughter's love for me in jeopardy for such a sum? If I were to she would never forgive me, and rightly so. Take your Spaniard, do whatever you like with him, all I ask is for my daughter's safe return. If you don't want me to know where the Spaniard is hidden, I'll wait here and you can bring her to me."

Jane stared at the orchard trees with their firm young fruit beginning to form. "That will be difficult," she said. "Return here in two hours and I'll see whether I can take you to her. There are people who have to be persuaded."

"Persuaded? She is being held against her will?"

"Of course not," snapped Jane Mordaunt. "Persuaded that you can be trusted not to betray them. Your daughter is not the only one who's risking her life over this escapade."

***

"Your daughter claims you are an honourable man," Jane Mordaunt said on his return. Once again they were walking in the orchard. "If you say no harm will befall Diego, then she says we should believe what you say." Her face softened slightly. "She also says that at this moment there is no one in this world she would rather see."

"And I her," Henry said with feeling.

"Those she's with have also agreed."

"Where is she?"

"On a foreign ship, bound for Spain."

Henry was shocked.

"Calm yourself," said Jane Mordaunt. "It has not yet sailed and when it does your daughter will not be a passenger: she does not desire it. Though I cannot say the same for Diego. But have no fear: it's an infatuation on his part that will soon pass once he's safely home."

"What of my daughter's feelings?"

"She sees her duty done. As to her feelings, I cannot say.

You'll have to ask her that. At the moment, I'm instructed to bring you to her; but I must warn you, give the captain and crew away to the authorities and they will come and slit your throat and dump your body in the River Fal without a second thought."

"All I want is the safe return of my daughter." Henry was tired of repeating the fact. "So, do I gather from what you say that she's so wounded she cannot come here, to me?" he asked, guessing what the answer would be.

"Yes. That's the problem. Her wound has been cleaned and dressed but she cannot as yet walk. A lead ball has gone through the flesh and out the other side. She has lost a great deal of blood but no arteries appear severed and no bones smashed. Anyone carrying her will draw attention, the town is full of militiamen who are only too well aware that a young woman has been shot and is now missing, and who are still busy searching for Diego. Naturally, the ship's captain has no desire to draw them to his vessel."

"Why can't she be transferred here by cart?" asked Henry. "She could be well covered."

"The militia are everywhere. They know Diego must be either in Falmouth or Penryn, and they know his only chance to escape is to board a ship bound for Spain. The quays are being watched and they're searching every cart they see."

"That I can understand. But not one leaving a ship and bringing something ashore, surely?"

"The captain does not want to take any chances."

"When does this ship sail?"

"Tomorrow. Never fear, the captain has a plan and will explain it to you."

"Then I suggest we go and see him."

***

Jane glanced carefully around, making sure the area was free of militia. Two soldiers were lounging at the far corner of a warehouse, watching the El Cabah. Not for any suspicious reason but because they had been ordered to watch every ship tied to the harbour. Sooner or later Jane knew they would get bored and wander off to study the next moored vessel. Within ten minutes they did so. She nodded at Henry and quickly made her way across the cobbled quay to the El Cabah's gangplank, mounted it, and was aboard in a matter of seconds, Henry close on her heels.

A seaman led them to the captain, seated in his cabin. Captain Rashide greeted Henry politely, rose and led the way aft, to the cabin occupied by Bess and Diego.

Bess was lying in the single bunk; Diego was standing next to it, at her side. As soon as he saw Henry with Jane and the captain, he guessed who he was and stepped quickly aside. Henry glanced at him and saw a tanned, handsome young man dressed in Arab clothes that had obviously been provided by a crew member. He turned to see Bess, studying him with a worried look on her face. Henry smiled. "Bess," he said.

"Father."

Henry took her hand, bent and kissed her brow. Bess had been expecting to be admonished, instead Henry was full of concern. "We must get you home," he said. She nodded. Henry turned, looked at Diego and gave him a curt bow. "Your friend knows that?" he asked.

"Yes, he knows that," said Bess, and smiled at Diego. Diego smiled back at her.

"Good," said Henry. He glanced round the tiny cabin. Jane and Captain Rashide were standing in the corridor unable to find room to enter with both Henry and Diego filling the remaining space. "I hear you have a plan, Captain Rashide," Henry said.

The captain tried to enter the cabin. Diego stepped sideways, realised that wasn't going to work, and moved outside to stand next to Jane.

"You have a boat?" Captain Rashide asked.

"Yes."

"Bring it alongside the ship." His English was excellent if heavily accented. "We have a yardarm with a pulley we use for raising and lowering goods. We will lower your daughter, wrapped in sacking so that she looks like a roll of cloth, in a net and into your boat. We will make sure that she can breathe; you will then sail away and unwrap her when you are well clear of the harbour."

"Won't that look strange? Unloading goods into a fishing boat when you are already moored alongside a quay?"

"Why should it? Boats carry goods for us across harbours

287

all the time. Taking your daughter ashore at the quayside is much more of a risk. The militia are everywhere."

Henry wasn't too sure. "She has wounds. Will the net support her without making them worse?"

"I do not know. We do not usually move wounded women around in this way," the captain said wryly.

"Father," said Bess. "It is the best, the only way."

Diego, standing in the corridor listening to the conversation, wanted to say that the best way was for her to stay aboard the El Cabah and sail with him to Spain, but held his peace.

Henry sighed and nodded. "I'll fetch the boat," he said. "Say goodbye to your friend while I'm gone."

Bess nodded. Everyone left the tiny cabin and Diego came back inside and closed the door. "If you will not come with me," he said. "I will come for you. This war cannot go on for ever."

Bess, knowing only too well her countymen's depth of feeling against Spain, saw no sign of a peaceful settlement for decades to come. Diego might promise that his love would be enduring but back home he would soon forget. Tears filled her eyes. The same could not be said of her.

***

A rope hung over the side. Henry grabbed hold of it and glanced up. Captain Rashide and Diego were standing, peering over the ship's side, looking down at him. Rashide waved a hand and Henry saw a rope threaded through a pulley at the end of the yardarm tighten up and take the weight of his daughter on the other end. He muttered a quick prayer as the taut rope passed slowly through the pulley and a net rose into view. Two deckhands steadied the canvas roll the rope was carrying and guided it clear of the ship's wooden bulwark and out into space, suspended high above Henry and Lilybeth.

Henry raised a hand to show he was ready and the netted roll slowly descended. Carefully, Henry made ready to receive it, guiding it lengthways into the boat. He untied the rope and watched as a deckhand hauled the line back up.

"Keep the net," Captain Rashide called to him.

Henry was glad of that and gave an acknowledging wave: rolling Bess off it would have been impossible without causing her wound to open up. "Are you all right, Bess?" he asked in a low voice.

"Yes, I'm fine, father," came the weak reply

"You can breathe?" he asked.

"Yes, I can breathe." And immediately Bess was reminded of when they'd transferred Diego from Caerhays to St Mawes and she had asked him the same question.

Above Henry's head, Diego gave a wave. Ashore, Mistress Mordaunt was standing on the quayside, watching, making sure that Bess was leaving Diego for good. Further along the quay, two militiamen were also watching the canvas roll being lowered. Henry tried not to let their presence worry him. Bored, they wandered away and Henry gave a sigh of relief.

"Your Spanish friend is waving," he said softly.

"Don't worry," said Bess, "we said our farewells while you were fetching Lilybeth. He is waving to you."

Henry raised a hand. "If it pleases you, I've waved back," he said.

"Yes, it pleases me, father."

On deck, Diego watched the fishing boat move slowly away from El Cabah. "Goodbye, Bess," he whispered, gripping the handrail. "I will not forget you."

***

With virtually no wind, Henry was forced to row, and because Bess in her canvas roll was stretched out down the centre of the fishing boat, he had to stand and row from the stern, paddling the single oar backwards and forwards in order to propel the craft through the water. Soon, his back was aching and his arms throbbing from the unaccustomed posture. Tiredly, he glanced landwards.

Clouds, lying across the horizon were suffused with rose: a sure sign of coming rain. Gulls circled the boat, their beady eyes searching for a catch on board. They screeched and swooped, soared and turned, unsure of the canvas roll lying there, not knowing whether to stay or widen their hunt for a more profitable source.

Well out in the estuary mouth and away from any moored vessels, Henry shipped his oar and gazed down at the canvas covering. "Can you hear me, Bess?" he asked. "I'm going to try and unwrap you. I want to make sure your wound hasn't opened."

"Yes, I can hear you."

Whoever had wrapped Bess up had done it with care, knowing that he would want to ease the hessian away easily and there would be no one to help him. Bess's face appeared and Henry could see that she had been crying. "Is it painful?"

Yes, it was painful. But not in the way her father meant. She tried raising her body to get one last glimpse of the El Cabah.

"Is that it, over there?" she asked. It was too far away to see anyone standing on the deck.

"Yes, that's it."

Bess looked at him. "If I hadn't helped him, father, he'd be dead by now."

"Is that what it was, Bess? Care of the wounded? Charity? Succour?"

Tears filled her eyes again. "What did you think it was, father? Love? If it was, it was love for my fellowman," she lied.

A deep feeling of remorse swept over Henry. "Aye, you were always full of that," he said chokingly. "Now let me look at your wound."

23
Strange Fruit

The sun was behind the headland; the valley floor purpled in deep shadow, the surrounding hilltops aglow with pink fire. On a granite outcrop, high above the cluster of stone cottages, Bess sat and gazed down at her village, remembering another day, another time.

Slowly she switched her gaze out across the sea to the far horizon. So much had happened. The Armada had been defeated, its ships driven round the north coast of Scotland, foundering on rocks, sunk by storms. A few reaching the coast of Ireland only to be lured ashore, their remaining stores raided, the ships broken up by Irish brigands, the crews massacred. The war with Spain was over - though no one truly believed that it would remain that way long - her brother, Thomas, his mustering finished, now back on the sea fishing from Lilybeth with her father. Robert Williams, also called for military duty only to find himself released within weeks of reporting to The Citadel at Plymouth, was now on his way home and expected to arrive any day. Will Bligh, gone from St Mawes this past two months, transferred back east to Dorset where he'd come from.

And Diego? He was now but a memory, recalled often and with deep and lasting affection in her most intimate thoughts, never to be forgotten.

So, had it all been worthwhile? Of that she had no doubt.

She'd saved a life and learned what love was all about.

Out of sight, round a bend, the sound of a cart, hooves clopping softly on the dirt lane, drifted up to her. Will Trudgeon back from Truro. She stood and watched the bend in the lane leading to Treviskey, hoping that Will had picked up the one she was waiting for. For that's the way her Robert would come, making his way the seventy miles from Plymouth where he'd served his short muster, arriving dirty and unkempt from sleeping in hedgerows, glad to be home, glad to see her.

Yes, her Robert. For once again that was how she now thought of him. There was even talk of their betrothal. Robert, who had sat with her every moment - when not out fishing - until his time came to join the militia in Plymouth. Every moment while she was slowly recovering from the wound in her side. A wound that was now a puckered scar. A wound that her father had told everyone had been caused by a fall from the cliffs to the west of Portscatho, where he'd found her lying on rocks.

Down in the valley, the figure of Will Trudgeon, seated alone astride the fish cart, rounded the bend. He glanced up, saw Bess outlined against the sky, stood and waved a hand. She slid down the hillside, through the winter browned bracken, to meet him, hopes that he might have met Robert on the road now past. Ah, well! Another day's wait wouldn't hurt.

"There's a barrel for you," Will called as she approached.

"For me?"

"Aye, so the man said."

"What man? Who's it from?"

"How should I know? A sailor brought it to me in Truro. 'Are you from Porthloe?' he asked, though he must have known to single me out. 'Aye,' I said. 'Well, I've a barrel for someone there.' And that's all he knew. It'd been given him by a merchant."

Bess climbed up on the cart. The barrel stood in the back: small, no more than a foot and a half high, with a rope wound round, more to form a handle for carrying than anything else.

"Well, aren't you going to open it?" asked Will.

"I don't know. I don't know who it's from. Come to that, I don't know who it's for. There's no name attached."

"'For the Trevanions,' he said. "Didn't say which one. I asked but he didn't know one member of the family from the others. 'Just the Trevanions,' he said."

"A sailor you say? Where did he pick it up? From a merchant in Penryn?" She had a sudden thought that it might be from Robert, though he'd never be mistaken for a merchant - he looked like what he was a fisherman, born and bred. She asked anyway: "Or from Plymouth?"

"Cadiz, he says."

"Cadiz? Cadiz in Spain?"

"You know of any other Cadiz?"

"Was he Spanish?"

"No, Flemish. But spoke fair English."

Cadiz. It must be Diego. Her heart sang a little song. Two months ago, it would have given a lurch that all but made her faint with joy.

"Do you want me to take it up to the house? It's heavy."

"How heavy?" asked Bess. She turned and lifted it by the rope handle. "It's not so heavy that I can't manage it. Drop me off at the fish store. I can roll it up from there."

"Sure you don't want to open it here?"

Bess could hear the disappointment in his voice.

"I'll open it when I'm sure that it's for me. It could be for Thomas. Or my father. Something he doesn't want others to know about."

"What kind of secret is it that he's likely to want to keep from his own daughter?"

"None, probably. But I don't know that for sure."

"Be a mite strange if he did."

"That'd be his business, Will. Not yours, or mine, or anyone's but his."

Will's face darkened. "Aye, well you know best," he said gruffly.

Bess touched his arm. "I'll not forget your help. And if I can tell you what it is, I will. You'll be the first to know."

Will brightened. "Aye, it's probably of no importance, anyway."

He dropped her off at the fish store. Bess rolled the barrel up the hill. As soon as Will was out of sight, she pushed the container into a clump of withies and stared at it, unsure what she should do with it. Supposing it was nothing to do with Diego? But then who else did she, or anyone else in her family, know in Spain?

She untied the rope, picked up a rock and knocked an iron hoop off. The wooden staves sprang apart enough to allow her to prise out the lid. Inside, the barrel was packed with wood shavings. In the top layer was a note sealed with red wax. Bess broke the seal. 'I have not forgotten' it said. 'One day I will come.' She shoved it down her bodice to study later, in the privacy of her bedchamber.

From the barrel a strange unknown aroma was drifting up. She rummaged in the shavings and her fingers closed upon a round globe-like object. She pressed - it felt both firm and slightly soft. She withdrew her hand and saw an orange.

She rummaged further. Altogether there were more than four dozen large fruits packed inside the barrel, Diego's disbelieving voice drifted through her head: You have never tasted an orange?

She laid the fruits out on the grass. Picked one up and sniffed at it, and put it down again. An unfamiliar smell, an unfamiliar fruit, from a person who was far from unfamiliar. For just three weeks she'd known Diego. That was all. Three weeks that she would carry in her memory for the rest of her life. Three weeks where she'd entertained notions of love.

Alone in her bed at night, the dreams, the memories of

their loving tended to resurface once more, raising desires and driving sleep away. Her Robert would take care of that...

She studied the oranges. What should she do with them? Take them home and her mother would want to know where they'd come from and why. It was no good throwing them away, pretending they didn't exist for everyone entering Will Trudgeon's alehouse would immediately be told of their existence.

Her father might guess, but would say nothing. Nicholas would settle for just eating them without a care as to how they had arrived, or why.

Will Bligh, that was it. She could say they were from Will Bligh; that Cadiz was simply Will Trudgeon mishearing. Or Cadiz was where the fruit had originally come from before Will Bligh had acquired them. The fruit, a thank you from him to them for their hospitality. Write a brief note in his name and drop it in among the shavings and hope that her brother, Thomas, never planned to stay in touch with the gentle Dorset giant.

But the first taste, the first secretly enjoyed segment, would be hers and Diego's.

She smiled, picked up a fruit and began peeling.

THE END

Author's Note

My wife and I lived in the village of Portloe for eighteen delightful months, and sitting up on The Jacka, like Bess, I used to visualise the Spanish Armada's huge invading force sailing past Gull Rock and anchoring off The Dodman, wondering at the fear and trepidation this must have caused the local populace. Then I thought that the Elizabethan Cornish were a far from timid people, who feared no one, loved their queen, and refused to bow to anyone but her. The same was true of their heroes, such as Francis Drake, Hawkins and Howard, and so, slowly, this novel was born.

From the cottage we lived in, we could see the Eddystone lighthouse winking away at night. In Bess Trevanion's time, of course, there was no light, just a rock sticking out of the sea. But the cliff top and the village are still very much as they must have been four and a quarter centuries ago: the stream still runs down through the valley to the sea, passing through what was then our garden; there may be a few more cottages, the village itself may now serve tourists more than catch fish for the local markets; and the inhabitants no longer live in fear of a foreign invasion - in fact, today, they positively welcome it!

The Roseland peninsular, if you've never visited it, is very beautiful and the villages mentioned in this novel all exist. Nankersey is now called Flushing; the two castles still guard the entrance to the River Fal, and Falmouth, of course, has overtaken Penryn in size exactly as Diego predicted it would. Otherwise, except for population growth, it is all very much as it was and one can easily track Bess and Diego's intrepid travels across the peninsular from Porthloe (as it was then called) to Falmouth and the dangers they faced on the way.

Visit the area and see it for yourself. The Cornish love visitors, indeed many now make their living from them, and I guarantee you won't be disappointed.

Ray Murray, Oxfordshire, 2013

About the author

Ray Murray, born in London, was creative director of a large American advertising company, working in both their UK and New York offices where he won numerous awards for his creative TV advertising, and saw his work exhibited and acclaimed in London, New York, Chicago, Los Angeles and Tokyo.

More recently, Ray has focused on writing novels for children and adults. His Arabella Parker series of children's books has been well received by young readers and their parents. The novels are available as ebooks and paperbacks.

Happily married, Ray lives in Oxfordshire.

Previous titles

Arabella Parker and the Primrose School Revolt
Arabella Parker and the Chinese Snakehead Gangsters
Arabella Parker and the Rhino Horn Poachers

For more on Ray Murray's previous titles go to
www.bluejacarandapublishing.co.uk